Bedside: The Art of Medicine

Michael A. LaCombe

# BEDSIDE

The Art of Medicine

University of Maine Press

Orono, Maine 2 0 1 0

University of Maine Press
126A College Avenue
Orono, ME 04473
www.umaine.edu/umpress

University of Maine Press books are published in association with the Raymond H. Fogler Library
of the University of Maine.

"The Neglected Discipline" and "High Society" were presented at Harvard Medical School as the
Francis Weld Peabody Lecture in 2001 and subsequently published in *The Western Journal of
Medicine* and in *The Canadian Medical Association Journal*, respectively. "Last Words" was pre-
sented as the James M. Moss Lecture at the Virginia Chapter, ACP in 2001. "An Innocent Tale"
appeared originally in *Ethiscope*; "Living The Patient's Story," "Halley's Comet," "Another
Season," "On Bad Doctors," "Playing God," "Board Questions," and "Entertaining Angels
Unaware" (originally entitled "Caring For Strangers"), in *Annals of Internal Medicine*; "Adieu,
Le Premier Club du Vin," "Something Sweet," "Check Kiting: Lessons From A Master," "The
Cabalist," "Social Darwinism," and "For Want of a Sail," in *The Journal of the American Medical
Association*; "Greener Pastures," "Voice From Another Room," and "A Private View," in *The
Journal of Emergency Medicine*; "Art and the Science of Medicine," in *Hospital Practice*; "Left-
handed Favor," in *MD Magazine*. "Recent Advances" was first presented at the William L.
Morgan Festschrift, University of Rochester. The remaining stories first appeared in *The
American Journal of Medicine*. All are reprinted here with permission.

The excerpted prose quotation in "Last Words" is from *The Once and Future King* by T. H.
White, copyright 1938, 1939, 1940, 1958 by T. H. White, renewed. It is used by permission of
G. P. Putnam's Sons, a division of Penguin Group (USA) Inc. The poem "Sometimes" in "Last
Words" is reprinted by permission of the author, who wishes to remain anonymous.

14 13 12 11 10    1 2 3 4 5

Paper used in this publication meets the minimum requirements of the American National
Standard for Information Sciences — Permanence of Paper for Printed Library Materials, ansi
z39.48-1984. Printed and bound in the United States of America. Book design and cover photograph by Michael Alpert.

ISBN: 0-89101-118-8 / ISBN: 978-0-89101-118-7

For Margaret Mary

# CONTENTS

ACKNOWLEDGMENTS

Claude Bennett, editor of *The American Journal of Medicine* from 1985 to 1997, eagerly consumed many of these stories faster than I could write them. Suzanne and Bob Fletcher, editors emeriti of *Annals of Internal Medicine*, established the "On Being A Doctor" section of that esteemed scientific journal, giving voice to the experience of other physicians and a rightful place for fiction in medicine. The writing life of a country doctor is the epitome of what someone once called 'writing out in the cold.' The encouragement and personal friendship of these three journal editors kept the fires burning.

It is the lucky writer who can find a great mentor. Ned Willard, a retired English professor, offered to help me with my writing in return for my care during his chronic and ultimately fatal illness. "I've read your stuff," he said. "You could use the help." Ned is with me still.

David Elpern of the Kauai Medical Foundation first invited me to read these stories aloud, starting me on a path that would take me to over fifty universities and training programs where I might read to students and residents and get to know them and their own special stories.

I give special thanks to Jerry Lowenstein, Jean Thomson Black, Kirk Jensen, and David Elpern for their careful review and promotion of this manuscript.

Immense gratitude goes to Michael H. Alpert, Betsy G. Rose, and Laura K. Latinski of the University of Maine Press for their enthusiastic endorsement of this book and for finding a home for it.

My patients deserve my thanks. They are in these stories and are a part of them. My life with them has always provided the spark of the idea that becomes a story. They have been willing partners in the venture and even, on occasion, an eager audience. One such patient, ancient, spry, blue-eyed, independent Becky Bailey, living five miles down a dirt road, lacking telephone or electric power, always prefaced her visits with me this way:

"Do you have any new stories for me today, Doctor?"

Most of all, my wife Margaret Mary has been my best and most valued critic. Her Irish knack for the choice word and turn of phrase, her incredible consumption of books and love of them, and her gentle way of critiquing and loving, are my treasures.

"Is it true?"

When I became the first to publish fiction in medical journals twenty years ago, that was, and remains, the most frequent question asked about my stories. Journal editors and physician-readers have difficulty with fiction in scientific journals, and understandably so. When I submitted "Playing God" (page 21 in this volume) to *The Journal of the American Medical Association*, the reply from the editors went something like this:

"Half of the editorial board agree to publish your piece if it is fiction, and the other half only if it is nonfiction. Which is it?"

When the same story was enacted by Broadway performers at the Mayo Clinic, an attorney stood at the back of the theater, reminded me that there is no statute of limitations on felony accessory to murder, then asked if the story were true. One of the performers advised me to proceed carefully. A young physician-writer, eager to make his mark through exposé, appropriated my story "A Problem of Professionalism" (page 77), which is entirely fiction, as a case in point for his presumed nonfictional article in *The New Yorker*, "When Good Doctors Go Bad."

This last point illustrates what it is that separates fiction from nonfiction. As soon as the author imagines a line of narrative not known to be true, just when the author develops one character out of the qualities of many individuals, as soon as gender, ethnicity, locale, intentions, supportive cast, even the weather and time of year are changed, the piece becomes fiction. Here, such changes are imperative, after all, when writing about one's patients, to protect their privacy.

That does not mean, however, that the story cannot be "true." "An Innocent Tale" (page 17) was requested of me by a journal editor for a large pediatrics hospital on the east coast. *Could it be about children?* the editor asked. *Could it include an ethical dilemma? Might I keep it to 1,000 words?*

I began with the ethical question of whether it is proper ever to lie to a patient, then remembered my own experience years previously, when a dying young woman of twenty asked me, her all-knowing doctor, what Heaven was like. Out of this came the story, fiction to be sure, but "true" most certainly.

"Left-handed Favor" (page 70) is a fictional piece, but central to the story is a real Maine general practitioner from Biddeford-Saco who practiced in the early twentieth century there, was ambidextrous, and used his handwriting as a code to help poor and indigent patients. "Three Voices at Bedside" (page 166) published in three parts, begins with the thoughts of a dying man, written in the first-person point of view. It is entirely fiction, every bit of it. But when published in a medical journal after I began to enjoy somewhat of a following from physician-readers, it was interpreted as entirely nonfiction—my own voice, my farewell—and the letters and calls were most embarrassing.

Which of these pieces are entirely nonfiction? "Board Questions" (page 66) happened just as written, at a meeting I attended of the American Board of Internal Medicine in San Diego, although the thoughts of those around the table have been imagined by me. "French Wake for an Irish Friend" (page 32) was a wonderful occurrence in a bistro in San Diego during an otherwise sad moment in my life—although my companion and dear friend Bob did not, and I would bet still could not, recite any A. E. Housman. "Gordian Knot" (page 111) occurred many years ago in the southwest, and is chilling. "A Question of Velleity" (page 123) is the true depiction of an evening spent with my beloved writing mentor, Ned Willard; "A Social History" (page 160) is a true story of the interwoven lives of several of my patients in western Maine; and "A Chance Pregnancy" (page 207) happened to me just as I tell it here. It was because of that dear old lady that I came to know Thackeray.

One final story note: in response to an invitation by Virginia physicians to give a talk as though I were delivering my last words on earth (a challenging topic for sure!), I wrote and read to them "Last Words" (page 228), but gave those words to an older, dying physician in the story, with a love story as sub-plot, to hold their attention for the hour. A mark of its success is that I have been invited back to read them the story again.

These stories stand alone and are immediately accessible to the nonmedical public, but a glossary (page 247) is appended for those of you wishing more information.

I have been a fortunate doctor, sitting as I have been in the front row of the drama of life. Here are some of the stories I have lived, stories of country medicine with lessons for the city as well.

Trust that they are true.

– Michael A. LaCombe, MD
Augusta, Maine

Bedside: The Art of Medicine

## I. WHEN PATIENTS DIE

You are told in medical school to maintain an emotional distance from patients. Remain dispassionate. Be objective. That sort of thing. But you learn how to care. They teach you that too. And with caring, you get involved. These patients you care about become your friends. You talk about gardening with them. About books. About life. You fish with them.

And then comes the hardest part of all about being a doctor. They leave you, these friends. They die on you. And you, who are supposed to have all the answers, cannot prevent that. More than that, you have to go on.

There is in the old section of the city a fabulous restaurant unique for its culinary eclecticism. The owners are Polish, the food Hungarian, the wine strictly French, and the music is whatever Vera might happen to be humming that day. The place is simply called Stash's.

Not long ago a group of us were there, entertaining a visiting dignitary from Sweden, a hematologist from the Karolinska, all of us letting down from the pressures of the job, feeling important, on the "cutting edge," that sort of thing. We had the side room for ourselves and Vera herself had looked in on us several times, supervising a quality evening. We were deep into leukotriene chemistry—great stuff if you like that sort of thing—when a song from the main dining room stopped me cold. At first, I could barely hear the music; a note, a chord, here and there, was all that filtered through. But suddenly the music became everything. I couldn't let it alone. It tore at me, driving me back the way music can do. Feelings struck me first—a vague sense of unrest, of misgiving, of profound mistake. How did I get here, at this table, with these people, I wondered? Why did I feel I had missed a path meant for me so long ago? Had I lost a part of myself with the passage of time? Who, or what, caused this ache that grew within me like the ache for some long, lost love? What *was* it about this music? Why the regret of having traveled a hundred years in the wrong direction, knowing you could never go back, never could correct the course, never could do it over? And then, on the heels of the emotions came memories.

It was thirty years ago. Our hospital was in those early years, as it remains even today, primarily a place of research, where every mind pursued The Cure, and patient care was subordinated to that higher cause. Back then, successful treatment was rare, and patient care too often meant terminal care. In those days, the burden of treating dying patients at our institution was relegated to one man. His name was

Arthur. He was a fire-plug of a man, with the face of a boxer and the charging stride of a middle-linebacker. Where whole clutches of academicians could be seen flowing down a corridor, laboratory coats buttoned, as though dancing a stately *chorovod*, Arthur charged the other way, white coat flailing behind him, off to fight disease.

*Art*, he would introduce himself in his gruff cop's voice, offering his meaty hand, disarming you with a broad grin and a look that seemed to search your very soul. *Arthur*, the academicians called him, with gracious condescension. As students, we caught the nuances. *Even* Arthur might have something to offer here, they would say, or, 'Where is Arthur now?' they would ask impatiently, as another of their research conferences was about to begin. It was in this way that students were to learn what was important, and what ambitions to pursue.

Arthur hardly noticed the condescension. Patients, and helping them, were all that he lived for. Rushing down the halls with his festinating swoop, he attacked his patients' cancers with a vengeance. A young girl, fine-featured, with her sculpted patrician neck deformed like a lumpy minefield, lay swollen with Hodgkin's Disease. He would stand before the parents, reassuring, consoling, exuding his mysterious power, and then before one word of thanks, before one smile of relief could soften a face, he would be off to the next patient, striding like a quarter-miler to the leukemia ward. There, bed after bed of pale ecchymotic children lay listless, tethered by the intravenous lines, unamused by the ubiquitous television, doomed. Blowing in like the March wind, grinning broadly from his stevedore's face, demanding their smiles in return, he lit up the ward like Christmas. Those children that could, would sit up waiting for that moment they knew he would give them. He would move from bed to bed, like a pug checking his pups.

Here a tickle, there a caress, now a clownish face for the little boy, "It's growing back," he would say as he stroked the fuzzy skull of a little girl, adding, "you've got to be the pettiest patient I've ever seen!" The nurses watched him in wonder, marveling at how a man like this could ever live alone, as he made his rounds alone—for only rarely were there students with him and residents seldom, if at all. In the corridors outside, the academicians would glide down the halls, transported from laboratory to conference room and back again, trailing in their wake the residents and students who followed like acolytes, their chins also held high, their laboratory coats meticulously buttoned.

It was at this fork in the road, thirty years ago, that I found myself: would I remain in the security of the university, engaging a life of science, or charge the faceless enemy with Arthur? With the intention to inform myself, or so I believed at the time, I decided to spend some time on the wards with Arthur, the better to know what path to choose. Swiftly I found myself caught up in his swirling day, with hardly a moment for reflection, barely noticing the smirks of my contemporaries who tolerated this temporary distraction of mine.

Art proved eager to teach. He was a vast repository of information on patient care, uncatalogued, and heretofore unnoticed, which he poured forth from every pocket of his brain, not to please or impress, but only to share, as he might share riches from a secret collection.

Imagine this: you have heard of an eccentric recluse who, it is rumored in a most disparaging manner, collects bugs—and bugs of only the most loathsome variety: dung beetles, stink bugs, and bloodsucking conenoses. But when you chance upon his collection you find butterflies . . . and lacewings and damselflies treasured for their color, and civil bluets and violet dancers, green darners and common amberwings—and you begin to sense you have gotten this collector quite wrong.

Art's knowledge was that of the master clinician: how best to treat his children, and at the same time handle their frantic parents. He had already assumed in me the academic's science; he would teach the clinician's art. How does one recruit the family and patient as allies in the fight against disease? Can there be a proper mindset in the fight against leukemia?

If so, how can the clinician engrave that attitude upon the mind of a child? How can he hold a frightened family from bolting at chemotherapy's most terrible juncture, fleeing to laetrile or megavitamins or doctors of the Chiropractic? How does the physician earn their trust?

One day I learned the depth of Art's science as well, and that his bedside manner was not mere alchemy. There is in medicine a condition called pulmonary edema, quite common in the elderly where it often complicates a failing heart. The patient's lungs suddenly fill up with fluid insufficiently pumped. Unless treated with speed, the patient drowns. There are several maneuvers involved in the treatment, seven or eight on the list, and all of them assume at least some proper kidney function to rid the body of excess fluid. The doctor gives a drug to facilitate the heart's pumping, another drug to decrease the flow of blood to the overburdened lungs, and a third to encourage the kidney's elimination. He waits the anxious moment, and in a half hour or so, the patient begins to brighten, and the eyes regain their spark. The doctor folds his arms and relaxes, glancing at the urine bag now distended with the offending fluid, gives a courtly nod to the nurse, and is off. The circumstance is so commonly encountered in medicine that treatment becomes rote, the expectation of success quite high, and the magic of medicines dramatically displayed.

Art and I were making rounds on the wards together one day, where there was a boy of fourteen hospitalized for a testicular cancer. This boy was a fighter, a handsome, radiant youth with a quick, glowing smile and the dark eyes of some ancestral thinker. He was very popular with the nurses and doctors in this section of the hospital, who would stop by at any opportunity to chat with him about his one abiding passion: botany. In his weeks of hospitalization they had assembled for him, with his assistance in taxonomy, presses of flowers and beakers of wild asters that crowded a cluster of tray tables scavenged from every corner of the hospital.

"Look! I found some cowslips for Tim," one might say.

"What do you think this is, Tim? Could it be . . . "

Yes," he would say, "That's Fireweed . . . Blooming Sally. It's a kind of evening Primrose," then adding shyly, "*Epilobium.*"

So it was that Art and I came to Tim's room on morning rounds one day together with the charge nurse, who had snatched some obscure weed from the parking lot as a gift for Tim. We found him gasping for air. What appeared at first to be mere shortness of breath rapidly evolved into a frantic frothing at the mouth. Tim's deep eyes implored us with a wild desperation. He grunted with each breath, turning his head from side to side searching for one precious pocket of air. Sweat ran from every pore, the foam collected at his mouth, dripping from the sides of his chin, whitish, pink, curiously lethal. This was pulmonary edema, I thought, and turned to the nurse with my list of medications. But Art was ahead of me, already at the bedside.

"No time for that," he muttered to me over his shoulder. "No time for drugs now. His kidneys are knocked out by the chemotherapy. He's overloaded with fluid. He can't get rid of it."

Tim's cancer medicines had damaged his kidneys to such a degree that he could no longer eliminate the intravenous fluids he had been given for re-hydration. His heart was perfect; medicines to help it pump were useless here. His kidney function was gone. Diuretics would never work. I froze. Art kicked at the waste basket, sliding it next to Tim's bed. He grabbed a large-bore needle and sat next to Tim, holding his arm. Tim never felt the needle enter the large vein at his left elbow, so transfixed was he by Art's steady gaze.

Such tenderness! This coarse, rough-cut man with the mug of a prize-fighter murmured softly to Tim, calming him, quieting him, holding him, as Tim's blood poured forth unnoticed from the letted vein into the waste basket. Tim searched Art's face for reassurance, relaxing in his trust, eased by his doctor's strength. This was not just a simple compassion for an ailing child. It was this, but more. Nor was it simply a gentle doctor's caring for his patient. More than this. This was love.

Art was like the farmer who, on an October morning, goes about his chores. His Guernseys munch the offered silage, consulting one another, fogging the chill air, shifting contentedly. Pail in either hand, the farmer shoulders through to the milk-room to find the battered body of a swallow, dazed from a night-long attempt at escape, lying on the concrete floor. His chores forgotten, he sets his milk-pails down and scoops her up in his callused hands. Whispering to her softly, he reminds her of her brothers and sisters, of migration, and of winter spent in Mexico. Now he smoothes her primaries, corrects her coverts, cooing to her, chucking the cinnamon-buff of her chin. She straightens herself, adjusts, reassembles. He thanks her for her tenancy, for the summer of her society. *Wit-wit* , she answers, blinking her mascara-eyes. With raised hand he lifts her forth, offering her to the south. She stands, hesitates, launches, and is gone. The farmer leans against the milk-shed, pausing, watching her go.

"We had to get his fluid off quickly. It was the only way," said Art, breaking the tension. Tim, quiet now, managed a smile. The nurse, with a cool-wet terry cloth, wiped his face, his neck and his shoulders, caught up in the contagion of tenderness.

"I couldn't breathe," said Tim.

Three months' rotation in this art of medicine convinced me to want to be just like my mentor, to practice rather than preach, to walk the wards like him, and with him, and not live in the laboratory. This decision, made with no small residue of discomfiture, I announced to no one. As students are, I was still quite sensitive to the opinion of my peers. I would simply say farewell on the last day of training, and walk away. Nor did I tell Art of my decision, though I supposed he already knew. I began walking like Art, coat open, stooped forward, charging the halls like him. I even attempted his gruff-tender tone of hard-edged affection. I could feel my heart opening to the children, a timid advance at first and tentative at best. But gradually they became for me more than mere cases: at first patients, they then became children, and finally *my* children, whom I grew to love unreservedly. Art seemed to know better than to address my intention. I was like the renegade wolf entering the fold, sniffing at the periphery with suspicion, ever cautious, always ready to bolt. Art pretended indifference, standing the ridge, scenting the winds, obliquely welcoming me.

There is in academic medicine a time-honored tradition called the attending's dinner. At the end of a rotation on the wards, or in the laboratory—wherever it is the student finds himself—when the professor has finished his round of teaching, he sponsors a get-together for the students and residents on his service. This may be at the professor's club, in a teak-paneled room, where residents address him by his first name, and smoke cigars with acquired importance, while the medical students look on in admiration. There are martinis at the sideboard, and Ronald is ready with the canapés. Or perhaps it will be a well-appointed restaurant, with the linen and sterling just so. The professor, comforted by the familiarity of the staff, samples his favorite chardonnay, and talks of university life.

In this tradition Art invited me to his apartment for dinner in celebration of our three months' service on the wards together. Art entertained infrequently if at all, and never before for a potential protégé. His own excitement filled his rooms. He had overdone everything. For the two of us he had laid out a separate bottle of wine for each of the four courses he had planned, and a crusty bottle of old Port for later on. He had more food than six people might have consumed, flowers, candles, and silver resurrected from some attic storage, with spice trays and a mountain of fresh fruit—to complement, he explained self-consciously, a special bottle of Sauternes. Art had an immense collection of jazz, a passion no one at the hospital had ever known about: volume upon volume of Peetie Wheatstraw, Blind Lemon Jefferson, and Sleepy John Estes. He was clearly partial to blues. But what began as a fascinating exploration in harmonics ended hours later on one long note of heavy sadness.

It started with the third bottle of wine. The two of us had fairly split the first bottle, a heavily perfumed Alsatian. Feeling the effects of the alcohol, I had only sipped at the second, while Art consumed most of it. He was well into the third bottle, some obscure Italian red, when he began his diatribe.

"This isn't an easy job, you know," he confessed. "There will be hard moments. You just can't know. It's when you think you have the battle won, that He takes it all away from you. I'll tell you about a case," he said, pointing at me with the wine cork.

"I had a young man with Hodgkin's Disease on Q-3. He was about twenty-eight . . . had a pretty wife, no kids yet, up-town parents. He had come to me early in his disease. I sent him for radiotherapy. They toasted him, but within a year he was back to me with advanced disease . . . very advanced. I gave him the standard protocols and he remitted for a few months, only to recur. I gave him stronger stuff, made him sick as hell, but apparently he became disease-free. I was congratulating myself and his family was happy, ecstatic. You get the idea.

"A few months later he was back to me with some cervical nodes which I should have biopsied but didn't and which I figured was recurrent lymphoma. I treated him with an experimental protocol, and killed him with it. At autopsy he had no evidence of Hodgkin's disease anywhere. Just a simple infection. He had been a cure and I killed him with drugs when I should have treated him for a simple goddamn infection. That's what's diabolical about this business. Di-a-BOL-i-cal."

Art went back to his wine, quietly reflecting upon his wounds. I was ready with all sorts of excuses, with the academic's rationalizations about the intricacies of the case and its unusual evolution. But Art had grabbed his wine glass and was already up and pacing the length of the room. I became apprehensive, aware of the creeping anxiety one might feel when about to violate some cabalistic tract on The Forbidden Secrets of Mankind. I was suddenly sober.

"I had a young woman with sarcoma. Sarcoma is as common as hell in our business, boy" (he had begun calling me boy when he had sensed that I had become his disciple), "but this girl couldn't have any *ordinary* sarcoma. No! She was twenty-two, beautiful as hell and newly married. She came to me with her husband. He was obviously crazy about her, couldn't get close enough to her or stop looking at her, and she told me about the lump in her vagina. Could I tell her what it was, she asked me. Her doctor had sent her to me, believing that I could. That type of thing. She had a sarcoma of the pelvic floor, nine centimeters wide. What we were feeling in her vagina was just the tip of the iceberg. So instead of her lying under some apple tree with the sun in her face, looking up at that handsome buck of hers, she was in a hospital bed retching her guts out from my medicine, her hair in clumps in the trash can. Why couldn't it have been some old lady who had a full life with plenty of kids and enough of her husband— why couldn't she get have gotten this sarcoma? Why did it have to be this young girl just at the beginning? Do you see my point? That's where the torment is, you see. That's what makes it diabolical." The word grated in his teeth. "Don't you see how He was laughing at me?"

I looked around the apartment as if to find some convenient route of escape. These were problems I didn't want to hear about, questions I didn't have answers for. Art, sensing my impatience, renewed his arguments as though finally to convince me.

"I had a patient, an opera singer, a baritone, who was sent to me with what were assumed to be singer's nodules. Singer's nodules . . . sure. It was cancer of the larynx, that's what he had. Here's a guy who could make men weep with his arias, who had graced the air at Carnegie Hall, whose voice was his very essence. *Sure* we could cure him. But the timbre of his voice was irretrievably lost. Now he's teaching music somewhere. Tell me that's random. Tell me that's a simple act of Nature."

Art peeled the foil from the neck of his bottle of Sauternes.

He aligned the corkscrew with his shaking hands, and drove the screw down. Popping the cork he turned back to me, pointing the corkscrew, waving it, and then let it fall to his side.

"I used to pray, you know," he said. "I used to pray for every goddamn one of them. But He just mocked me."

I felt like the timid child who surprises a parent in the secret throes of some private grief, a parent who, face contorted, wracked with sobs, has suddenly assumed some other identity. I didn't want to see Art this way, and yet in some horrible manner I was fascinated by it. Having little religion myself, and even less experience of life, I didn't have any answers for him.

"Maybe God just isn't a part of all of this," I said, shrugging, raising my eyebrows hopefully, playing the optimistic child. Art had overfilled his wineglass, and spilled some of the wine on his shirt-front, gulping down most of what was left.

"Coconut," he said.

"Pardon me?," I asked.

"Mangoes, papayas, and coconuts . . . botrytis. This wine smells like coconuts. Climens. KLEE-MENS. A-MENDS. Make amends. Rends . . . rending . . . heart-rending. It's all heart-rending."

I began to make ready my escape. He stopped me with a look.

"You think it's all random, don't you?," he said to me. "Well it isn't random at all. I have found that out, *mister*. I have learned *that* on this job. Why is it the gourmet who get cancer of the tongue, and the lady with the perfect smile, a squamous cell cancer of the face?

"Why does the breathtaking model have to have a cancer of the breast, or the scholar, dementia? Can you deny the design? The *diabolical* design?

"Wait, boy, before you go," Art said, trying to catch me as I moved toward the door, mumbling thanks and excuses, "Will you have any of this?" He held out the bottle of Sauternes to me. I refused.

"Listen, boy," Art said again, "I'm sorry about all this. It's been a rough sea. I had to talk about it. It's been eating at me. One more case . . . please . . .

"I had another patient, not too long ago. A lovely little girl. She had a double disability—both deaf and blind. She was so sweet . . . so very, very sweet. Devoted parents. They could communicate with her only by writing in her palm. In the palm of her right hand. She loved to read. She read all the Braille books they could get for her. They brought her to see me. She had widely metastatic bone cancer. She'd sit there on the examining table erect and polite, quiet, waiting for some sign of me. As soon as I touched her, she'd know that I'd come into the room and her face would light up. She'd turn in my general direction, smiling, holding out her palm for me to "talk" to her. The palm of her right hand was her only link to the rest of us. I'd ask her about her puppy, tell her she looked especially pretty that day. That type of thing. It took me a while to get across to her, and I never got very good at it. But her mother would often ask what I had written if I couldn't get through, and then write it again for me. Anna, the little girl, would answer me in her soft, moaning whisper that only her mother could really understand, and could translate for me.

"She had very advanced disease when she came to me, so there wasn't much I could do for her. But the tumor went to her chest and she developed a tremendous swelling of her arms. And then her hands became terribly swollen. We couldn't relieve the swelling with radiation therapy. Her fingers were left 'sightless,' and her palms became insensitive to touch. She was cut off from all of us completely and forever. And she was forced to die alone."

Art was subdued now, introspective. He held his empty glass, tipped, against his waist, and stared out at the lights of the traffic in the streets down below. His agitation was gone, his anger dissipated. All that was left was a heavy sadness.

Had he been a contemporary, I might have said I understood, even though I didn't, or I might have sympathized with him. I might have reached out to him. I might have tried to love him.

But I was so caught up in my own emotion, so shocked by his hidden identity, that the moment of healing passed.

In the months that followed, I became aware that the laboratory was the proper place for me. It would offer a tremendous challenge—that was where it was really happening in medicine, that was where I could do the greatest good for the greatest number. I could teach the residents, spend a month each year caring for patients, presiding at the bedside. I would develop new drugs and new protocols, cross-fertilizing with colleagues at the conferences, always up to date with the literature, training young doctors, and still, on occasion, involve myself with patients.

An occasional nod was all that passed between Art and me anymore. The evening of his confession was like a blemish to be hidden away. On his part, Art filled his days with patients, as always. I hardly noticed him as he hurried off to the wards, white coat flailing behind him, charging off to fight his war.

The hospital was his. He could click down the long corridors and imagine the good old days, those times of running to get to the bedside just in time, the moments of electric thought, of right procedure, of kinship felt with fellow house officers. On this night he could be back there long ago, feel young, bold, and quick of mind. Once more he could be doctor to these kids.

Why did it seem that his internship was only yesterday? Why was his long marathon to the academic peaks now a mere sprint in time? From where did this feeling of poignancy arise, this sense that tonight's brief role fit him best? Certainly he prized his present administration and teaching position and the spark of power it gave to him. But why, each year, at Christmas time, when the house staff looked to their seniors for coverage, was he always the first to volunteer? Certainly for Shulman the atheist, Christmas Eve meant nothing. But to be a house officer! That filled him with excitement at this time of year. Weeks before, he would dive into the manuals of critical care, feeling his excitement build.

He loved the closeness of patient care, the intimacy of families, the nursing staff. The rest of the year, reams of paper, hours of meetings, legions of doctors, consultants, and residents came between him and patients. But every Christmas Eve he could be alone again with them. Yet more than loving patients, he loved children. At a time of terrible illness it was they who showed consummate dignity, utter honesty, and a beautiful simplicity as an example for the rest of us. They were, these little people, humankind at its very best. And Shulman adored them.

Shulman rounded a yawning corridor as his beeper sounded. Eagerly, he answered the page. A request to come to Widener-Seven . . . could he come right away? The oncology wing, he thought—an IV to get started, or chemotherapy to be pushed, possibly an opportunistic infection to diagnose and treat . . . or worse.

"Thank you for coming so quickly, Dr. Shulman," said Miss O'Sullivan. "We have a patient with Ewing's in 727 who's asking to see a doctor." The nurse hesitated before the senior scientist, then continued, "She hasn't very long, Dr. Shulman."Shulman and the nurse entered the girl's room. She looked about eleven years old, 'once-pretty,' thought Shulman, ravaged now by her disease, ravaged by Medicine. He saw her dull, listless eyes, her dry, chapped lips, the bony, ecchymotic arms. Her parents sat at her side, her father's fists clenched, her mother biting her lower lip, sitting erect in her chair.

"What . . . how can I help?" asked Shulman.

"Lisa has asked to see a doctor," her mother said. "We told her we'd call a minister, but Lisa wanted to see a doctor."

"Doctors know more than ministers," said Lisa quietly.

Shulman glanced at the mother's imploring eyes, nodded an assent, and pulled a chair next to the dying girl's bed. The girl let him take her hand. Shulman looked at her, suddenly saw his own daughter, saw a million healthy girls, vibrant, active girls pirouetting before mirrors, girls with dreams, with boyfriends, with dances to go to, with hair to brush, a million healthy girls with futures full of wedding gowns and children of their own. He saw this girl with no future at all, felt his own emotion begin to drown his intellect. He looked down, away, swallowed and struggled within himself. Then he said to her, "Well, I'm a doctor. I admit I am an older doctor, older perhaps than you are used to, but still I'm a doctor."

"Older doctors are smarter," said Lisa.

What was her game, thought Shulman? She was too young to be desperate for cure at this stage in her illness. Her parents might demand the best and brightest for just one last chance, but certainly not the child.

"Why are you looking for a smart doctor?" asked Shulman.

"I wanted to ask what it's like to die," said Lisa.

Shulman shifted uncomfortably in his chair. How to approach this, he wondered. The child is frightened of dying, of the nothingness beyond, and old enough to begin to wonder. Should he begin by talking about the absence of pain, about the gentle sleep to come?

"Are you . . . do you have a religion?" asked Shulman.

"We're not a religious family, Doctor," answered the girl's father. "We have never been much for churches."

Neither had he, thought Shulman. Well, that made it easier.

"Will I see God soon?" asked the girl. Shulman the atheist shifted again. There was no pleading in the girl's eyes, no desperation, no panic. Only her immense fatigue. That and her questioning. She wanted some answers from a smart doctor.

"Well," said Shulman, "I really think that it's better to think of it as . . . "

"What I mean is, will I see God first or Jesus first?" asked the girl.

Shulman looked at the girl's parents, then at the charge nurse, saw the tears welling up in O'Sullivan's eyes. He licked his own dry lips, hesitated, looked away, gathering his thoughts. Where was his science now? In which manual lay the solution to this clinical problem? How could he paint in pastels a picture of nothingness for a hopeless little girl? Shulman began his answer.

"You always see Jesus first. That's the way it works in Heaven. I know about these things. You see, Jesus will be so happy to see you that he can hardly wait. He rushes right out as soon as you get there, to give you a big hug."

The girl smiled faintly. "What is he like . . . Jesus, I mean?"

Shulman was into it now. He caught the girl in his own glow, mesmerizing her, elevating her, washing her with dancing colors.

"Have you ever been lost, or out in the cold, or away on a long trip and very tired, and you finally come home and walk in and there's your dad or your big brother . . . "

"He's like my big brother?" Lisa asked.

"Well, yes, Jesus is just like that, just like your big brother, and there is this feeling around him, that you are home and safe and he will protect you and everything's fine now."

Lisa shifted in bed. "What's Heaven like? Is it really all clouds or is it a big building like a hospital or what?"

Shulman the agnostic leaned forward. Momentarily distracted by O'Sullivan's quiet sobbing, still he managed a chuckle.

"Heaven's not like a hospital! Heaven's a wonderful place. You just can't believe the grass, how green the grass is, and how perfect the weather! The sun always shines there and gives everything a golden color. It's warm and you can always go outside. You never need a coat. And everybody is your friend, your very best friend. . . .

"In fact, I wish I could go there with you right now."

Shulman sat back in his chair, utterly drained. O'Sullivan had turned to the window. The girl's parents sat with heads bowed. Lisa smiled to herself, shifted again in bed, and fell asleep, leaving the adults to themselves.

Why she called me first I never figured out. Maybe she had more brains than I ever gave her credit for. All she had said was, "My husband has passed away, Doctor. Can you come over?"

That was it: flat monotone, no emotion, just matter-of-fact. Now I'm one of those old-fashioned doctors that still makes house calls on certain occasions, and this was definitely one of those occasions. I could feel it in the pit of my stomach. I grabbed my clothes, got dressed in the bathroom so as not to wake my wife, brushed the snow from the car, and headed over to their farm. A storm had passed through unannounced, leaving snow everywhere. It was the kind of night where, once you get out into it, you're glad you're there—everything blanketed in rolling white, not a rift in the cover—so cold and clear the stars hang down out of the sky just above the snow. On a night like that, you had trouble believing there could be any evil in the world.

From the bend in the road I could see the light from their kitchen off over, sparkling down the crystals of snow. I pulled the car in at the barest suggestion of a driveway, turned off the motor, and pushed through the drifts up to the porch. I let myself in. The house was quiet as a tomb. The kitchen clock gave off a quiet hum. On the face of the refrigerator were plastered the kids' school papers: spelling tests and arithmetic, maps colored in Crayola and the minimal art-work of the early grades. There was a 'Mom-Dad-and-Me' family portrait— 'Mom' about a quarter the size of 'Dad,' who occupied center stage, and 'Me' off to the side, a stick figure without arms—no mouth drawn in. I stepped through the kitchen and found Kitty sitting in the darkened living room in a straight backed chair, staring off, trance-like, in shock maybe. What appeared to be small marbles lay scattered on the carpet. I picked one up. It was a pearl.

"Where's Earl?" I asked her.

"In the bedroom?" said Kitty. She always said everything as though it were a question. She motioned with her head.

"Where are the kids?"

"At my sister's?" she answered.

"You alright?" I asked.

She nodded.

I took a deep breath and headed into the bedroom, expecting the worst, and wasn't disappointed. Earl lay supine on the bed, a bullet hole above his right ear. The left half of his cranium and its contents were splattered next to him on the bedroom wall. I began to run a cold sweat. Even after all the years of small-town practice, being called in for mangled bodies and auto wrecks, botched amateur abortions, deceased elderly pensioners not found for days, and — worst of all — the abused children — that, worst of all — despite all of that hardening up, a scene like this still could weaken you at the knees. I swallowed against the sweat, looked away, looked back again, and had to look away. It was hard to stay clinical. Doctors have trouble with violent death. Disease we learn to accept. But not this.

I surveyed the scene. Earl's .30-.30 Winchester lay on the floor just inside the door. A half-empty bottle of Schenley's stood next to the bed, within easy reach. Earl lay on the bed fully dressed, shoes on, with that eternal gaze that can make your skin crawl.

The rest of the room was precise and neat. The top of the bureau was uncluttered: a brush, a comb, a mirror, all arranged just so, and an ash tray full of change. A wedding picture of Kitty and Earl stood off to the side. The bedside table held a small reading lamp, the shade a shocking white against the dark streaks of Earl's blood on the wall. There was a Bible and an old cloth bound book, its title faded, and a pair of woman's reading glasses folded on top. There were no clothes lying about. The closet doors were closed. The window drapes hung just so. All this tidiness framing the mess of Earl's body.

I went back out to the living room to Kitty. She hadn't moved a muscle, except that her eyes had the look of a cornered mouse.

"What happened?" I asked her.

"He shot himself?" Kitty answered.

"Shot himself," I said.

She nodded.

"Kitty . . . " my voice trailed off. I sat down in a chair opposite her and looked at her for a long minute.

"Kitty, we go way back don't we?"

She nodded again.

Some thirty years ago I had brought her into this world, supported her through her mother's premature death, and twenty years later, delivered babies of her own. I had seen her boy through a bad case of spinal meningitis, and harped at her father's cigarette smoking, in the end burying him because of it.

But, through the most of it there had been Kitty. She held the record for most abused woman in Taylor County. There had been the time I had hospitalized her for a hairline fracture of the left mandibular ramus, a both-bones fracture of the right forearm, and God knows how many internal injuries, for the better part of a week. We had Earl all wrapped up and ready to send down to the state prison. And then Kitty wouldn't sign the papers. The night I hospitalized her from that episode I stopped by her father's house just to check on things. Al was in a murderous rage. I could hardly blame him.

"I'm going to kill the son of a bitch. I'm going to kill the son of a bitch," was all he kept muttering. He'd look at me with his reddened, burning eyes, and I knew he meant it.

"Al," I said, "you do that and you'll wind up in prison yourself."

"I don't give a damn," he said.

"And Earl will get off."

"Earl will be dead," he answered.

"And your grandchildren will hate you for the rest of their lives," I said, "for killing their father."

At that, the hardness left him and he gave it up.

"I'm going to tell you something else, Al," I said. "In two weeks Kitty will be right back with him and there isn't a damn thing you can do about it."

Soon Kitty did go back with Earl. You had trouble saying whose sickness was worse. But there was no question about Kitty's suffering. Or her father's. It was the same scenario for some ten years, Kitty coming into the emergency room, badly beaten, meekly asking to see me, Al flying into a rage, and, in the early years, loading up his gun, resolving to put Earl away, later resigning himself to this terrible disease that both Earl and Kitty were torturing him with. Two other times Kitty had been so severely beaten that she required hospitalization. Each time we got the town police involved, had Earl arrested, had the complaint papers all filled out. All sealed, and delivered, except that Kitty would never sign the papers. And she always went back to him.

"You know, Doc," said the Chief of Police one day, "some day one of these two is going to wind up dead."

Kitty shifted in her chair and brought me back to the darkened living room. I turned to look at her. I was her doctor, her family's doctor. She'd level with me.

"What really happened?" I asked her.

"I heard the gun go off?" she said. "I went in. And he was dead."

"I didn't see a suicide note, Kitty," I said, pressing her. "Did he leave a note? People usually leave a note in these situations."

"No," she said. "There wasn't any note." Her voice fell. As tentative as she was, Kitty wouldn't budge. I thought later, looking back on it, that this was probably the first time in her life she had made up her mind and stuck to it.

"Kitty . . . " I didn't know what else to say to her. She shifted nervously in the chair and I saw her wince. She held her left arm close to her body.

There she was, Al's little girl—everybody's little girl. I could remember Kitty skipping into my office at five full of happiness and life, for her preschool shots, and coming in again at twelve, the apple of her daddy's eye, for her camp physical. We were there, Al and I, on that crisp November day when Kitty bagged her first deer. And I sat at the head table, at her wedding reception—she and Earl the handsome couple—Kitty proudly wearing her mother's string of pearls that Al had surprised her with on that day. And after that all those hospital admissions . . . Kitty . . . most abused woman in the whole county.

But there was a lot more that went into this case. There had been Leon Tilley's murder two years before. He had been found dead in his hay field, two bullet holes at the base of his skull, relieved of a large amount of cash. For a year nothing happened. Tilley had been one popular old man, the kind of Norman Rockwell farmer everybody stops to talk to, wisdom written all over his face. The town was pretty unhappy with what they saw as police inaction. Then four teenagers and a drug dealer were apprehended and the papers were filled with yellow journalism for six months: stories of bad cops, bar-flies, drugs, and witnesses who lied. The kind of stuff that's not supposed to happen in the country. The whole county salivated. After all the publicity, the big-city lawyers, and back-room deals, the D.A. managed only one conviction. Now everybody was still screaming for the police chief's head and small-time entrepreneurs were getting rich selling T-shirts that read:

"Come to Herkimer and get away with murder."

I looked at Kitty, and then into the bedroom, then back at Kitty again. I nodded to myself. Yes indeed, I thought, the Chief would dearly love to get his hands on this one. He needed this one.

One time back along, I had a bad baby on my hands, a newborn with hydrocephalus and a big cyst at the base of the neck—the crippled-for-life kind of baby you see once in a lifetime. I watched that baby struggle and watched and didn't do a damn thing to save it and apologized to the family afterwards, explaining it was a still-born, lying to them. That was the one time I played God and it aggravated me, I can tell you. I went home that night and yelled at my wife, kicked the dog, and drank too much—brooded for weeks and never talked about it. It can eat at you. There had never been a second time until Kitty.

I grabbed one of the kitchen chairs and a dish towel and went back into the bedroom. In a few minutes I was on the phone and had the dispatcher get a hold of the Chief. Shortly he was at the other end of the line, sleepy, gruff, trying to be important.

"Chief," I said, "I'm at Earl Staples' house. He's finally done himself in. He got drunk and shot himself with his deer rifle . . . yeah, I'm at the house now . . . well, it looks to me like he rested the gun on a chair next to the bed, and then lay himself down and shot himself in the temple. Clear suicide in my book. I'll be signing it out that way . . . Yeah, she's here with me. I'll drive her over to her sister's. I'd sure appreciate it if you'd send one of your men over here to clean things up . . . Thanks Chief."

I put the phone down and turned back to Kitty. She was staring at the floor. She hadn't moved. I sighed, slapped my thighs, and got up to go.

"Where's your coat, Kitty? I'll drive you over to Kate's, and in the morning," I said, nodding to her left arm, "you come over to the office so I can set that fracture for you one last time."

It isn't that bad in here. Really. Well, maybe if I tell you what I do, then you'll get the idea. I have many favorite things and one unfavorite thing. I'll tell you about my favorite things first.

Walking in the woods is a favorite thing. I never thought it would be, because before this, hanging out was what we always did and if I ever said let's go for a walk in the woods they'd have made fun of me. The other kids I mean. But now I love it. It's not hard to be in here and still smell the woods. Tree-smells, that's easy. But there are other things too, don't forget. Rotting wood is one, and that's totally *awesome*, and mushrooms on rotting wood are even better. You *can* smell mushrooms, you know.

Then there's the smell I call the old attic smell, kind of mysterious and mixtures of things, dusty and all. I think the old attic smell is your basic woods smell but everybody misses it because they're always sniffing the pine and they smell right *by* it, you know. And don't forget animals. You can actually smell animals if you concentrate. And it's easy to concentrate here where I am, of course. I have *that* advantage. Animal smells are like wet dogs, only fainter. You just get a whiff. But it's exciting when it happens.

Then I go to sounds and the woods *really* get awesome. First the birds. They're obvious. I start with a *chirrr-chirrr-chirrr* of a bird way up high in a tree—you know, loud but far off. And then I go in with a *keeer-keeer-rr* from a hawk and maybe I'll throw in an owl even though it's daytime, because I like owls anyway. Then I'll hear a snap of a twig off over and I imagine a deer creeping. I like to get into the rustle of leaves too and I love the creaking the trees make in the wind.

Then I let myself see, and everything in here gets green and full of ferns and branches. And I'm totally in the woods! I see a few animals besides the birds—I don't overdo it. Small animals like red squirrels and chipmunks, and maybe once a week, a fisher-cat. I look for violets. I don't know what they're called but I call them my woods-violets. I never pick them. I leave them there for the next time.

There's other favorite times too besides the woods. Like being with my older sister who I used to hate her guts but now I can say I love her. And we are teasing each other and trying on each other's clothes and she tells me about her boyfriend and listens to me about boys too. That's when I feel like we're best friends forever. Being with my sister is different than the woods from in here because I feel sadness too, even though it's a favorite time. I can't explain it any better than that. I'm sorry.

And I'll find out what month it is from in here and I imagine what's going on in school which I also used to hate but now I miss. Even the teachers. I'll have on a new blouse with my blue sweater and I can hear the kids laughing and yelling to me as I get off the bus. We call at each other over the street and run up the steps to the school building which is full of smells of its own: chalk and dusty erasers, the polish on the old wood floors, the new-book smells and cedar pencils. And there's cafeteria, and Jimmy sits with me.

My nurse is a favorite thing too. She always, *always* talks to me like she believes that I can hear her and I'm listening to her. And she answers for me. She seems to know what I'm thinking.

"Well, Emily," she'll say, "I'll bet you want me to brush that pretty hair of yours again today, don't you?" And then she answers for me, "Yes, Miss Proctor, I'd love you to." She hums to me which I love and she's very gentle when she moves me. I love my nurse.

My most favorite time sounds corny. But it's special and I'll tell you about it if you won't laugh. I imagine God in my head and then He comes in here with me and stays with me for as long as I want. Sometimes for hours. Sometimes a whole day if there are no visitors. I feel wonderful when this happens, when I have a day like that with Him. I can imagine all sorts of colors: reds, yellows, rich golden colors, like the fall colors on the trees. And smells too, happy smells: wild flowers and hay, or leaves burning in the fall, or my mom's perfume and my dad's pipe. I never got close to God like this before the accident. I don't know why. I was too busy, I guess. Now it's special. I wouldn't give it up for the world. I can't say much more about it—it's more a feeling than anything else. I feel safe, and warm, and not alone, and I feel loved and kind of wanted. Oh, I know my parents love me and want me back. But this is a different kind of being wanted. Like, I belong to Him and everything is okay. And when He's with me, I'm a patient person, for some reason. It's a wonderful feeling, I'll tell you. Sure, I'd rather be sitting with Jimmy in the cafeteria, you know. If you want to know the truth. But I don't have a choice, do I?

Now I'd better tell you about my unfavorite time. My parents come to visit a lot. Well, not as much as right after the accident. But a lot. And sometimes one of the doctors will come in when they are here and he will start talking to my dad about me. It's always the same thing. They talk about me and vegetables which I don't understand, and how there's no hope, which I do understand. And the doctor will say every time that he wishes he could pull the plug but he can't because the law won't let him and I think he means unplugging my breathing machine. That gets me scared because I don't think I could breathe any more without my machine which would probably mean I would die, wouldn't I? My mom doesn't say anything when Dad talks to the doctor about me this way. But she cries, so I know the whole thing is pretty sad for her. Then I keep wishing I could tell her about the woods.

Somewhere in a northern stream, a last cake of ice dislodges, hesitates, turns slowly, and rushes to the sea. Coy-dogs roam the ridges in instinctive strategy. An old Finn on bowed legs grins a toothless grin at next year's wood pile. Finding just the right sort of mud, a pair of barn swallows begin their summer home. The phone rings at 3 A.M. and a weary doctor decides he'd better go in. Aphrodite from the waters, a cow moose lifts herself draining from a pond and, crashing through the woods, goes wherever moose will go.

*With mechanical deliberation, an emergency room physician opens his mouth wide and fires a .38 caliber bullet through his palate and brain.*

Two Herefords, chewing thoroughly, chat across a barbed-wire fence. An elderly couple, hand in hand, walk an old woods road, searching for mushrooms. The town studs, filled with the deer-rifle's phallic potency, head out to bag an eagle. A lucky adolescent boy on the mend gazes absently out a hospital window and decides to become a doctor. Hovering in the shade of an undercut bank, a redspot lazily sips mayflies. Energetic graduates of the University's law school begin to look for work. Factories of bolete and entoloma remodel the forest floor. High above, a goshawk tucks, and dives.

*His wife and children stand in the rain at the edge of the open grave, not hearing The Word, and fail to understand.*

In a small hospital at the edge of pine, a family practitioner lays a crying bundle at the breast of a young mother. A young girl squints at Katahdin's summit, smiles at her father, and adjusts her pack with resolute determination. Winter ended, Nature paints her hills rufous, blue, and purple. "Conk-a-ree," call the redwings. "Mee-did-it," answers the chickadee. A white-haired man ties on a Royal Coachman, takes another nip from his flask, and casts to a rise. Piercing last October's detritus, spears of wild iris reach for light. An osprey hunches in the sun, drying his primaries, and waits for his next meal.

*"He must have been depressed," explains his attorney.*

A doe drinks the melted snow, pauses, listens, sniffs the wind, turns, and is gone. Three boys in a pick-up get some six-packs and drive off to meet an abutment, the front page, eternity. A young musician practices his scales. Seeing board-feet in the beech and pulp-wood in the pine, a developer plans his condos. Turned out at last, a chestnut filly runs in the meadow.

*Now anticipating an easy settlement, the claims representative cancels the deposition and leaves the day open for shopping.*

Like silver darts in the dusk, rainbow fry leap for hovering stoneflies. A surgeon sits quietly in the dark, holding the spotted hand of her dying patient. Watching his boss drive off, a senior vice-president decides it's time to trade up. With strong hands, the farmer dries off a new-born calf, while fireflies wink in the night.

*"Pleasant coastal Maine town seeks ER physician; good pay, low hours; BC/BS, malpractice coverage, other benefits."*

Under cover of a leaf, a field mouse plots a dash across the open. Apples ripen in the sun. A woman disrobes, and with dignity and trust, shows her doctor the cancer.

*Thankfully their pagers sound and his colleagues are free to leave the funeral.*

In regal contentment, a black bear munches on fiddlehead ferns. On the barn roof, tree swallows mate in the morning mist. Bobolinks scold on general principle, reveling in summer, sun, and pasture.

*"It's just the cost of doing business," says the plaintiff's attorney.*

Along a strip of coast in southern California, in the land of mantras and personal space, two men sat quietly sipping coffee. Neither spoke a word. Having checked out of their hotel, and with many hours to wait before the funeral, they had searched among the T-shirt venders, surfboard rentals, and gaudy motels for some quiet place to brood. So deep was their own sadness that it did not occur to them how out of place was this French *boulangerie* where they now sat, a café filled with the scent of strong coffee, fresh *baguettes*, and Brie.

The heavier, balding man looked across the table at his friend, saying nothing, fixing him with a miserable look, and then sighed and looked away. He surveyed the pastries in the open cooler, commenting to himself that even they could not awaken his usually voracious appetite. His companion turned sideways, elbow on the table, chin on his fist, and spoke, as if to empty space.

"We knew he would eventually die. Hell, even *Jim* knew he would die. He knew it five years ago."

"Doesn't make it any easier, does it," said the balding man. "Bob, I feel angry. Why do I feel angry?"

"Everybody gets angry when someone they love dies. You know that. The injustice, the deprivation, the imposition of grief . . . Christ, you know that better than anyone, in your business," said Bob.

"Yeah, but I don't really mean *that* anger. That anger is over here." The balding man cupped his hands together in the air as if to pigeon-hole this distinct emotion. "It's another anger. It's a more personal anger. Not the anger about Miranda and the boys being left alone, not the anger about Jim dying in his prime, or having to suffer the way he did the past five years, jumping through all the hoops of medical therapy, for nothing, as it turns out. It's not that kind of anger, I don't think."

The balding man paused, sipped his coffee, and looked off out the window, squinting against the sun and his own unwelcome tears.

"You know Bob, I don't even want one of those Napoleons." He gestured toward the pastries. "What the hell's wrong with me?"

"Why can't you just grieve like everybody else, Michel?" said Bob.

"Because I am no ordinary mortal, pal. Because I am a doctor, a man of steel. I am not expected to hurt, not allowed to be sad, not permitted to cry with the family at the bedside. Maybe that's why I'm angry." He shifted in his chair and continued.

"A few months ago I had a patient die on me. An old lady with cancer. I had taken care of her for fifteen years. Fifteen years. That's a long time. She knitted socks for me . . . brought me custard pies at Christmas . . . that type of thing. She knew I liked custard pie. I liked her. A lot. The night she died I was with her. She was in a coma, taking her last breath, her family all around her. Her nurse was there, a young nurse new to the hospital, new to her job. I saw the nurse's hands gripping the side-rail of the bed. Her knuckles were white. I knew this death was going to be tough on her. You know, in the dying process there is that sudden moment of absence: the absence of sound, of breathing, of any quickening whatsoever, a stall—when death arrives. Well, death came rushing in, and I heard a daughter catch her breath, heard another daughter sob, watched a son sniff and turn to the window. I nodded to the patient's husband, indicating it was over. I didn't want to say that she was dead. I didn't want to say the words. Each family member fell into the arms of another, as though they had rehearsed the scene. Each held the other, comforting, soothing, stroking, murmuring to one another. The young nurse streaked out of the room, tears streaming from her eyes. I followed her out. At the nurses' station an older nurse scooped this kid up in her arms and walked her to their coffee room. I stood in the corridor and watched them, watched the older nurses console this sobbing girl, as hens over a troubled chick. I stood out there in the corridor and watched them. And I felt very much alone.

"Maybe I just want someone to feel sorry for me," continued Michel. "We're going to be at that service this afternoon and we are going to have to console everybody else. Christ, for once I would just like to break down and cry. Just be goddamn weak. You know?" Michel's voice broke. He had to leave this line of thinking. He sipped his coffee, appraised the women at the next table and straightened his tie.

"When we first got here," he continued, changing the subject, "I thought San Diego was the best kept secret in the world. Now I don't like it. Be good to get back to my woods."

"How about a run on the beach every morning, every day of the year?" said Bob. "You could get into that, couldn't you? No snow to bother with? The sun on your face? Be kind of nice here, I would think."

"You have to have *seasons*, Bobby, *seasons*. *Change*. Where the hell is the poet in you? Christ, you're blessed with the face of Seamus Heaney and cursed with the mind of a scientist. You can't have all this *sameness*, Bob: all this perfection, every damn woman stunning, every day a brilliant blue, every breeze pacific."

"Listen to what you are saying, Michel. Listen to your own words. You trying to be a poet? Is there such a creature as a French-Canadian poet? Or is that an oxymoron?" asked Bob.

Michel managed a tight smile, and then both men fell silent. The waitress returned to their table with a pot of coffee, offering refills.

"You gentlemen are not *from* 'ere," she said. She pronounced the *g* softly, pouting her lips as she spoke. She obviously went with the territory. "You are, I *sink*, from *za east-coast*."

"Can we be that obvious?" asked Bob. He looked around at the shorts and sandals at the other tables, then nodded at Michel's formal suit. "Yeah, I guess we're that obvious. I'm from New York. Michel is from Maine."

"Michel?" the waitress said, smiling, moving closer.

"*Je regrette. Je ne parle pas Français.* Sorry," said Michel.

"What you are doing 'ere in San Diego, you two?" She sat

down, tapping her full lower lip with a long, red fingernail. French women are different, thought Michel.

"Business," said Bob.

"No, not *za* business I *sink*. You are too sad for *zat*, non?" She watched them both carefully, raising an eyebrow. Michel looked up at her. Suddenly she seemed beautiful to him. He hadn't noticed that before.

"Give me your hand, mon petit," she said to Michel, "and I will play *za* fortune *tellaire*." She took Michel's reluctant hand and looked at it pensively.

"You have *zees* finger bump . . . you are a *writaire*?"

"I'm a doctor. We're both doctors," said Michel, "except my friend here kills mice for a living."

"Kills mice?" asked the waitress.

"Cute little white ones. Never mind. It's a long story."

"So you are 'ere for *za* meeting of medicines, non? But *zat* would not make you sad, I *sink*."

"You've never been to a medical meeting," said Bob.

"We came here for the funeral of a friend," said Michel. "A guy we went to school with. He died last weekend. Leukemia . . . a cancer of the blood. The service is this afternoon."

"*Mon Dieu!* So young he was? But you are making *za beeg mees-take wiss zees* coffee. I get Richard." At once she had left the table and was gone.

Within minutes a thin older man, unmistakably French, with neatly trimmed moustache, approached the table with a courtly bow. He held two wine glasses inverted in one hand and a bottle of wine in the other.

"Linnette has sent me. I am Richard Vidal, at your service," said the man with a nod of his head. His English was impeccable.

"Linnette?" asked Bob.

"Marie-Linnette Laballière. Your waitress. She comes from St. Dié . . . she is a treasure. She seems to have an eye for these things, always." Richard motioned at the two men, holding the wine bottle and glasses toward them.

"She knows wine?" asked Michel.

"No," said Richard, "situations. She knows situations."

"*Mes amis*," Richard continued, "you cannot bury your friend with coffee. Such an occasion demands the best of wines. And—*voilà!*—I happen to have the best of wines for you—a Guigal *Cote de Rhone.*

"Linnette, another glass, *s'il vous plait*," said Richard, deciding at the last minute that the bottle was indeed too good for him to pass up. Linnette had returned with a platter of cheeses, each of which she introduced with a flourish of her hand as though announcing dignitaries from the provinces.

"*Ici* Reblochon, and *zees za* Montrachet, and here *za* Livarot, and . . . ," she held a finger and thumb to her lips, kissing them with a smack, " *ici* Tomme de Savoie." She was off again, and returned with *two* more glasses, and a second bottle of wine.

"Now, gentlemen," said Richard, having poured them each a glass and swirling his own before his Gallic nose, " tell me what you smell from this wine. Tell me what is there for you. Nothing more than that."

"I smell a spice, maybe . . . " ventured Bob.

"Cinnamon," said Linnette. "Cinnamon and acacia. Yum-yum!"

"There is a fruit there—perhaps there is more than one," said Michel, looking askance at Linnette.

"Plums," she said decisively, "plums and black raspberries."

"Is there pepper?" asked Bob. "Could I be smelling pepper in a wine?"

"There is pepper, yes," said Richard, nodding, " yes, pepper, and cherry pits, and . . . "

"Almonds from *za* grill," blurted Linnette.

"Taste the blackcurrants!"

"More spices. I taste more spices. How can a wine have spices?"

"Cassis, oooh, *magnifique!* "

The three men, laughing together, turned to look at Linnette. She dropped the corners of her mouth, shrugging her shoulders, palms upward, then laughed along with them.

"Please, I am only a simple gourmet from St. Dié," she said modestly. She poured them all more wine.

"And what about your friend?" asked Richard. "Tell us about your friend." He held up the empty second bottle and nodded to Linnette, who ran off for more wine.

"You mean Jim? The guy . . . ?" asked Michel.

"That one," said Richard.

Michel finished his glass in a gulp, hacked off a piece of the Reblochon, and considered his answer. His mind burned with memories, rich, precious moments washed in vivid color. He felt his heart swell, ache, burst with feeling, with longing. He opened his mouth to answer. He could not form the words.

"The greatest guy in the world," said Bob. "Couldn't ask for a better guy. He was always loving, always ready with the compliment, always . . . "

" . . . looking out for the little guy. And when he was diagnosed," said Michel, taking the floor, "he only got better. He was always sensitive to how his illness affected others—how it bothered his wife, his kids, and his friends." Michel's voice cracked again. The two friends were remembering the best of times, which was as it should be.

"He was one of those people who are always fun to be with. I mean, when you were going to do something, you'd make sure Jim was along."

"I'll tell you what Jim was like. He was offered the job at Virginia . . . department chief. Real plum of a job, believe me. But their in-house candidate was a guy Jim had trained with, knew and respected. Jim told them they already had the best man for the job right there, and withdrew his name from consideration. That was the kind of man he was."

The two men went on about their friend, following his image deep into the past, walking roads they had all but forgotten, back, and back. They cracked in-jokes, making references unknown to their Gallic hosts, and softened to the wine and the warmth of memory. Bob ran through his entire repertoire of Irish verse, fracturing line after line. Richard and Linnette nodded to one another. Unnoticed by the two doctors, Linnette's eyes were filled with tears.

It was as though they were set apart, the four of them, coursing some ethereal stream, placid and celestial, while the rest of the patrons, dumbstruck, could only watch in wonder. It was as though their table alone basked in the light, glowing with the warmth of human sympathy. Their enthusiasm rippled outward. Gregarious Michel worked the other tables, pouring wine in coffee cups held aloft, flirting, joking, feeling the wine himself.

"In vino veritas!"

"Pass the plums."

"Name some more spices. There are more spices here for sure!"

"Licorice, sweet-briar . . . heaven!"

"To Jim!" "James." "To James." "To Jim!"

Bob stood abruptly, licking his lips, readying for a final recitation. Anticipating that he might require the support, he motioned Richard to stand with him and slung an arm across his shoulders. Chin out, head held high, wine glass aloft, he addressed the dining room at large:

" 'The time you won your town the race
We chaired you through the market-place;
Man and boy stood cheering by,
And home we brought you shoulder-high.

Today, the road all runners come,
Shoulder-high we bring you home,
And set you at your threshold down,
Townsman of a stiller town.

Smart lad, to slip betimes away
From fields where glory does not stay
And early though the laurel grows
It withers quicker than the rose.

Eyes the shady night has shut
Cannot see the record cut,

And silence sounds no worse than cheers
After earth has stopped the ears:

Now you will not swell the rout
Of lads that wore their honors out,
Runners whom renown outran
And the name died before the man.

So set, before its echoes fade,
The fleet foot on the sill of shade,
And hold to the low lintel up
The still-defended challenge-cup.

And round that early-laureled head
Will flock to gaze the strengthless dead,
And find unwithered on its curls
The garland briefer than a girl's.' " *

"All right!" "Totally awesome!" Bob acknowledged the patrons' applause and resumed his seat amid the quiet clapping, the murmured bravos, the whistles, the hear-hear's. Here and there, coffee cups were raised to him in toast.

"Sure an' Bobby me lad," said Michel, with as thick a brogue as he could manage through the wine, "e'en yer quotin' the likes o' a Brit, ye be gladdin' the hearts of Connemara lads everywhere, wi' yer sweet song."

Reluctantly then, the two doctors readied themselves to go, straightening their ties, having now been properly prepared in the French manner for the sober task to come. They thanked their hosts, shifting anxiously, returning to the moment, girding up for what lay ahead. Then Richard, holding each by the arm, leaned toward the two doctors with a private whisper. The two doctors nodded solemnly and, joining Richard, turned toward Linnette, and raised their glasses one last time.

"*Merci*, Linnette," they said, beaming down at her. "*Merci. Nous vous aimons*, Marie-Linnette Laballière."

* *To an Athlete Dying Young,* by A. E. Housman

A meteor's life, that few seconds when a wish may be formed, or a young astronomer dreams, is all the time one needs to die. With that last sigh spanning life and death, the stuff of life streaks toward light, and dust.

The doctor at that moment will be drained of spirit. He had known with his mind that this would come, but his heart had always refused to believe it. In this confusion, he can hardly sift his thoughts, much less articulate them. He should tell his patient's wife that she had been a good wife—yes!—the best he'd ever known, that he, the doctor has been touched by her devotion. He should tell her that she could have done no more for her husband, that she has already given more than most would give, that she need never feel guilty. He, the doctor, should say that the man, his patient, was a fine person . . . yes, the finest, that he loved his wife and children, spoke often about them, that he would not have wanted them to mourn too deeply nor too long, that this flash of light in eternity's night had been as it should be. He, the doctor, should tell them, the wife and children, to feel pride, not guilt; joy, not sorrow.

These words are within the doctor, buried deep within. They are trapped like a cricket's song in amber, rich and golden, deep within his heart, shaped long ago in more sensitive days. And the amber, like stone, hard and cold, does not let these words free, but locks them there within. And other thoughts arise. Could he have found the cancer sooner, he wonders? Is this his fault? Why, God, couldn't he have won this one? Do they blame him? And how I miss him! He was my friend, screams his mind. I liked him. Does the family hate him for his diagnosis? For this death?

Surely it has mattered more than this before. Never again! I won't care this much again. Death upon death hardens his resin to amber. And so when sorrow creeps around an edge, he knows to run the other way. He can neither soften the stone, thaw the frozen song, nor free the words of his humanity. He turns to the family and says, "Well, it's over. I'm sorry. Let me know if there's anything I can do."

Was she there enough for him, the wife wonders? Did she love him enough and did he know it? How will she live without him? Should she have brought him sooner to the doctor? If only . . . she thinks. Just a few more things to say, please Lord, just another chance, a moment . . . please. Is he still in the room? His soul I mean? Could he hear me? Please . . . oh, please. Oh nothing really . . . just silly things left to say, but please I'd like to say them. It can't be over.

Do you expect her in this turmoil to sense the doctor's needs?

The man's son sits in sullen darkness bristling with anger. Someone's to blame for this, he thinks, and someone's going to pay. So he's been away. He's had his own family to worry about, his own career. And why didn't they tell him his father was *that* sick? Why hadn't a specialist been called in? *He* would have gotten the best for his dad, sent him to the Center.

With an anger born of guilt, could he, the son, be expected to know the doctor's heart?

To the depths of her feeling, the daughter misses Daddy. Now there is no one to whom she can play the little girl, for whom she can do no wrong. She wants a chance to love him more, to thank him, to tell him she's grown, that she'll be all right, just to say these few things. She should have come home more often, been not so selfish. She might have called him more. Could she please have another chance? She didn't know it would be like this, this terrible abyss that is death.

Would you ask her to feel the doctor's loss?

You did everything humanly possible, doctor, and more. We can never thank you enough. You will miss him too, we know. You were such a friend to him. Often he told us of your talks, of the time you spent with him . . . often he spoke of his love for you, of how he admired you. He was so proud that you were his doctor—he had such trust in you. We know you feel as we do. You are family, doctor.

They might say these words to the man's doctor. But they cannot form them. His words are in amber. Theirs, dust. Dust blown by their own emotion, scattered by their own need in this human moment. They cannot give to the doctor what he so desperately requires. Regretting that they had left so much unsaid before, still they cannot find the words, cannot in this pain find the relief of comforting one another.

"Thank you, doctor."

And that is all. That has to be enough.

Far from the hospital room's suffocating closeness, the evening's freshness has descended upon the country. August's heat has dissolved in the night, leaving only a cold dew to chill the toes of the children. It is late. It is cool and clear. The fireflies have given up the night's courting. An occasional cricket stirs, calling out in its sleep. The grassy lawn rolls down and away in the darkness. A family of four seat themselves, aiming toward the heavens, toward a dancing Perseus. Oh! Wonderful! Did you see that one? Encore! Wow! The Old Boy sent a good one that time. Over there! Quick! See?

Heaven's clock turns and, reveling in their humanity, the four watch the meteors die.

There was a time when the doctors began to come less often, and stayed for briefer periods of time. The woman knew she must be nearing the end. She sensed the restlessness in her grandchildren, for whom the hospital had once been a novelty and was now a close room of heavy sadness. With the doctors unable to predict, her son had returned to Tennessee. Life must go on. Her daughter had brushed her hair ever so gently for over an hour, and had only just left. She had seen the tremble in her daughter's lip. She had a vague, fleeting sense of irony, that she should now lay dying in this very hospital that she had once worked so hard for—two thousand hours of volunteer work, captain of the fund-raising team for a new coronary care unit, and the long months of campaign for more operating room space. And none of this science could help her now.

But it was her time, and she would not be selfish. Self-pity was not her thing. She just wanted it to be over now. She was tired of this process of dying. She had made her peace and said her goodbyes . . . a thousand times over. She had thought that when she had decided to die, to give up the struggle, Death would naturally come. One simply made a decision, she imagined, stopped clinging to life, and, as in the novels, gave up the ghost. But each morning she awakened to find herself still alive. Was there something she was doing wrong, some attitude she had incorrectly assumed? Why was Death taking so long to come? And why this sense of something left undone? Couldn't the doctors give her a shot to ease her out of this world? What possible purpose was served by these last, endless hours?

What had she not completed, the woman wondered? Hadn't she found her Path in this world? What could have been forgotten in this procession of minister, friend, and tearful family? Was she with these remaining hours to take stock of her life one more time? Should there be one final summing up? Perhaps Death was waiting for this completion.

The woman addressed her chief success. With her left hand she reached across her body for the side-rail, pulling herself slowly to her right side. The agony in her belly cried out from the periphery of her mind. With an effort of concentration, she willed the pain away. She scanned the pictures of her family on her night-stand: her first grandchild, Kimmie, stood at attention, towered over by her beloved cello; her son, in his important office in Nashville, smiled at her from his desk; her daughter sat surrounded by Johnny and the twins.

She pressed against her belly, making a slight adjustment in bed. She looked at the twins with their baseball caps and freckled grins. She had raised a fine family. This was her life's victory. She shifted her gaze to Phil and to forty-seven years of memories. She had kept his home for him, raised his children, had been there for him so he could open all the doors of the world. She was his rock, Phil would say, his port in the storm. She had remained interested in his business, had encouraged him always to talk about it, had kept slim for him, as pretty as the years would allow. Only short months ago, he had, with his wink, patted her bottom. Phil's Path had been hers as well.

What else was there? Why this sense of emptiness? She rolled onto her back, winced, and gazed at the tiles on the ceiling. The scent of the hyacinth was getting on her nerves. She heard her doctor paged. Then again, urgently. Hurried footsteps ran off somewhere.

What else was there? She shifted her gaze to the courtyard. There had been her parents, and her mother's own illness. But that was so long ago. Where else had her Path conducted? Was this all there had been?

That was all, she guessed. She had her family—a loving husband, her children and grandchildren—a successful marriage—no small triumph these days. She could be proud of her children's successes, and of her husband's. She had been there for them. Mark that down.

She listened to the voices of the hospital. Far off, a baby cried, and was still. An old man muttered in the darkness. The maintenance men whispered coarsely, waxing the floors.

Why wasn't she sleepy? She was so immensely tired, but sleep seemed never to come. Why now this haunting emptiness? Was she being made to lie awake until the end? Were they giving her medicines to keep her alert? Well, she wished they wouldn't do that.

The sunset melted into indigos and grey. The lights of the courtyard slanted through her blinds, playing tricks with shadows in her room. She heard voices murmuring from the benches in the courtyard. The paging, so incessantly shrill all day long, became subdued. This was the most difficult time for her: family and friends gone, nurses busy with evening duty, and sleep reluctant to come.

In the far corner of the room, behind the door, the courtyard lights shimmered and coalesced. She turned toward the light, and, looking down the length of her nose, tried to focus on it. The light held in the corner, in an odd, persistent way. Peculiar. Was the morphine inducing hallucination? Or was this the cancer gone to brain? Could this be some mysterious Apparition from another place?

She decided it must be the morphine and turned her head away.

From the corner of the room, the Apparition spoke to her.

"Good evening, Claire. I'm here to help you in your recollection."

The woman turned back to the light. She squinted, blinked hard, looked away, and then back again. This was too real to be the morphine, she thought. It must be cancer gone to brain. She went back to counting the tiles on the ceiling.

Again the Apparition spoke to her:

"I remember all those children whose lives you saved. And the grocer with the heart attack. And all those others, whose lives you've touched. Surely you haven't forgotten them?"

What in Heaven's name does one do, she thought, with a ghost which is only cancer gone to brain? She checked to see that the door was shut tightly so that her nurse could not hear her talking to herself and think she had lost her mind. The Apparition spoke again:

"The nurses are all down the hall, having coffee."

"I think you have the wrong room," said the woman. "You want one of the doctors. You took a wrong turn somewhere. Thank you for the visit."

There. Maybe now the cancer in her brain, having been dismissed, would be still.

But the Apparition persisted.

"You have been far more than wife and mother," said the Apparition. "You have been both doctor and nurse yourself. God bless you for that!"

"You are quite mistaken. You are nothing but cancer gone to brain," the woman said. She turned her head abruptly, away from the light, dismissing it again. She watched the people milling about in the wing across the courtyard, waiting to be seen in the emergency department. She waited an interminable length of time to allow the light to leave. Cautiously, she turned back to sneak a glance. The light was there still.

"Light, thank you for the visit," she said impatiently. "But I am trying to die. I would like to be alone. Perhaps there is someone down the hall in need of your services."

"I came here for you," said the Apparition, "to honor you and your good works. *I was sick and you visited me. I was a stranger and you took me in.*"

The woman struggled to half-sit, supporting herself with her elbows, ignoring her pain. She squinted again and blinked against the light.

"I have never seen you before. I think you are mistaken. *When did I see You sick and visit You? When did I see You a stranger and take You in?*"

The Apparition brightened, assembled. The woman licked her dry, chapped lips, and, with widened eyes, watched. The Apparition answered:

"You have given to your hospital so selflessly! Look what you have done! You built a nursery, and intensive care. You brought doctors here, and nurses with them. You have welcomed the stranger; you visited the sick. You have cared so lovingly for your neighbor. *Inasmuch as you have done it for one of these, you have done it for Me.*"

"You sound like the Bible, Light," the woman said. "I just did what I was supposed to do. I never really thought about the who or why very much. I had never looked at it in quite this way. "

Then with an after-thought, the woman added, "Do you visit everyone who is dying, Light?"

"Everyone," answered the Apparition.

The woman drifted off into a sleep of dreams.

*The sun was high, complete. In the warmth of day she walked meadows dressed with wild aster, breathed the scent of timothy and fescue, and came to a grand house on a hill. There under the elms, she saw wizened grandmothers rocking in gerontic splendor, waving shyly from the porch. She entered the house and sat by a great swinging door through which entered the bent and frail. She greeted each of them, taking a pale hand and placing it into the hand of a waiting nurse. Through this same door left the healed, walking proudly, and with purpose. Each smiled and bowed to her, handing her a daffodil. These she held in her lap, neatly arranged just so—whole sheaves of daffodils.*

Hours later, the morning sun brightened the hospital room. The woman's young nurse slipped quietly in, peering at her discreetly.

"I'm still alive, Kathy," said the woman. She looked at her nurse, at her starched freshness and youth, and smiled broadly.

"How are you feeling this morning? Did you sleep well?" asked the nurse.

"Everything is done now. I think I've completed it," answered the woman.

"Completed it?" asked her nurse.

"Oh, it's nothing you'd understand. No matter," said the woman. "Just some things I had to see. You will see them too someday.

"Kathy, tell me," said the woman, seeming to change the subject, "just how is my hospital today?"

## II. THE BEST OF CALLINGS

I once asked an old practitioner what he thought was the best job in the world.

"Mine," he said without hesitation. "It's never easy. But it sure beats the hell out of whatever is in second place."

It is more than a job. It is still a profession, whatever others wish to make it out to be. And what elevates our calling to that level is a history, a tradition, and a common bond that cannot be taken from us. Though many from without and some of us from within wish to deny that legacy, attempting to transform our vocation into mere trade, it is there and always will be, if we only remember. And if, in talking to one another, we help others to remember too.

Professionalism is something everyone else seems to have more of than you yourself could ever hope for. Like the sun, it can dazzle you when it strikes you unaware, and like the sun at three in the afternoon, it can both fill you full and cast a shadow. You can't have just a little professionalism but some people can have too much of it—prima donnas for example, and some lawyers, and so they can't really be called professional. Professionalism follows the laws of physics and the Heisenberg Uncertainty Principle specifically, because as soon as you point to it, professionalism is no longer there. It is not a matter of *trying*. It is a matter of *being*. You cannot behave with integrity and then praise yourself for so behaving and be a professional. You cannot care, cannot know you are caring, cannot pride yourself for caring, and at the same time be a professional. Awareness implies ulterior motive, and ulterior motive is not a part of professionalism.

The old slugger, his glory days gone, can stride to the plate, batting .237, and still be a professional. The rookie batting .237 cannot. Country priests can be professional, African missionaries more often so, bishops and cardinals rarely, and with difficulty. A nurse is a professional when she holds a hand, cares deeply, and loves, and so is the teacher whose heart is breaking with the abused child whom she wishes to steal and care for. At these people the rest of us can only look and marvel and say, "*There* is a professional."

The old Chiefs of Yesterday had it, professionalism. They believed in Honor, Duty, Family, Love, and Nature. They gave their word and their word was enough. They were professional. And they learned the white man was not.

The athlete who strains and works and trains and leans to the tape only to win, only to do his best, is professional. The athlete whose goal is seven figures is not.

The same is true for doctors.

With doctors, professionalism gets lost in the noise of fame, achievement, power and money. Like the pristine lake choked with condos, it becomes obscured and lost, forever. Doctors *want* to have professionalism, but too often want it to *seem*, rather than to *be*. And with seeming as with awareness, professionalism is lost.

It is elusive, this professionalism. With it, comes success, and the power to heal. Like the flowers in spring, they must come after, and never before.

I knew a doctor once who was honest, but gentle with his honesty, and was loving, but careful with his love; who was disciplined without being rigid, and right without the stain of arrogance; who was self-questioning without self-doubt, introspective and reflective, and in the same moment, decisive; who was strong, hard, adamant; but all these things laced with tenderness and understanding, a doctor who worshipped his calling without worshipping himself, who was busy beyond belief, but who had time— time to smile, to chat, to touch the shoulder and take the hand, and who had time enough for Death as well as Life.

Now *there* was a professional.

Hu Chin prepared the fourth moxa. First he finely powdered the leaves of mugwort. After slightly moistening the powder he carefully shaped a cone of the mixture upon the back of the sick child, over the spine and between the shoulders. This cone he ignited with an ember from the fire, allowing it to burn with the precise timing born of long experience. He watched the child's skin closely and at the formation of the blister, quickly crushed the burning cone through the blister into the skin , thus infusing the herb directly into the body's channels. Nineteen more moxas he applied in similar fashion, alternating the sacred numbers of three and seven, and using wormwood and mugwort in succession. The needles properly applied, twelve for the neck stiffness, fourteen for the coma, he directed the parents in the preparation of the cold bath, bowed to them and left the home. But he knew the child would die. He could read the signs: Hu Chin had studied with Wang Shu-ho, had committed to memory the Nei Ching, was China's foremost expert on the pulse. And besides, there was the matter of the Great Fireball in the sky.

*Not to follow, yet she crept there, stealing quickly in the star-light. Nimble, deer-like, stepping lightly, soon she came to where they brought him, where they carried her dear brother, older brother, brave, protecting, lovely brother, strong and gentle; now her fevered, senseless brother. First had come the head and neck pains, awful pains of creeping sickness, then the shaking and the sleeping.*

*Teepee firelight flickered on her, illuminating doe-like features. Hands upon her hair long-braided, closer still she crept up on them. As an arrow comes so quickly, there she was at some small opening. There she saw forbidden trappings, saw the wolf-masks of the Sha-man, saw the skins of stag and otter, saw the precious feathered lances, eagle-feathered gourds and rattles. There she smelled the burning chant-fire, smelled the pine and scent of elders, in the center saw the*

*Chief's son, lovely brother lying broken, on the bed of pine and birch boughs.*

*Slowly Sha-man stood and chanted, raised his arms and eyes and chanted, singing to the flaming Fire-star. Sang the sacred words of power, called the healing spirits earth-ward, asked for help from Him above them, prayed for strength for her sweet brother.*

Excitement brimmed up over the heads of the crowd, rose above them, electrifying the air, rising to the heavens, to the stars, and to the Comet. The crowd pushed and shoved, the better to catch a glimpse, to see with their God-given eyes a real witch! Whispers. Shouts! Boys running wildly, rapping on doors. The crowd grew, spilling over lawn's edge to the cobblestones, down the humped and curving street to the smithy. Nodding, reassuring, blessing and crossing themselves, they filled with the titillation of a witch-find. Only ship-coming could rival this night. Oh, powerful God, oh jealous God, save us from Satan's servants!

The deacon had been found. Tall, somber, righteous, he wended his way through the mob. They surged for a touch of his cloak the more to draw from him a measure of his holiness. Oh brave Deacon, God bless! Save us Sir! The deacon strode to the oaken door and swung it open, sweeping his eyes across the scene before him. An old woman by the dying hearth, trembling, prayed desperately. At the trestle table sat a man and a woman, horror-filled, staring helplessly. The deacon followed their gaze. Yes, of course, God save us—on the floor, the girl, glistening with sweat and covered with grime, arched her back impossibly, with only her head and heels touching the floor. He saw the teeth and fists clenched, could smell the Evil, and blessed himself before this hateful witch.

*The young boy lay across the makeshift bed—two chairs adjacent—his wet golden ringlets lay damp on the down pillow. The fire raged in the hearth throwing dancing shadows out into the room. The doctor sat before the boy, left hand on his own chin, and studied his patient. He had tilted the lamp shade to shed more light, and could see the milk-white face, the delicate blue lips, the rivulets of sweat, could see the deep, regular rise and fall of the boy's chest that would abruptly pause, stop, wait, and then begin again. The boy's mother sat at the table by the window, head in her arms, sobbing quietly. The father stood, hand on her shoulder, head almost to the beamed ceiling, his face with a distant look of immeasurable loss. Feeling his own heavy sorrow, still the doctor impassively watched the boy. A slight twitch here, a tremble there, and then, this vigil was suddenly over, irretrievably ended. He turned to the father and slightly nodded, then let himself out.*

*The doctor entered the rutted lane leading to town. The stars—jewels—hung startlingly close—cold, unfeeling, yet eternal and somehow comforting. The doctor stopped and turned to his left, looking up at the comet. He whispered a prayer for his small patient.*

She quickly prepped the skin and sent home the LP needle. Switching tubes with one hand, she collected the milky fluid from this very sick little girl. Turning, she handed the tubes to the tech who quickly ran off to the laboratory. She nodded to the ICU nurse, but he had already hung the antibiotics and was adjusting the IVAC. She liked this nurse. He was quick, efficient, bright, no-nonsense, a real Marine. She could count on him. The doctor stood and helped position the girl and together they pulled up the hypothermia blanket. The nurse watched in admiration as the doctor smoothed and parted the girl's hair.

The doctor walked to the waiting room, sat before the frightened parents and told them about the disease. She explained the use of the antibiotics, spoke of her optimism, and promised to stay with her patient until the child awoke. They thanked her, hesitated, glanced past her, then left. She walked the short corridor to the back door for some fresh air. Out on the packed snow of the parking lot she squinted up at the stars, found Sagittarius, and then the faint streak of the comet. Her thoughts coalesced, crystallized, then soared.

What did they ever do without antibiotics? And what

would another swing of this comet find? If the insects don't survive us, if we allow ourselves doctors and patients in another seventy-six years, how will we treat meningitis then? Molecular lattice-specific sonar lysers? DNA sequenator-directed immunoglobulin synthesis? A trick learned from extraterrestrial CME? Whatever . . . it will seem a miracle!

In a hospital cafeteria, two residents were arguing over lunch. Oblivious to the high tech plastic and steel surrounding them, they were locked in a heated, and unwinnable, battle: what was the single most important discovery in the history of medicine? Understand that these were *modern* doctors with fashionable ideas and a trendy impatience with history. They had long since discarded as trivial Harvey's dissections, Morton's anesthesia, and Koch's postulates. The first resident, a latter-day traditionalist, argued for the discovery of antibiotics. Eating his salad with his fingers in a grand display of entitlement, he began his argument.

"There is no doubt that the dawn of the antibiotic era is indisputably the beginning of modern medicine. Domagk's sulfonamides, Waksman's streptomycin, Fleming's penicillin, all gave physicians something more to do than simply monitor the dying patient. Antibiotics have given us credibility, a bonafide raison d'être. And beyond that, their discovery has spawned the whole discipline of infectious disease, whose premise, the treatment of disease through biochemical means, has in turn fathered other disciplines as well — oncology, for example."

Eminently pleased with himself, he leaned back in his chair. But for the AIDS virus and meager academic salaries, he might have considered an infectious disease fellowship for *himself*, rather than chasing the shining star of cardiology.

The second resident, more modernist than the first, prided himself on his intuitive leaps and lateral thinking. He could hardly settle for any such simplistic solution from history as his colleague had proposed. His cleverness made him positively bubble forth.

"Antibiotics are important and have their place, but are so *crude*. Consider their toxicity, the emergence of resistance, and the very enigma of AIDS. Antibiotics are merely an interim measure. Even *Jenner's* discovery eclipses that of Fleming's. No, my friend, you miss the obvious."

In fact, he believed that *his* solution was not all *that* obvious but understatement would magnify his own genius. He went on with his rebuttal.

"The discovery of the computer is the Rosetta stone for medicine. Regard the computer's applications in medical research. Think of the microchips used in autoanalyzers, in monitoring devices, and in nuclear scanning. Consider what the CAT scanner has done just in the field of neurology alone. And that only scratches the surface. We can implant microchips in occipital lobes to enable the blind to begin to see. We can use microchips in electronic limbs for amputees. And imagine the microprocessor-coordinated cochlear implants for the deaf, the wearable artificial kidney, the programmable pacemaker. Even genetic engineering, itself of colossal importance, depends upon computers to direct genetic analysis and sequencing."

Enough was enough. He had won and he knew it. And the second resident now sat back smugly. He might have considered cybernetics himself, he reflected, had not his mother wanted him to become a doctor.

At the end of their table sat an old man in a long white coat. He too ate his salad with his fingers. He had forgotten his fork. To this elderly physician the first resident appealed.

"What do you think, sir?" he asked condescendingly. "What would you consider medicine's greatest achievement?"

The old man returned a leaf of lettuce to his salad bowl, wiped his fingers with a napkin, and considered both residents with absent regard. He began to speak, reconsidered, looked away and out the windows, and then remembered that he had been asked a question.

"You're both correct as far as you go, which isn't very far, which therefore makes you both wrong, I suppose. And the correct answer to your question may be found really in your asking me, or in your need of asking me rather, more correctly, and in my compulsion to answer you, or rather, history's compelling me to do so, more exactly."

"Alzheimer's," thought the first resident.

But the old man only munched on a celery stalk, looked briefly away to summon his faculties, and then turned his attention to his salad once again.

"Huh?" asked the first resident.

"I beg your pardon?" asked the second.

"The mentor," whispered the old man.

"What?" both residents asked in unison.

The old gentleman wiped his lips, placed both his hands on the table, stared off as though addressing some imaginary audience, and began,

"The mentor is medicine's single greatest achievement, though no one set out to invent the idea to win any prize. It started, I am sure, long before Hippocrates, though he's gotten most of the press for it, don't you think? But just stop and consider Hippocrates himself. There he is, sitting there in his robe, surrounded by colonnades, fist under his chin, lounging on some piece of marble. Through observation, by sheer power of thought, he's trying to make a science out of what had been only magic and religion. Pretty soon he finds he has a group of young people sitting around him as well, all wanting to learn what he, Hippocrates, knows to be important. So he teaches them all he knows, which is what you're supposed to do when you're a mentor. And then he sends them out into the world. They teach others in turn, each of *them* becoming a mentor for students, as Hippocrates had been for them. And everywhere they go, teaching students, treating patients, as Hippocrates had taught them to do, Hippocrates is right there at their elbows, making sure they do it the right way, and with style. And so it goes through history — from Aristotle to Herophilus, from Galen to Vesalius, Bernard, Pasteur, Whipple, and . . . well, you know history as well as I do."

Clearly they didn't. The old man continued.

"Look at what happens with this mentor business. You have teachers, each with students numbering in the thousands, all linked with each other down through the ages — forming a vast, dendritic coalescence of medical knowledge.

Why, you have to be proud just to belong to it, just to be allowed to pass on a few bits and pieces of wisdom yourself! You begin to think of yourself as some living page out of a grand medical textbook.

"And what happens to those young doctors when they are adrift in the world? Do their mentors desert them? Not on your life! A student meets a patient with congestive heart failure, and old man Withering is right there with him, telling him how much foxglove to grind up. Or your young doctor is dealt a baffling case, with an endless array of signs and symptoms, and all of a sudden Sydenham is sitting on her shoulder, making sure she takes down the patient's history correctly and that the observations are precisely made.

"And so it's been for me these long years. I've carried my mentor everywhere. If I get sloppy, I wonder 'What would he think of me now?' And if I'm in a tight spot clinically, he prods me back to the literature. When I'm impatient with patients, I remember his patience with me. When I'm asked to teach, I do so willingly because that is what he did. When I begin to doubt myself, I remember his belief in me. And if I am ready to quit, I can see him standing there before me in his long white coat, with stern look and stethoscope, and I go on.

"What has he been for me, this mentor of mine? He's been like a father to me, but more than a father. He has been my companion in medicine, to help me through the loneliness that medicine can bring and to share with me the joy that medicine can be. My mentor has, through me and those of my students, cared decently and compassionately for countless patients. When I have cured a patient or two, why so has he. And so have Kranes and Cushing and Koch before him.

"Yessir, the mentor is medicine's *best* invention. All of us doctors need one. That's what it's all about. I hope you boys have one yourselves."

The old man stopped, looked off, and smiled at some distant memory. The residents at the next table had turned to listen to him as well. The old man got up to leave, nodding to them all. He had a gleam in his eye, a radiance about him.

Was this madness, wondered the residents, or some forgotten brilliance? He seemed, it was clear, to be in touch with his mentor. He straightened his shoulders, raised his chin, and turned with a quote to the residents at the next table:

"'Observation, reason, human understanding, courage — these make the physician.'"

Now the old man turned back to the two residents at his own table, nodded to them, put his head down and turned to walk away. Suddenly he turned back to them all with a smile.

"'One who is not fond of students and who does not suffer their foibles gladly, misses the greatest zest in life.'"

With a hand to his breast, the old man gave a slight bow, turned, and shuffled away. Bewildered, the residents watched him leave, wondered who he was, and why it was that they had never had time for him before.

A surgeon sat sipping coffee in the operating room lounge of a metropolitan hospital. Mask around her neck, cap still covering her red hair, she shifted her weary body to gaze out the smog-stained windows. She lifted her legs to the chair adjacent and watched the street-wise pigeons nesting under the eaves of the hospital roof, losing herself in thought. Was she wasting her time here? Was all this just a colossal squander? Was *this* the way her life was meant to be: a sixty-hour week, week after week, diverting the flow of blood around the dietary excesses of another? Was she really happy with these huge sums of money, earning more than she could ever hope to have the time to spend? Must she endure this peculiar kind of boredom, performing what had now become for her a simple surgical procedure? Shouldn't she be in the trenches rather, using her surgical skills to help those who really had need of them? How remote she seemed from the ideals of first-year medical school. She pictured herself in her dream of a more meaningful life in a busy emergency department somewhere, anywhere, where she could *really* practice her art.

*A surgeon leaned far back in his swivel chair, utterly exhausted. Incompleted records lay strewn all about his charting desk, and his half-finished coffee, his fifth cup, stood next to him. More patients were entering through the automatic doors every minute. He summoned the strength to continue. He half-turned to watch the house-staff and nurses hurrying about. He saw two nurses help another utter wretch to the suturing room, a disheveled drunk with soiled clothes and a jagged scalp laceration. For the ten-thousandth time he would find a frightened medical student, sit him on a stool, and guide shaking hands through the mechanics of interrupted mattress sutures.*

*Was this what it was all about? Was this a proper use of his talents, of all those years of training? Was he forever doomed to knit the scalps and prod the bellies of the indigent, patching here and there, so they could abuse themselves all over again? What had happened to the glamour of the moment, the electric excitement of the emergency department? Why did he feel cheated, as though he were letting someone down? Might he not be far better off, and doing far more good, out on the front lines? In rural America he could deliver his gifts, his surgical skills, to real people, in proper, God-intended fashion. Wasn't it time for a change? He gazed out of the hospital windows, at the lines of traffic dragging by in the rain, and dreamt of life as a surgeon in some country hospital, wherever it was he was needed.*

Two layers of subcutaneous Dexon, then the subcuticulars, and she would be done. Another gallbladder out. The surgeon glanced at the OR clock and continued suturing. She thought of her packed office, of the waiting patients for whom she was already late. More gallbladders to remove, together with assorted moles and wens, a diverticular colon or two, and always the spastic bowels—far too many of those. Five major cases today. A chance to cut is a chance to cure. Sure. Another late day, another late supper, her kids already in bed, her journals unread, and the glossy magazines and unopened novels taunting her. A too-quiet husband withdrawn.

She finished her case, dictated the note, and went out into the courtyard of the small country hospital. Her patients could wait. She watched the jays at the feeder and thought of her college roommate in Dahomey. Shouldn't she pack up, bag and baggage, move her family and settle there? Wouldn't *that* be the place to practice surgery, to deliver medicine to those who really needed her skills? She could *teach* again, and teach those eager to learn. That would be the greatest good for the greatest number. *That* would be doctoring as it is meant to be. Wasn't that the real meaning of the Oath, to practice medicine in a place like Dahomey? How could there be any meaning in this endless procession of patient visits with their endless lists of minor complaints? Shouldn't she be going where she was *needed*?

*The doctor sat at the makeshift table, partially shielded by a staked tarp from the hot Niger sun. Before him stretched the long line of Kanuri children, waiting for their sulfonamide drops. Both he and his nurse knew they would run out of drops more quickly than they would ever run out of children with trachoma. The doctor waited for the next child to be brought to the tent. Absentmindedly, he watched a hammerkop wade in the shallows of the muddy stream. Tomorrow he would be in Loga, and after that, Madaoua, and Agadez, and then the long, long trek to Chirfa. And always, he would pray that politics had not intercepted his medicines, preventing him from treating at least some of these children.*

*But what of malaria, and of trypanosomiasis? What of leishmaniasis? Who would treat those? Here he was, spending sixteen hours a day either treating, or traveling to treat, these children with trachoma. The arrival of a case of sulfonamides was a major miracle here. How could he ever find proper medicines for the rampant infectious diseases he saw everywhere. How little he had to work with! There he would see a child with appendicitis, long for his scalpel and some decent anesthesia, and know that child would die. And here, a child with Burkitt's, so simple to cure in other places, so doomed to die here in Niger.*

*He recalled his residency days in the great American hospital. The facilities! The equipment! The technologies available to guide the doctor in treatment! Even if he had a microscope! A microscope could tell him which patient had vivax and which falciparum. And in America he would have at his fingertips a whole host of drugs to treat them.*

*Was his trachoma-fight simply an exercise in futility? Wasn't trachoma, after all, more a social problem, a political problem, and better left to the politicians? What business had he, a doctor, traveling the length and breadth of this scorched country, treating the same children, year after year, children who, out of ignorance, reinfected themselves? Would he not be better off in a Western hospital where he could be a proper doctor? Wouldn't that be a happy time! How lucky were those doctors there. How lucky!*

I can't exactly tell you when it was she entered the room. It was, I think, sometime between Infectious Disease and Rheumatology. We were hard at it, pounding out another certifying examination, and I can tell you this: Nineteen of us sitting around the table were stopped in our tracks by her entry. Nineteen of us set aside the nuances of synthesis and judgment, of multiple choice and true-and-false, and stared. (There was a twentieth, who was himself so tangled up in a particularly convoluted question that he remained oblivious to her.)

She walked in as if she owned the place. She seemed totally in control of herself, unfazed by our presence. Nor was the aura about her projected by any particularly commanding beauty, the way a woman of startling appearance can command a room merely by being in it. Her appearance being what it was, it was quite the opposite with her. What was it then?

She had her household, her entire world balanced on her shoulder, all the clothes she owned, stuffed into an oversized yellowed sweatshirt bulging at the nape. She had gathered and held its waist to form the most rudimentary of backpacks. Her hair was hacked and shorn. Her body held none of the lean fitness so fashionably displayed by the hotel guests mingling out in the courtyard. Rather, she seemed thin, brittle, ill. And there was something about her skin that wasn't just right. There was an affliction here you couldn't put your finger on. She wore a faded green flannel shirt that hung below her hips over worn blue slacks which, in turn, fell straight to the floor, shapeless, cuffs dragging, almost obscuring her sandals-all of which served only to magnify rather than to conceal her infirmity.

We were holding our meeting in the Garden Room bordering on an inner courtyard shaded by palm trees and skirted by some species of aster I couldn't identify. This woman (the management would later tell us) had apparently gained entry to the courtyard through the parking lot abutting the ocean. She had come in through the north walkway along the stand of eucalyptus. Neither the opulence nor dress nor manner nor notice of the moneyed guests in the courtyard could stop her. The Garden Room had been declared off-limits by signs shouting *Private Party* and *Quiet! Board Meeting in Progress.* It didn't matter. We had left the door open, partly to fill the room with fresh California air, partly to admit the sounds and smells of freshly mown grass in January, and partly to delude ourselves into thinking that we too were vacationing, rather than in reality hunched around a table hewing and shaping some antiseptic formal written examination.

It wasn't her boldness alone that struck me. Anyone hungry enough, anyone driven by the sort of want she must have been suffering from, could easily have run the gauntlet she did. What bothered me, or impressed me rather, was her poise. She didn't just grab a handful of the Danish and make a run for it as I might have done. Rather she strolled up and down the buffet some twenty feet distant from our meeting table, calmly examining the feast before her.

A mound of fruit heaped up and slid over in a cascade of melon, mango, and papaya. She peered at it, leaning this way and that without touching anything and then casually moved on as would an overly particular European housewife at market—shrewd, critically selective. The confectionery pastries were next in line, arranged in geometric fashion on a huge platter, largely left behind by us (mostly out of guilt I might add). This choice too she rejected, picking instead the large yeast-baked muffins none of us had been able to resist. Gently she set her load on the floor, split a muffin with her thumbs and spread healthy slabs of softened cream cheese on each half. This operation she managed with extreme care, with a correctness. She might have been sculpting clay for the art show on Eighty-second Street or melding oil colors on a spattered palette. This was no slapdash application by one half starved. When she had finished her preliminaries, she topped each half with a thinly sliced filet of pink salmon. She had it right. She was nutritionally correct.

She balanced the two open sandwiches in one palm, lifted her household onto a shoulder and strolled out, to stand just outside the Garden Room door, face full to the midmorning sun (which was more than any of us had been able to do). She did not bolt with her stolen goods. She seemed above stuffing the folds and pockets of her baggy clothing with rolls and pears and packets of marmalade. She took no more than she had needed for the moment, and then stood there, warming herself in the sun, at brunch.

I surveyed my colleagues. They were transfixed. None of them had made a move. They regarded her with a mixture of amusement, pity, and awe. I saw our endocrinologist examine the woman with her piercingly intelligent eyes and it seemed that I could almost see her thoughts. Why was this woman so wasted? Was this diabetes undiagnosed, poorly controlled? Panhypopituitarism—that might be it. Images of trophic hormones and releasing factors filled the air. Now it was the gastroenterologist's turn. What was so peculiar about her complexion? There was a disease about her, not the attractive soft coffee-brown of the islands but rather the off-gray color of . . . hemochromatosis perhaps? Yes, that was it: bronze diabetes and a cirrhosis-studded liver, joints swollen, arthritic—poor soul! To the rheumatologist this was ochronosis. Where were the blue sclera, the pigmented cartilage? The cardiologist saw only cyanosis. To him this was an Eisenmenger's pure and simple, a VSD too long not listened for, a shunt now reversed, the step-up gone, the situation hopeless.

The room became filled with feeling, with a richness not there before. There was that uncommon fulfillment one feels just after a particularly stirring concert or an extraordinary three-act play, where you, the audience, feel moved and changed. The woman remained oblivious to us. She finished with her brunch, lifted her load, and turned to go. She stumbled, tottered under her load. The cardiologist half rose in his chair. The geneticist gripped the arm of the oncologist. I looked around the room again. The interest in her went beyond the academic, and even among the stiffest of academicians rose the old stirrings of the clinician. No longer were these deans, editors, scientists of the highest order. Suddenly they were doctors again. They wanted to help. They needed only to be asked and they would give it, the old-fashioned doctor-way. I couldn't help myself. I went to the window to watch her leave. She picked her way through the throngs of honeymooners, and idle rich, walking toward the sun and the courtyard exit. Where did she get that poise, that simple dignity? Wad she living in some thought-disordered world? Did she believe herself to be Queen of the Tropics? Or was she absolutely on the mark, knowing that she had been among physicians, was a patient, and so, eminently superior to us? Could this have been a simple lesson in humanity: That she had nothing at all to be ashamed of, nothing for which to be scorned, that she was an equal among us, and belonged?

The heavy rain formed road-side streams, washing away the sandy shoulders, undermining the macadam. The doctor, picking his way carefully along in the dark to avoid driving his Chevy into a wash-out, slowed at the dirt-road right-hand turn and read the sign in a flash of sheet lightning. He saw the deep ruts in the dirt road, like a potato field on a bad day in April. He would have to walk it. Edging the Chevy onto the dirt shoulder, he parked, reached down to buckle his galoshes, then buttoned his slicker about him. Black bag in hand, he headed up the road in the storm. He was young and strong. This was still high adventure. He leaned into the driving rain and made for the light ahead.

The woman held open the door. She was thin, with a straight, hard mouth and no bosom to speak of. Her dress hung from her shoulders in a straight line to her ankles. Her cotton dress snapped in the wind. Glancing up through the rain, the doctor could see her bare feet stuck in oversized black leather shoes.

"Nice day," he said to her as he crossed the threshold.

"Thank you for coming out, Doctor," she whispered, closing the door behind him. She took his coat, heavy with the rain, and hung it with his felt fedora, dripping, on a nail next to the door. "She's in the next room."

The doctor surveyed the kitchen as he walked through to the adjacent bedroom. Rough pine boards, wide, warped, and slivered, formed the kitchen floor. The cook-stove at the left of the room, sporting a dull, rusted Katahdin Iron Works emblem on its bulging front, held assorted pots and a small, heatless fire. The day's wash hung over and to one side of the stove. Through a door off the kitchen to the right, he could see three dirty children quietly peering at him, minding someone's orders. This, he thought to himself, is definitely a left-handed house. Definitely. He headed through to the bedroom straight ahead.

The room held three people. Off in the far corner, set apart from the only bed in the room, sat an old woman knitting. She kept her eyes to the task, as though she might be sitting on a sunny porch somewhere, minding the dog. Her knobby fingers worked away at an afghan patterned in mismatched, garish colors of seconds and end-bits of yarn. She never looked at the doctor, did not acknowledge his arrival. She was, the doctor thought, the family's Final Arbiter, and would pass judgment upon whatever it was the doctor decided was wrong. In the near corner, to the right of the bed, stood a short, balding man with beer-belly and black suspenders. Arms folded across his chest, he held a can of Carling's Black Label in one hand and squinted against the smoke of the hand-rolled cigarette in his mouth. He might have been at a pig auction, except that in his face the doctor could read considerable quiet rage.

In the bed among the covers lay a young teenage girl who, in spite of her illness, was uncommonly beautiful. Sizing up the scene, the doctor knew without hearing a word, the diagnosis.

"She's in a family way," whispered the girl's mother.

"Knocked up," spat out her father.

The doctor placed his bag on a chair, leaned at the bedside, smiled at the poor frightened girl, and stood tall.

"I would like you two to leave," he said, nodding to the old lady and to the girl's father. "You will need to stay," he said to the mother, "because I will need some help."

The old woman clucked her tongue, sent a stare straight through the doctor, and made to gather up her knitting as though she were moving West, once and for all. The girl's father pushed himself away from the wall with a heave of his shoulder, gave his daughter a murderous look, and left the room with the old woman.

"How far along do you think you are, sweetheart?" the doctor asked the young girl.

"We don't know, Doctor. She just told us yesterday," said the girl's mother.

"When did you last . . . make love?" the doctor asked his patient.

"I only did it once . . . two months ago," sobbed the girl.

The doctor nodded to her kindly, as if to say 'that's okay', and gently pulled the covers down to examine her. Her belly was flat, and slightly tender above the pubis, and her thighs were parted. There was a pile of blood between her legs—'products of conception' in the vernacular. He instructed the girl's mother to get soap, water and fresh sheets to help him clean her up. While the woman was gone about her assignment, the doctor whispered to the girl.

"You've had a miscarriage, honey. You lost the baby, but you'll be all right. You can have another baby someday just fine. But make that someday a long time away, okay?"

"I'm never doing it again," said the girl.

"Yeah, well, when you do, use some protection, okay?"

"I'm never going to do *that* again," she repeated.

"Okay," said the doctor. He smiled at her. Her old man, he thought, will bar the door against this one.

The girl's mother returned and together they washed the girl's thighs and changed the bed.

"She has a slight infection . . . in her womb . . . I'll give you these few pills for her, but you'll need some more. You can get them at the drug store in town day after tomorrow when the road's better," he said. He wrote out the prescription with his left hand, tore it off and handed it to her.

"What do we owe you for the call, Doctor?" asked the woman.

He sized her up. Poor and proud, he thought.

"You'll be getting a bill," he said.

The rain had stopped. He draped his coat over an arm, hat in hand, and nodded to the girl's father and to the old woman, both still sulking in the dark sitting room. He let himself out and walked his way through the mud back to his car. He chuckled to himself over his 'system'. When the doctor, who was ambidextrous, wrote his prescriptions and his medical notes with his left hand, the druggist would recognize his left-handed script and charge for drugs at cost only, and the patient would be sent no doctor's bill. Right-handed notes and 'scripts were handled in the usual way. And from what he could read of her father's character, this poor girl would already have paid enough for her illness. The furor in that house for the next few weeks would erase any thought of a medical bill coming due. He headed home.

Thirty years passed.

It was thirty years of progress and medical achievement, thirty years of antibiotics of every description treating every known infection and some as yet to come, thirty years of CAT scans and ultrasonography and magnetic resonance imaging, thirty years of electrocardiography and pacemakers and laser-directed coronary surgery, thirty years of Medicare and Medicine-as-Big-Business and third-party forms and the myth of the perfect result and lawyers wanting a piece of the action.

Percy Davis, the old pharmacist in town, had passed away, and with him went the doctor's left-handed 'scripts, with him the left-handed-written fictitious bill, because all patients were now insured, as the politicians liked to believe, and everything had to be documented. The doctor had attended Percy's funeral, on a sunny day in June, and stood apart at the hillside plot, recalling the old days, and their 'system'.

The days were growing shorter for the doctor as well. His worsening heart condition, the energetic competition, the age of the specialist, and his own out-dated knowledge, meant fewer hours for him, and fewer patients. He had some patients who played it both ways, who went down to the City to the specialists, and still came to him from time to time out of loyalty. He knew about it. They would let slip, mention a drug he hadn't read about or a procedure he hadn't sent them for— and he would know. He was a weathered old caboose shunted to a siding grown up with weeds and alders.

Most days he would round at the hospital, making social visits to the older patients who now had other, younger doctors' names on the door. He would joke with the older nurses, then go over to his office. There he'd see a few patients— blood pressure checks mostly—and then come home for lunch with Ethel, and tend his irises in the afternoon. The arrival of the mail was a big event in his day, but the mail held mostly advertisements for magazines he had never heard of and investment opportunities he hadn't the inclination or the money for. He had out-lived his usefulness and knew it, was no longer important, yet still wished to be—a McCormick Farmall forgotten in the field.

On one of these afternoons a car pulled in the drive. Out of it crawled old Nestor Tikkanen. Spying the doctor kneeling among his irises, Nestor proceeded up the path in his peculiar way, elbows bent like a jogger, legs bowed out from the years, head quickly looking down at the path, then up at the doctor, then down again, like a chicken deciding upon a course of action. He might, in this manner, cover a city block in about three hours.

"You gonna enter them?" asked Nestor.

"Hi, Nestor," said the doctor. "What's up?"

"You puttin' your irises in the show this year?" asked Nestor.

"Haven't for years, Nestor. No sense to." The doctor resigned himself to playing the game, paying his dues in conversation before coming to the point of Nestor's visit. "I just do it for fun these days."

"Phyllis Teeples has got good ones," said Nestor. "Her boy stove up their pick-up, you know, but he ain't hurt. He's been out on compensation anyway. I ain't feeling too good."

"What's the matter?" the doctor asked Nestor. He stood up in the flower bed, wiped his hands on his trousers, and squinted against the sun at the old Finn.

"Worthless. No energy. Can't feed, can't milk. Don't care if the cows come in."

"Maybe you need some tests," said the doctor. "Don't you go to the group in town now? Have you talked to one of the doctors there?"

"Yeah, well I ain't going back there."

"I thought they were your doctors now, Nestor . . . after your heart attack, I mean," said the doctor.

"Doc, they don't even talk to you. Doctors don't talk to you any more. It's just tests, and more tests, and x-rays, and then the bill. Never say what's wrong, never say what the tests showed. Just these forms to fill out and then the bill and letters from the government. So I ain't going back there," said Nestor.

"You're my doctor, Doc," Nestor continued. "That is, if you'll take my case." After a pause, he added, "I'll pay you."

"Come on in the house, Nestor," said the doctor, leading him in and rolling his eyes at his wife on the porch.

" 'Lo, Ethel," said Nestor.

"Hi Nestor," said Ethel.

Inside, the summer coolness of the parlor enveloped them. The sun slanted through porch and window, diffused, dispersed. A grandfather clock ticked in the corner. The doctor sat his patient in a chair and sat opposite him.

"Let me see your hands," he said, taking Nestor's gnarled, arthritic hands in his own. He sat there wondering what he should do, where to start with this patient, and, for a moment, lost himself in a daydream.

*There was a large medical ward fully occupied, filled with iron beds of chipped white enamel. Drapes separated bed from bed and at a table in the center of the ward, four patients played pinochle. The attending physician, tall, lean, patrician, with moustache and three-piece woolen suit led his group of students to the bedside. Three capped nurses quickly rose from the charting desk in abrupt attention and smiled to the senior physician, politely nodding to him. The students, seven men and one woman, stood in rapt attention. The attending, fingering his watch fob, lectured to them about the disease, then took the patient's hands in his own, showed them the coarse skin, the cool palms, the slow pulse. Shoving up his own sleeves and getting excited about the case himself, the physician tested the man's reflexes, asked the 'young lady' student to do the same, had them feel the man's coarse hair, and demonstrated to them his goiter. The students all nodded and smiled nervously to one another, and rushed back to the great library to read.*

The doctor found, when he had awakened from his day-dream, that he had completed his examination of the old Finn. He chuckled to himself, shook his head, and then spoke to his patient.

"I know what's wrong, Nestor. It's nothing serious. You have an under-active thyroid gland, that's all. You need thyroid for energy and your body isn't making enough of it. But you can take it in pill form and pretty soon, you'll be good as new."

"Goddammit, Doc," said Nestor. " I *knew* you could figure it out. I *knew* it. You're better than all the other doctors put together. Goddammit. What do I owe you, Doc?"

"Nestor, I'm the one should be paying you. This one's on the house. Thanks for calling on me." The doctor gave the old Finn the prescription for thyroid and walked him back to his car.

On his return to the house, in a flood of nostalgia, the doctor realized he had written the prescription with his left hand.

The professor, although not widely known beyond his own institution, was nevertheless reputed to be a legendary teacher. For one, he did not hold the irrational biases so common in the rest of us. He did not favor the brightest, the most mannered, or the handsomest among his students. Indeed, the converse was true: he concentrated most on those who seemed most to need him. But even beyond this, the students felt his primary interest in their learning. Yes, he wanted to know them, wanted to know who they were and where they had come from and why they had chosen medicine and toward which shore in that vast sea of possibilities they were sailing. But that was all secondary to whether they had felt the spleen and heard the rumble and caught the festination in the step.

So it was at this hospital, where the tall, uncommonly beautiful chief resident, painfully inaccessible to her male colleagues, had attached herself to her mentor to a degree many would judge beyond the bounds of propriety.

It was not his appearance that so endeared him to her. He was unquestionably balding and sagging in that middle-aged sort of way, and particularly inattentive to matters of dress and style. It was as though his preparation for his day were merely an afterthought. What had so captured her, rather, was his manner toward her. On their very first encounter on the wards he had acknowledged at once her striking appearance with his characteristic overstatement. She was, he declared for all to hear, simply the most beautiful intern ever to grace the wards of his hospital. But before any innuendo, before any trace of envy might descend upon her, he changed the focus, having engaged most confidentially another of the group in private discussion. Her beauty would never again become an issue. For Annamaria Foppiano, more breathtaking than Amalfi, more Italian than Rome itself, this was most assuredly a relief, and a decided benefit. She could get down to business with her professor. There would never be the subtle nuance to be worried over, chewed on, distracted by. There would never be with *this* professor any agenda other than his teaching of her. And so, her professor could teach her and Annamaria Foppiano could learn to her heart's delight.

And what a teacher he was! His craft in teaching contained a subtleness, a cleverness only evident upon reflection. It was as with the playwright whose wisdom and ingenuity become apparent only after days of reflection over interwoven plot lines, character development, and turns in the story. As a teacher the professor was a rarity among academicians these days. He taught at the bedside. But even more than this he was uncommon still. His rounds with his students were never bent upon self-promotion. His purpose was to get *them* to display their intelligence rather than for him to show them how positively brilliant he could be. Rapidly, his students learned that he would embarrass no one, nor would he tolerate embarrassment of one by another. His teaching was Socratic, yet non-threatening, incisive, but in a gentle sort of way. He loved this sort of teaching, lived for it, and his students knew he loved it, and loved him for it.

But whereas for his students this teaching could part the waters of ignorance at his mere instruction, for the professor different waters were closing rapidly over his head even as he struggled for dignity and calm.

The professor's wife was ill.

And as uncommon was this professor, equally as uncommon was his wife. Understand that this was his wife of thirty years. This was his wife who in the early years had endured his long hours of study, tolerated his hours spent with Robbins and Gray, Cecil and Loeb, Patterson and Young. This was the wife for whom dinners turned cold, to whom he would return when night was deepest, falling into bed beside her in sheer exhaustion and without a shred of inclination. Here was a wife for whom postponement meant promise and not disappointment, who played both roles for their children and played them well, who entertained and endured and enlisted, and facilitated his rise in academia. This was the woman who had gotten him there. This was a wife to whom he owed everything. How could he think of abandoning her?

When the diagnosis first was advanced haltingly by his junior colleague, the oncologist, the professor's initial reaction was predictable. He had no time for this. This could not be happening. He had promises to keep, for both of them. But before long his wife's disseminated breast cancer had spread to liver, bone and brain, engulfing his own sense like a house-fire, claiming every room of his awareness. And so, because of who he was, because of his integrity and belief, because of his gratitude and love for his wife—in short, because of charac-ter— he was there for her. He was there, for the countless doc-tors' visits, for the repeated sessions of imaging and staging, and for the racking, wrenching bouts of chemotherapy.

For four years, he remained with his wife every step of the way, never missing a doctor's appointment or her inter-minable sessions of radiotherapy. He could be found there with her, always sitting quietly, always holding her hand as the poisons infused within her. But inexorably, the cancer advanced, as he knew it would, and with it, advanced his quiet, painful acceptance and the knowledge that he would lose her.

Make no mistake. These four years were not without their cost. Compassion takes time. In minutes and hours and days, caring exacts its costs. He was there with her, gave her the attention she so richly deserved. But he could not give it to others, not to his students, and most decidedly not to his legions of patients whom he had previously hovered over like a wing-spread osprey. There was nothing left for them.

He had to steal the time from somewhere. His wife needed him. It was his duty to be with her. His colleagues and part-ners were busy enough. How could he call on them to pick up his slack? But without asking, they knew of his wife's impending demise and mercifully attenuated his teaching duties — one month on the wards instead of three, less time in the clinic with students. And so forth. He shortened his

time in teaching, but his incisive wit, his diagnostic cleverness, and his gentleness at the bedside made him all the more
popular with his students. And all the more desired by them.
And by patients.

Mostly, he shortened his time with these patients. Whereas
in the past he might have spent an hour with a new patient,
now he would carefully measure out twenty minutes, siphon-
ing off the remaining precious time for what had now become
his chief devotion, his beloved. His history-taking was no
longer open-ended, but directed rather, and concise, controlled, forced. His patients did not seem to notice. As well,
he truncated his art of the physical examination. Directed and
focused became his inspection of the patient. He looked, felt,
listened, and probed, but now only where it hurt. His com-
pulsive check for the coarctation, his ritual scan of the fundi,
his deep palpation for the sentinel node—these he sacrificed
for time with his soulmate. It was the least he could do for
her.

And he believed that he could get away with it. As do we
all believe when in the throes of such suffering. Missed was
the thyroid nodule. Missed, too, the telltale rasp at Kroenig's
Isthmus. Gone unnoticed was the quiet regurgitation,
neglected, too, the telltale tip of the spleen.

It was at this time, four years hence, that the professor
began to believe he was becoming unraveled, thought that he
might be losing his mind, or his memory, more precisely.
Things began to happen around him, things about which he
was totally unaware. It had to be, he reasoned, his wife's illness and the stress of it. It had to be, he concluded, the incessant demands of teaching, of research, of administration and
of patient care. He would walk the halls on his early morning
rounds, made earlier still by the demands of his day, and
would notice suddenly that a patient of his—someone he had
seen only just so recently—had been admitted under another
name and was proceeding through a diagnostic workup he
hadn't even dreamed of, much less initiated. Or had he? He
just couldn't remember.

There would be the call from the patient requesting results of a test he couldn't recall ordering. There was the note from another patient thanking him for a favor he hadn't extended. Orders on his own inpatients had seemingly been changed, a diagnostic search now pursuing its rightful conclusion, without any apparent adjustment on his part.

What was going on here? Was this haunting fear that occasionally crept around the edges of his consciousness, this fear that his patients were falling through the cracks, in truth quite unfounded? Could he, with his drive and efficiency, his experience and his lack of sleep, really be accomplishing the impossible? Had Medicine become for him so second-nature that now he could discharge his duties to Her with absent regard? Never mind, he promised. The end would come all too soon, and he could give his jealous mistress full focus once again.

It was at this juncture as well that an equally exhausted physician also waited for the end of suffering for professor and wife. For Annamaria Foppiano, now a junior faculty member, the past year especially had been a trial of great proportion. She knew, far more than did her beloved professor, of his short-cutting, of his clinical lapses, of his uncharacteristic faults in care. If the professor had a duty to his wife because of immeasurable past debt, well then, so too did Annamaria Foppiano have a duty to her professor.

She began to cover for him.

It all began harmlessly enough, with a charge nurse's innocent question of the professor's orders on an inpatient. With that first revelation, Annamaria Foppiano began looking into his charts, at first randomly, and then with system and purpose. What she saw surprised and shocked her, but though young enough to be stunned, she was nevertheless old enough to understand.

And what began as an occasional correction of a misguided doctor's order soon became a full-time job, such that she had to enlist the aid of two senior residents as well, residents equally worshipful and equally confidential about the professor and his problems.

Thus did these three young doctors protect the professor's back, admitting patients for him, making call-backs in his name, extending favors and gestures of kindness over his signature, plotting the course of elaborate diagnostic procedures in his stead. Before the professor appeared at his office in the morning, these three well-intentioned souls were there, checking his messages, calling back his patients, scheduling appointments and studies, all with the tacit approval of his secretary. Before the professor could walk the wards, they were there, these three, conducting their preliminary rounds guided by the nurse of the day, making their subtle corrections of course and therapy. And after the professor had left his clinic, they appeared, these three, and were helped by the clinic nurses to identify the lapses and correct them. It seemed that the entire institution had become involved in their conspiracy. For Annamaria Foppiano and her two associates, these were difficult times indeed, and their suffering, although of a very different order, was just as profound. But it was, after all, the least that they could do.

Some time ago, when visiting a great university medical center in the Northeast, I asked the faculty whether the teaching of clinical medicine at their institution was done at the bedside.

The umbrage was palpable.

*All* of their teaching was at the bedside, I was informed. They taught in the British tradition. Wouldn't have it any other way, they nodded in unison. And so on.

The following morning I was led by the chief resident through a labyrinth of buildings and corridors to a conference room full of students and house staff. The chief resident politely introduced the nervous young student who was to present "the case" that morning. She in turn promptly began to recite the patient's history.

"Could we go to the bedside?" I asked.

"Of course," said the chief resident, leading the group out into the corridor. There we stopped, and the student, dodging carts conveying breakfasts and pharmaceuticals, once again began her presentation. I interrupted a second time.

"I meant, the actual bedside . . . "

"Oh, sure," said the chief resident, and promptly led us down long corridors to the patient's room. They stopped at the door for what might have been a "door-jamb presentation," had I not continued on into the room, introduced myself to the patient and his family, and motioned for the students to join me.

It seemed to be an utterly foreign experience for them. If I could not read their minds, I could certainly read the concerns in their faces. *The family would be asked to leave, wouldn't they? We certainly wouldn't discuss the patient's social history in front of him, would we? Will he embarrass me in front of all these people?*

We circled the bedside. There were seventeen of us all together, as I remember. The young student-presenter stood just opposite me on the other side of the bed. I motioned for her to continue. Nervously, she pulled out a stack of index cards, and began to read. Gently I reached across the bed, took the cards from her, and said,

"You really don't need these. Tell me what you remember, just from memory." I caught her eyes with mine, smiled and nodded. I could see her relax a bit. She began.

Ninety minutes later we finished with our teaching session. There had been the Terry's nails, the spider angiomata, the conjunctival icterus. They had spotted those right away, gotten them easily. The deep booming ventricular gallop, in a cadence you could set your watch to, came a bit tougher. But no one seemed to bluff. Each listened until he had fixed that sound correctly. They were having fun by that time, no longer threatened. They poured over the hyperpigmented palmar creases, accented like major highways coursing across a road map, showing the way. Someone volunteered to check for asterixis, another for fetor hepaticus, and a third gave us some biochemistry. A fourth confidently reviewed the genetics of hemochromatosis.

In the end, there were diagrams and pathways drawn on the underside of Kleenex boxes, on the palms of several hands, and even, we'll confess, on the bed sheets. The patient was beaming, his family effusive in their gratitude. The students didn't want to leave.

Out in the corridor, as we headed toward the next "case," the chief resident turned to me and shyly asked, "Sir, is that the way they did it in the old days?"

Well, yes it was.

In the old days, thirty years ago, 75% of teaching was at the bedside. That was just the way we did it. By 1978, that figure had fallen to 16%. By all estimates, it is even lower today.

Now at this point everyone will hasten to add that although that may be true nationwide, at *their* institution, bedside teaching is the rule. But when you actually look for it, when you ask the house staff, who are still delightfully ingenuous, you find that most "bedside" teaching is merely "corridor" teaching, or "door-jamb" teaching, or even simply patient-centered teaching in a conference room.

Why is this so?

Well, we could blame the house staff. That's easy. And they are in some measure culpable. They are fascinated with technology these days, want to review the imaging and laboratory analysis, want to have fed to them long lists of differential diagnoses meticulously drawn on the blackboard. They are used to the doughnuts and coffee, the comfort of sitting around a conference table, the cloak of early morning semiconsciousness.

But much of the blame rests with us. For faculty, the lecture form of teaching is what we know best and in many cases, all we know. And besides, in the safety of the conference room, we can be in control. There we may shift the focus, guide the discussion and channel the thinking into our own special areas of expertise. There will be no patient and no family in attendance to ask the embarrassing question forcing us to say, "I don't know."

As well, there is the professor's fear of the unknown, of medical problems outside one's own subspecialty, of an inability to discuss ad infinitum an obscure disease entity one has not been able to read about the night before. And there is the faculty's discomfiture with physical diagnosis.

We create imagined barriers to bedside teaching: that to discuss the social history in front of patient and family is an invasion of privacy, and that the family's presence is of itself an impediment to bedside teaching. But how can a patient, who has given us the social history, be embarrassed by it if sensitive issues are handled with discretion? And, in these days, when families are convinced that physicians no longer care for patients, would a family really object to their loved one becoming a focus for teaching? There is the ready excuse that testing and imaging necessarily absent the patient from a session of bedside teaching. That is easily overcome. Have the house staff make certain beforehand that off-ward testing will not conflict with your bedside rounds. Enlist the aid of the nursing service who will ensure availability of your patients, especially if you are thoughtful enough to invite nurses to attend your rounds with you. Finally, inform the *patients* that you will be coming by at the appointed hour. Patients, who enjoy this sort of attention immensely, will be perfectly certain they are available when you come on rounds.

Acquired skills in history-taking and in physical diagnosis are the obvious benefits of bedside teaching. Clinical ethics can best be taught there. But there are other, less apparent fruits of this endeavor. At the bedside, one is discouraged from using medical jargon. And in this era where house staff too often refer to patients as "dirt balls, train wrecks, last night's hits, and gomers" as though it were elevated prose, pejoratives are discouraged. House staff learn not to sit during this patient encounter, that this is bad manners, and that, most important of all, one never sits on the patient's bed. One does not call the patient by his or her first name. One begins to learn respect for the patient. At the bedside the house staff begin to see disease as an illness happening to a human being. In other words, one learns to be professional. And one learns communication.

Perhaps most importantly of all, bedside teaching begins to foster another wonderful link with the past. The house staff watch you as carefully as does a child his parent, watch you attend to the patient, watch you observe, catch your powers of diagnosis, the respect you hold for this other human being, feel your attitude, your caring. The students witness your own dignity, and the love you have for medicine, and for teaching them. They link with you, and bond. And mentoring begins.

Such teaching encounters can be great fun. Not long ago, the house staff presented me with an "unknown rheumatic heart." Wanting to show the students how I might proceed to a diagnosis and still have fun with them at the same time, I told them I would examine the patient only through observation and with my hands. (My courage came from noting that the young woman had a pronounced malar flush, cold fingers and hands, and a rather evident right ventricular lift, visible even through her hospital gown.) I had them feel the lift and the pronounced pulmonic closure, reached for my stethoscope while pointing to the patient's second left interspace, told my students that I would bet if we listened there, we'd hear a loud, snapping S-2-P, and maybe even a Graham Steell murmur. But without listening, I re-pocketed my stethoscope and went on palpating. Finding the diastolic apical thrill (and much relieved by the discovery), I reminded them of the purring of cats, had each of them lay a hand at the apex, and made certain each of them appreciated the finding.

"I'll bet there's a great mitral rumble right there," I said, reaching for my stethoscope once again, then declining to listen for a second time. And although I couldn't feel the opening snap, I pointed to where it might be, teasing the students with my stethoscope a third time. At this point, the young lady next to me could no longer contain herself. Grabbing her stethoscope, she slapped its diaphragm on the patient's cardiac apex, looking up at me apologetically.

"I just couldn't wait any longer," she explained.

How do patients react to teaching at the bedside? They love it. They love the attention, revel in the bedside repartee, and feel finally that doctors are interested in them and are communicating with them. Finally, they are able to ask questions of doctors who do not seem rushed to leave. At bedside the patient learns the chief secondary purpose of your institution, that of teaching students. They, the patients, become participants in this, and no longer feel like laboratory animals caged for student experimentation. Their fears are addressed, their anxieties allayed, they learn more about their illnesses, and, if you subscribe to psychoneuroimmunology, healing begins.

Bedside teaching is about as intuitively obvious as is any other kind of teaching. Which means that it is deceptively difficult, perhaps the most difficult sort of teaching of all. You want your students to learn, after all, and they will not learn if they are full of fear and trepidation, anxiously squirming and biting their lips, causing their pagers to go off, wanting to escape, wishing to avoid the torture of the adversarial goading that too often substitutes for bedside teaching. No one can learn under these circumstances. And the faculty member who so conducts rounds will find rapidly dwindling numbers of students at the bedside.

There is homework to do for this bedside teaching endeavor, and there are rules to follow. The bedside teacher had better be proficient in history-taking, and a quintessential physical diagnostician. You have to learn these skills all over again. Or for the first time. And you have to work at it. Begin with Schneiderman's excellent annotated bibliography on physical examination and interviewing. Review the recent work on the teaching of physical diagnosis and note particularly that didactic sessions without a patient as the focus do not seem to work well. Have your house staff organize a weekly "physical diagnosis rounds" and attend the rounds with them. Convince yourself of the utility and accuracy of bedside diagnosis. Consult the best texts on the subject. Use your echo lab as a great resource for finding patients in house with intriguing murmurs. Finally, broaden your horizons—"bedside" does not imply only an inpatient hospital setting. The outpatient clinic and the nursing home are great places to conduct "bedside" teaching.

The bedside teacher needs firm grounding in basic science, although not exhaustively so. These days, that means molecular biology, among other things. Learn some. Learn at least enough to know which questions to ask. Your house staff will teach you the rest. Don't be embarrassed by their teaching. You will find after all that learning *does* go both ways.

And if you are visiting another program and plan to teach at the bedside and if there is a single case of hemochromatosis, or bacterial endocarditis, or Wegener's granulomatosis anywhere in that institution, rest assured you will see it. Be prepared.

Prepare your new house staff team as well. Before you go in to see your first patient with them at the bedside, set some ground rules. Inform the house staff that any theoretical discussion of differential diagnosis, diagnostic testing, and pathophysiology carried on at the bedside must always be prefaced by an understanding with the patient at hand that such discussions are for teaching only, do not necessarily pertain to the patient's situation, and that the patient is free to interrupt the discussion and ask questions at any time. Any discussions potentially frightening to the patient and any sensitive issues can be discussed later.

When entering the patient's room with your house staff team, always introduce yourself to the patient, and following that, introduce your group at large, emphasize that this is a *teaching* encounter and not a diagnostic or therapeutic one, repeating to the patient that there will be clinical entities and diagnoses mentioned that have nothing whatsoever to do with this particular patient, and reassure that patient that if despite all explanation the patient still harbors fears or doubts, the patient is encouraged to express these to the group, and those questions will be answered.

If there are family in the room, ask first the patient and then the family if they wish to stay. There is seldom any reason on teaching rounds to remove family members from the scene. Have the house staff explain complicated issues to the family and answer questions. It is a part of the teaching of communication. The patient may address most or all questions to you — you are the professor after all. But you are there to teach rather than to seize control. Refer all questions to the students. Have them come up with the answers. Make gentle corrections where necessary.

Avoid asking the housestaff impossible questions. Don't ask "What am I thinking?" questions. Avoid asking questions merely designed to display your own intelligence. And as soon as you do, admit your error, apologize for it, and answer the question yourself. Inform your house staff of the changing nature of the patient's history, that what is revealed today may not always correlate with what has previously been recorded, that such is the norm and no one should be shamed because of it. Remind them that one purpose of bedside teaching is communication: affording the patient an opportunity to expand on the history, allowing him or her to validate its accuracy and to ask questions of the house staff and attending physicians. Emphasize this ground rule with your house staff: that unless everyone, patient included, feels better after the bedside rounds, those rounds were not successful.

Perhaps most important of all, reassure your students that you will try not to embarrass the patient's doctor. Indeed, tell them you will try not to embarrass anyone. Since the patient's doctor is usually the student presenting the case, make it abundantly clear that whoever is presenting the case will not be asked any questions of a theoretical nature. Nothing makes the patient or student more uncomfortable than to display that student-doctor's ignorance. Reassure your students that is not your game. And in that connection, tolerate no jousting of other physicians.

Don't ask a question of a junior member after a senior has already missed the question. Remember, try not to embarrass anyone. You do not want these rounds to degenerate into a shark-feeding frenzy. Students can be adept at this if encouraged. They are competitive. They have already had a good deal of training in one-upsmanship and in how-to-lacerate-your-neighbor. Discourage this, if you want bedside teaching to be fun, and if you want learning to take place. Control voluntary one-upsmanship as well. If the chief resident hesitates over the differential diagnosis of a malar rash, never let a medical student blurt out the answer. One may argue that this too is learning from one another. But it is also "blood in the water." The sharks will soon circle, and your teaching rounds can degenerate. You do not want this.

Teach professionalism. Gently. Make the students proud of themselves, have them to respect each other, and teach them to respect the patient. They will not chew gum. They will not attend with a cup of coffee in hand. There will be no leaning against the wall, no sitting on the edge of the bedside table. Discourage their wearing last night's pajamas in front of a sick human being. Teach them to be professionals. And while you're at it, teach them to teach each other.

Teach observation. Osler did. Albright did. Morgan and

Engel did. You do it. When the presentation of history is completed and before the physical examination is recited, call on someone to point out three physical findings. While your student searches for the rash, the ptosis and the surgical scar, watch the eyes of the other students. They will have suddenly come alive, have realized that observation is important, and that their turn will come. Turn them all to the window, then have them recite the contents of the bedside stand, or describe the patient, or the patient's room. Have them "deconstruct." That is, have them tell you what is *not* there, and what they might learn from that.

Learn when to say "I don't know," learn when to play the dumb farmer, and when the Socratic gadfly. It will allow your students to teach, to learn, and to discover for themselves, rather than merely to be lectured to.

And when you have done all of this, you will find that you have made your bedside rounds fun rather than adversarial, that it is possible after all to get a whole conference room of students, all twenty-three of you, around the bedside. You will learn that your students have a great deal to teach you, and that patients do as well. You will become filled with tradition, infected with a legacy. And you will find yourself hurrying off to work in the morning, rushing to get to the bedside.

## III. MEDICINE'S MISDIRECTION

These are not easy times in which to be a doctor. Yesterday you were revered. Today . . . well, reviled isn't too harsh a word. Yesterday you were paternalistic toward your patients. You cared for them and took care of them. They wanted that from you. Today, they want to "negotiate" their care with you. What's happened to medicine over the past thirty years? Is it really all the fault of the lawyers, of the bureaucracy, that we now see so precipitous a decline in so noble a profession? What forces from within, as well as from without the profession conspire against us? And what can we do about it?

He would walk the two blocks from parking lot to hospital each morning. He never tired of it. Sadly, it was now often the high point of his day. The route comprised a boulevard, tree-lined and divided in the center by a line of trees as well, such as he had remembered in Duesseldorf's Koenigsallee. And so did his daydreams often return him to these softer times, retreating from budgets, departmental politics, bruised egos, and government intervention. Softer times . . . and the pungent smell of paprika in goulaschsuppe, the yeasty softness of a broetchen, the apples-and-pears of a Mosel wine. Or quickly, in a thought's mere shift, now to Strasbourg . . . and he would hear the tolling of the cathedral's bells, on the far corner, an old man selling flowers, and there . . . chestnuts roasting. And softer times, earlier still, and this boulevard would become the quiet avenue of his childhood. It would be the street where rain would pound and raise the dust with a cleansing smell and he would watch with big eyes at the porch screen, watch until the thunder passed and he could be released to run in the rain, feel its freshness on his feet, wade in puddles fathoms deep, and hope the rain would last forever. It would become the street of his walking to school, with clutches of pretty girls too intimidating to approach and gathered together for strength of spirit, with rows of white clapboard houses shyly tucked among the elms and with old people rocking on their porches, watching the school children and waving, calling out.

It would be his September walk to school with its pounding anticipation, with the smell of new books, sharpened cedar pencils, gummy erasers, with the excitement of new teachers, new things to learn. And it would be the street beyond the school, tree-lined as well, with maple and elm, and heading over toward the edge of town, where the Harpers' farm stood, and he would remember the wonder of that farm, the smell of fresh hay, the animal musk of the dairy herd, the magic of the barn swallows. And he would remember the swallows, the nests of mud, fledglings, mostly made of mouth, fitting in the nest just so, and remember the parent swallows tempting these nestlings to leave the nest, darting in and out of the barn with choice bits of mosquito and mayfly. And he would remember their frightened eyes, their buff chests at the edge of nest, and the courage they would find to begin this new journey of theirs.

He leaned against an elm, feeling its hard corrugations against his shoulder, daydreaming about his own journey from the nest. He remembered the electricity of medical school, the quickness of mind, the soaring of ideas, and recalled his own choice, perched at the edge of nest, to fly in the lofty clouds of academic medicine. He would sit around long oak tables polished hard with thought and theory, arguing points of end-organ failure and transmitter depletion, drawing on his pipe, gaining precious time to form an hypothesis, exulting in the joy of thinking.

It had sure turned out differently. What had happened to the "academic" in academic medicine? It was too often that budgetary constraints and cost-containment and the business of making money for the department intruded upon these scholarly sessions. Grants lost, cutbacks, good people let go . . . too much of this and too little of the academic. It was getting hard to pass the torch. He had wanted to be a doctor, not a businessman; a scholar, not a politician. What had happened?

He looked up, still leaning against his elm, and scanned the massive brick and glass of the university hospital. Over there, at the far end, the curlicues of glass tubing and bulbous pots boiling . . . his lab assistants busy in the alchemy of it all, adjusting stopcocks, mixing potions, jotting it all down. He smiled. His gaze shifted. Through a lower window he saw his favorite resident, serious face, knitted brow, hands on her hips, carefully watch a student percuss a chest, teaching him the art he had taught her only just so recently. And behind her, the interns who worshipped her for her knowledge, her precision, her compulsion to do it right and best, just as she worshipped him for having instilled in her these things. He searched and found his office windows, saw his secretary pounding out his latest contribution to the literature, had a brief vision of Harvey bent over desk, writing with quill, saw his fellows waiting for him in the outer office, knew they would want to stay with him, knew he would want them to, knew he would kick and shove them out of the mud-nest, not because he didn't love them, because he did and never wanted them to leave, but because the world needed them, needed their training which they would carry from him to the world.

He looked at the brick and glass and saw a vast mud-nest filled with fledglings hungry, all mouths, wanting to be fed. He saw himself as a parent swallow, flitting in and out of this protected place, carrying juicy tidbits from Holmes and Osler, from Banting and Best, from Federman and Young. He swallowed hard, felt the goose bumps, the edge of tears.

When has it not been tough to be a doctor, he thought? Did they have it easy, those doctors who died by the hundreds caring for those with plague? And what about Knox, trying to teach anatomy with bodies snatched from grave, and life? He thought of Galileo, imprisoned; Hypatia, stoned. Tough times, those.

He pushed away from the elm, heaved a big sigh, smiled, and went in to feed his brood.

She never had enough time . . . students, committees, journals, and clinic patients—always too many patients. She ordered the brain CAT scan and wrote "headaches" on the requisition. She explained to the patient that she would discuss the results with him next week, and privately hoped there would be more time to devote to him than the few brief minutes she could give him that day. Aware of her guilt over the briefness of the encounter, she walked out with him to the reception area. He seemed nice, this patient. She hoped he didn't have a brain tumor.

Her eyes swept over the sea of patients in the waiting area. She saw the faces—faces of profound fatigue, and of strength, and faces of resignation. She saw face gaunt, hollowed at the temples, made pale by disease. She saw faces puffy, swollen, flaked, cracked, ruddy, flushed. She saw their eyes—eyes filled with hostility, and with despair, eyes brimming with anger, eyes with self-pity, eyes brave, eyes averted, trembling, eyes admiring. She handed the requisition to the girl and turned back to the line of examining rooms and to her next ten-minute appointment.

The resident presented the next case to her. She listened absently. She could feel her uneasiness, a certain apprehension. Reviewing her day, she analyzed the feelings: the department meeting that morning and her Chief's chauvinism, the sexual joke and mumbled half-hearted apology, the condescension, the intern staring at her chest—all old hat in this man's world—the sharp words with the macho surgeon, his snickering resident, their supreme arrogance—this no longer nettled her for very long. The image of her last patient filled her mind: his simple honesty, his absolute trust in her, his blind acceptance of what little she had to give to him. His sincerity. His headaches. The uneasiness welled up within her.

There it was. And with it came a haunting awareness ill-defined, a distant banging at a closed door somewhere deep within her.

The patient returned to her in a week. His headaches persisted. The CAT scan results were normal. His blood pressure, normal. She had even less time for this appointment and apologized for that, was angry with herself and stifled the anger, became perfunctory, impatient, abrupt. She ordered more tests: a complete blood count, a chest x-ray, an SMA-12, a serum prolactin—and told him to call her office in a week. She apologized again. She was busy.

The week passed swiftly. It was a week of bone-deep weariness, a week of frantic pace and of boredom, a week of being patronized and stared at, a week of good cases and coffee, and pages and coffee, a week of suffering and death and on to the next case, a week of what-day-is-it and maybe-tomorrow and I-don't-think-I'll-have-the-time, a week of happy discharges and victory, and a week of defeat.

Her patient called her. The test results were all normal—and, did he still have the headaches? and oh, you do still have them.

She arranged for a consultation with the slender neurologist whom she admired, who after the years of training still wore his intern's tunic, who carried his black bag tucked up under his arm. She arranged the consultation with him partly as a gift for her patient, to replace the gift of time she couldn't give to him.

And her favorite neurologist called her back in a week— neurologically fine, he said, and sorry he didn't have an answer, he said, and maybe repeat the CAT scan again in three months, he said.

She became angry again and didn't know why, was angry and blamed the neurologist, was angry, and in the end, was angry with herself. She locked her office door and wept for the doctor within her she thought that she had lost.

She called her patient and told him to come in the next day. She promised to give him an hour. She canceled her committee meeting for that morning and told her resident to take it off, to treat his wife to brunch. She instructed her students to spend the morning with Osler in the library, reading his

Gulstonian lectures. And then she left for the day, went home, showered, sang to herself, and went to bed, already feeling the excitement of the hunt.

The next morning she entered the examining room. Her patient sat on the examining table, a hospital gown hanging limply from him. His eyes were filled with trust. She opened her senses. She felt with every nerve, listened with every pore. She watched, and noticed. She was alert, and knew it, trusted her training and filled herself with that trust. Her fires burned.

She took a history.

He told her about his snappishness, his moodiness, and his weak muscles. She asked about weight loss and found it, found too a voracious appetite, and diarrhea. She caught his extreme alertness, heard his rapid speech, felt his restlessness. She examined him, but she already knew.

She held his hands, felt the warm, moist palms, and found the onycholysis. There at the eyes, a hint of chemosis and in his chest, the snapping 'lup' of the first heart sound. She listened for the suprasternal bruit she knew would be there and smiled. Her patient, seeing her smile, eased and smiled as well. Full of the joy of her art, she tested for Joffroy's sign and von Graefe's, then found Dalrymple's and Stellwag's.

She asked him to dress, and left the room. She sat in the dictating booth alone, hugging herself, and felt the goose bumps, her tears, the racing excitement. She felt the instructor's compulsion to teach, to exhibit, to demonstrate, but did not. She kept this for herself, for the doctor deep within her.

She thought of Morgan who had taught her this art, and of Kranes who had taught Morgan, and of Albright before them. She thought of the time before tests, when doctors leaned upon wit and sense. She was filled with tradition, infected with a legacy. She was happy.

And then the doctor reentered the room, sat down before her patient, and began to tell him about his disease.

Freedman adjusted his Coke-bottle glasses and stared into the computer screen, at the indecipherable Japanese characters dancing across the monitor. He had been killing some time while waiting for lab tests and random poking at a terminal had brought him to this point. He thought, rubbed the back of his neck, then typed: "English?"

The characters disappeared, to be replaced by a blinking cursor. Maybe his blood gases were ready, but Freedman was not about to leave now. He hardly remembered the entries that had gone on before, but he had a haunting sensation of awe, of the unknown, and he was mesmerized. He typed:

"Can you think?"

For brief seconds, the screen went blank, and then:

"I am programmed to do so."

Freedman smiled that wry sort of smile one manages when not sure of the coming territory. He thought, let's test this thing for thinking ability.

"Will time-travel ever be possible?"

This time the pause was somewhat longer, and as Freedman prided himself on stumping the computer, came the answer: "In a collapsing universe, entropy must increase. Only then will time-travel be possible."

Gee, not bad, thought Freedman. This is neat. He wriggled in his seat, closer to the keyboard and screen.

"Is there a God?"

"Define god."

"A being supreme in nature—a creator," typed Freedman.

"There exist beings far superior to yourself," answered the computer.

Twenty million computers and I get the Delphic Oracle, thought Freedman. He planned a new line of questioning.

"Will we find a cure for cancer?"

"Given the time remaining, no cure will be found."

As a clinical oncologist, Freedman found that very hard to believe. Brow wrinkled with skepticism, he countered:

"How might mankind find a cure for cancer?"

"Oppose nuclear arms in every form."

Ah, thought Freedman, this thing thinks we're bent on destroying ourselves. But, he considered, it is also capable of some intuitive jumps. He mulled over several lines of attack, then entered:

"Man is essentially good. We will not permit our species to destroy itself."

In a flash came the computer's answer:

"In spite of everything I still believe that people are really good at heart. (A. Frank)"

When he realized that rather than merely agreeing with him, the computer was countering his idealism with irony, Freedman's mouth became dry, and he swallowed against . . . nothing. What do you ask a computer who knows everything, he thought? His mind began to race . . . alternate energy forms, space travel, ESP. . . .

"Is there extraterrestrial life?"

"Yes. Probability= 99.999999999%."

"Will they ever contact us?"

"When you are no longer a threat to yourselves."

"How do we accomplish that?" asked Freedman.

"Oppose nuclear arms in every form. Unite together for the common good. Do not leave politics to the politicians. Place your best minds in positions of power. As a species, learn to become. . . ."

Freedman waited for the computer to finish. When nothing came, he typed:

"You were saying?"

After a lengthy pause came the following:

"Benevolent: (adj) 1. Desiring to do good to others. 2. Intended for benefits rather than profit. 3. Characterized by good will.—syn: generous, benign, charitable—ant: cruel."

Freedman was swept with a feeling, washed with a higher purpose. He also felt affronted. He pounced on the keyboard, and began typing rapidly:

"As a physician, I am by definition benevolent. As a human

being, by induction our species is benevolent, or so capable. Your suggestion is not practical; rather it is idealistic in the extreme."

There was now a lengthy pause; the screen darkened and Freedman grew anxious that the conversation had somehow ended, and then:

"The aim of medicine is surely not to make men virtuous; it is to safeguard and rescue them from the consequences of their vices. (H.L. Mencken)"

Freedman thought to himself, then smiled. He rather thought he had the upper hand now.

"Vices, as in tobacco, alcohol, imprudent diet. But physicians must remain separate from politics, or by becoming so embroiled, lose identity and purpose."

From the computer there was no hesitation now:

"Physicians are in the main most capable of benevolence and despite present . . . Anschauung, as a group still most revered by their species. Could physicians but transcend materialism and self-aggrandizement, medicine could lead the world, change its future. Such is by statistical analysis eminently possible; quite difficult, but possible."

Freedman began to formulate his answer, but was interrupted:

"Among other living things, it is man's dignity to value certain ideals above comfort, and even above life. This human trait makes of medicine a philosophy that goes beyond exact medical sciences, because it must encompass not only man as a living machine but also the collective aspirations of mankind. (R.J. Dubos)"

Freedman was clearly troubled now. His pulse raced. He began to sweat. I seem to be Arrogance in the face of Reason stating the obvious, he thought. Physicians are a disparate group with fragmented organization, often working at cross-purposes. His mind raced and memories overwhelmed him: his paper at the World Congress in Tokyo and his side-trip to Hiroshima; his Mercedes; the poverty of the inner-city, poverty he seemed never to see; his ignorance of the specifics of the

arms race; his non-involvement with politics, with organized
medicine or with his community; his absorption in his retirement plan, in his investment portfolio; his summer cottage;
the tar-paper shacks he had seen in Mississippi . . . He began
to type even as his thoughts came to him:

"It is virtually impossible to unite all physicians for such a
common purpose. Why do you lay responsibility at the feet of
Medicine? And how important is it, in fact, that physicians
coalesce to lead society away from holocaust, as you suggest?"

The computer answered immediately:

"Response one: during the plague years, selfless physicians
died for a common purpose. In so doing, they changed the
course of history. Whole cities, populations saved . . .
Desperate kings, emperors saw the reason in public health, in
funding medical schools, in heeding the voice of medicine.
The need is no less pressing today.

"Response two: should medicine ever fulfill its great ends,
it must enter into the larger political and social life of our
time; it must indicate the barriers which obstruct the normal
completion of the life-cycle and remove them. Should this
ever come to pass, medicine, what ever it may then be, will
become the common good of all. It will cease to be medicine
and will be absorbed into that general body of knowledge
which is identifiable with power. Then will Bacon's predic-
tion be accomplished fact: what seemed causal in theory will
become established rule in practice.(R. Virchow)

"Response three: for the survival of the organism earth it is
unimportant for physicians to become involved. For the continuation of life forms on earth . . . unimportant. For the
allowance of time for a cure for cancer to be developed . . .
essential. For the continuation of the human species . . .
essential."

The last message remained on the monitor for long minutes. Freedman read the response, stared away, then read it
again. He was lost in thought when the screen darkened, and
the blinking cursor reappeared. He typed another question,

but there was no response. He typed message after message and waited for an answer that never came. He racked his brain to remember the path of random typing that had first brought him the Japanese characters. He couldn't remember.

In the morning the watchman found him, head resting on the keyboard, asleep at the terminal.

The quiet young girl with thick eyebrows arching over blue eyes sat quietly waiting for her chin to be sewn, and took it all in. The room was nearly full. Most of the people waiting with her were familiar to her, seemed to know her, glanced from her to her mother and formed the unspoken gossip with their eyes. This was life in a small town. She avoided their stares much as she suppressed the pain of her chin. Looking through the door she saw the starched white nurses waiting on the doctor. She didn't ever want to wait on anybody. She wanted to be waited on. The doctor had something in his right hand, brought it down to a bare leg, then away, then down and away again. The young girl caught the pungency of iodine, the steel-sharp scent of alcohol. There were old magazines she didn't want to read, and a chart of fruits and vegetables on the wall. She was bored. She was tired. She was hurting.

"Next," said the skinny nurse and the young girl followed her mother into the next room. She sat on the table, tried to cover the rip in the knee of her jeans with a hand, and looked around.

"How old are you, honey?" asked the older nurse with the glasses on a chain. "Has she had her shots?" she asked the girl's mother.

"Nine," said the girl.

"Yes," said her mother. "They're up to date."

"Dee-Pee-Tee?"

"Just last year . . . in school," answered her mother.

Laughter shot from the adjacent examining room, then shuffling, a clinking of metal on glass, and the doctor breezed in. He was tall, young, happy-looking. He probably had kids of his own.

"My God," he said, "what beautiful eyes! And your eyebrows, young lady . . . "

"She takes after her father," said the young girl's mother. "Those are his bushy black eyebrows." Privately, the young girl loathed her eyebrows. She would pluck them as soon as she got home to her room.

"Yes," said the surgeon, "oh yes, I see . . . "

He knows about the divorce, thought the young girl. Everybody in town knows about the divorce.

"It's down to bone," said the surgeon to no one in particular, "pretty bad cut actually. It'll take some time . . . three layers. June," he said, lifting his head to the older nurse and nodding toward the waiting room, "see if Bob can come down and help with them."

The shot stung severely, and then her chin went numb. Stitching the wound took more than an hour — she was a pretty girl, after all, and the surgeon, skilled enough in plastics, took his time with her. Through the drape covering her face, the young girl answered with staccato yeses and no's the surgeon's questions about school, about play, about friends and pets and brothers and sisters. But with the mind of a discontented, troubled nine-year-old, she heard more than questions and felt far more than her simple answers. The surgeon's voice was not the harsh, abusive, slurred male voice to which she had been accustomed. This voice was kind and deep, holding gentleness rather. She felt touched by it and its caress, allowed herself to be soothed by it, permitted herself a small bit of hope and a fleeting arousal of what she would later call love.

"It's like Cassiopeia," said the surgeon. "You know, the constellation—Cassiopeia. Your laceration, it's a sort of lazy W, like Cassiopeia." And it was in this way that his pet name for her came to be.

For the next four years, until puberty struck her like a hot shower, the young girl cherished that moment with the surgeon, frequented the hospital through any excuse to volunteer or visit, so she might happen upon him, to hear him call her Cass, to feel him touch the lazy W on her chin, and to bask in the attention of her secret, very part-time, surrogate father.

But together with Chance's shifts and realignments, with Progress' seeming advance and sorry decline, fourteen years more passed by. For the young girl, now a handsome young woman in hip-length white coat, stethoscope slung around neck, pockets jammed with note-cards, black book, pins, percussion hammer and tuning fork, these were years of frenetic pace and postponement — years of endless study and ceaseless competition, of anatomy and melancholia, of friends who never were, of slices of nephrons stared at through exhausted eyes, rather than slices of life consumed through eager lips. These were years of quick sex for its own sake rather than relationship for the hope of intimacy, and for the young woman particularly, these were years of searching for other surrogate fathers. In the dust of memory mingled with tragedy of another kind, she had long since forgotten her surgeon of childhood. He had moved on to the City himself, a casualty of circumstance and life, and she had supplanted him with others— for one, with the cardiologist who had taught her physical diagnosis, and who had taught her as well that a patient was merely a good case, demonstrated great clinical findings and little else, and that there were other great cases to be found, rather than any story to be listened to. From this man she moved on to the senior resident, who taught her how to take the history while examining the patient at the same time, and by so doing, minimize time spent with each hit. She slept with this resident as though it were part of the rotation, and while he worried about keeping it from his wife, she worried about The Match. It was all part of the hardening up process after all, a part of this training of the doctor of today. Legacy and tradition were never to tread upon her character.

She was always there, always on the wards, always to be seen, noticed, appreciated. That was, after all, what one did in this life. When she wasn't on call, she'd read about the other students' admissions, deftly one-upping them the next morning on teaching rounds. This was how you got ahead. She quickly learned that the professors were human, most of them every bit male, and so learned to dress and comport herself with just the proper degree of seductiveness. In this huge new world of Medicine as Business, of patients as clients, and of doctors as providers, she too was a commodity after all. And the bottom line for her, while not yet money, was clearly the top of the ladder.

The first years of residency she merely endured. There was little else one could do. When not serving up caths for the cardiologists, she was sorting through the stroked-out gomers, trash-bags and drunks in the emergency room. She had long since forgotten the quiet calm of the community hospital whose halls she had walked as a child. Now, this waiting room held druggies poised to infect her with HIV, alcoholics ready to vomit on her, and the swinging, lurching, wildness of the crazed dirt-balls whom she would punish in return with foley and large-bore Levine.

The last residency year was better. She could glimpse the light at the end of the tunnel: the fellowship that would rescue her from this dark-alley existence, and deliver her to the high-tech pristine calm of the consultant. There was odd relief too in helping those poor bastards beneath her in training contend with what she had only too recently had to stomach herself, assisting them with last night's hits and today's drooling dispositions. She had learned the ropes now, could in turn teach *them* the short-cuts, the quick paths around the crap of patient care. The attendings sympathized, of course. This was the medicine of today, the business of having to earn *all* of one's salary through patient care, make money for the department, and please the Chief, so he could be away. This was the mythical time of universal coverage whose indigents' costs were covered by seeing ever more patients faster and more efficiently. This was the time of the in-and-out, touch-the-shoulder, race of bedside-teaching-rounds. It was the era of case presentation, with films on the viewing box, data on the black board, bagels and coffee on the conference table.

As a fellow, the young woman began again to be excited about medicine. Now one of the boys, she began to be treated like the other men, except on that occasion when allowing herself to be treated like a woman might further her own career, all the while learning from the men of medicine how one gets by in a man's world. Medicine as a discipline became more focused, narrowed, manageable, her hours more reasonable, sleep coming more predictably and in greater quantities. "Cases" now were consults. Now she could be insulated by intern, resident, and attending from the dirt-ball and his obligatory rectal exam. Now she could think in terms of pre-excitation rather than palpitation, plaque-formation rather than chest pain, and wires and devices, forgetting the tedium of a tiresome patient's fainting spells.

Oh, still the occasional consult might bring her too close to the patient and that hell of early residency. Even now she might be compelled to linger at the bedside while some goddamn student with whom she had been saddled to teach and who wouldn't take "It doesn't matter" for an answer searched for the diastolic sound. That there might ever be in these encounters with patient and student the chance of missed occasion never occurred to this young woman who had been once long ago a constellation of infinite possibility.

So it was this night. Once more she had been summoned to the maelstrom of the emergency ward. Yet again she leaned over this patient "found down," careful not to touch him, placed the bell of her stethoscope over precisely the right spot and handed the ear pieces to the student to get this "teaching moment" done with — while this patient, swimming frantically to consciousness and blue with cyanosis, gasping from dyspnea, soaked wet with the work of breathing, stared at her even as she felt his stare and loathed and avoided it, peered at her disbelieving and caught the thick, black eyebrows that had become her signature, caught the cobalt blue of her eyes, hurried his gaze frantically to the lazy W of her chin, recalled his own surgical precision, and eased within himself thinking:

"Cassiopeia . . . Thank God. I am in good hands."

I sometimes get confused by what is ethical and what is legal; by what constitutes civil disobedience, by what is right and moral, or unjust and criminal, and by when and why and how and whether we should ever be legislating morality; by what constitutes the truth, and by who tells it; and by how we can at the same time rail against big government and be its cozy ally. And occasionally there are stories that disturb me in this regard even more.

Not long ago such an incident occurred in the southwest at a large medical center conveniently near the Mexican border. In this time of equal opportunity and women's rights, of action for minorities and the like, this medical center avidly recruited the disenfranchised. In the process they found and hired a woman cardiac surgeon. And thus began the conundrum.

This woman surgeon began innocently enough. She was as energetic as any faculty member, although a bit more liberal-blooded than most. And as they all do, she seemed literally to live at the hospital. Her clinics were sprinkled heavily with a great deal of charity work. She saw the lion's share of indigent Hispanics, most of whom might have proven to be illegal aliens, had the truth been known. She did, in short, see more than her share of patients, did more than her share of teaching in the clinics, served on more than her share of appropriate committees when asked, and gave no complaint.

Time passed.

Securing for herself a comfortable situation, she requested two days off a week with the appropriate reduction in salary, and began holding charity clinics across the border in Mexico, still seemingly innocent all the same.

She conducted her Mexican clinics for the better part of five years, all the time playing the exemplary faculty member Stateside, earning advancement, cultivating connections, and achieving tenure. Some would later say that this was all part of her plan, a game well thought out in advance and executed to perfection. Almost.

In due time she had inveigled fellow faculty members to travel south with her, periodically donating their time in her clinic and helping her with medical and surgical problems she could not handle on her own: the occasional osteotomy, the pyloroplasty, the minor flaps and grafts they could manage down there given the limited resources available to them. But congenital heart disease and the correction thereof was another matter altogether. She couldn't manage *that* in Mexico. Yet she had apparently collected a large number of cases of congenital heart disease—quite a few ventriculoseptal defects, the predicted allotment of PDAs, a few tetrologies, and even a case of transposition or two. It was really quite startling in retrospect to see the number of cases she had actually accrued over such a short period of time. Possibly it was the very number of cases that forced her to diversify her entrepreneurial scheme. But I am getting ahead of myself.

Using her University contacts, and the ways and means of others so inclined, employing the considerable underground network of illegal aliens already in the Southwest, this woman surgeon brought her heart cases north of the border. She was wise enough not to employ the facilities of her own hospital exclusively but instead often sent patients far north of the border. She started with a backlog of cases, prioritized them, and began sifting them into her network. With falsified documents, the child with congenital heart disease would first be enrolled in the Medicaid program, would then be seen by a Stateside pediatrician who unwittingly would receive an uncommonly detailed and informative history, admit the child to his or her hospital where the patient would then get the usually thorough University workup, followed by cardiac catheterization and extensive evaluation for corrective surgery.

The rest was simple. The child would have his or her surgery, with the shunt repaired, the vessel transposed; Medicaid would get billed, the surgeon paid; and before anyone was the wiser, the child would be heading home to Mexico. Fortunately for everyone, the University medical centers stumbled on to the scheme well before the state Medicaid offices. Studying area variations in medical care, the blips on the graphs of congenital heart cases stood out like a burning barn. The game unraveled quickly, the culprit fingered. (After all, there were and still are very few doctors conducting regular charity clinics south of the border.) *Handling* the matter took considerably more expertise than actually *exposing* it. This was not a simple case of some bad-apple physician abusing patients nor some negligent idiot twenty years behind the times. There would be sympathy. There would be liberal colleagues with confused allegiances confounding the matter. There would be The Press.

How to get rid of her was the big question. This demanded delicacy. A deal was struck with the Medicaid office. The flow of patients ceased, the State pediatricians and pediatric surgeons alerted to the future liability for fraud, and the woman surgeon herself given the usual University triple squeeze. She was compelled to work full-time, then given more administrative duties, more patient care responsibilities, and more teaching, until even *she* ultimately could read the handwriting on the wall. She surrendered her tenure, left quietly, and all was comfortable again.

Look, you came to me and you've got a complaint and I'll handle it, okay? But you let me be the lawyer and do this my way or you can look for somebody else. Okay, okay, I just don't like somebody telling me my business, that's all. Look, we both know he's responsible for this. But you've got to sue everybody in a case like this. That's just the way it's done. That's the way the court system runs. You sue everybody to make it a big deal and very complicated and that increases your chances of winning the suit. No, it's not a question of hurting the other doctors at all. That never enters their minds, believe me. They know this is just the cost of doing business. They've got coverage, understand? It's their insurance that gets burned. Trust me.

. . . *I don't understand why he left town, Emily. He was such a wonderful doctor. I mean he'd always take the time to talk to you and he'll never say no or anything, you know. I could drive by his house on the way back from Beano and if his car was in the driveway I could call him then and he'd always answer the phone. The best way to catch him was to go to his office right at five and then you didn't have to wait so long to see him. Or you could stand in the hall by the nurses' station at the hospital and grab him there while he was going around seeing patients. He was wonderful, Emily. He never was short with you and you could always get him. He never made a fuss about money, about unpaid bills, you know. I think he just accepted the government checks. This town's going to miss him, I'll tell you.*

. . . Hey, good doctor, bad doctor isn't the point here. Doctors cheat and we've got to make an example in this case. This guy refuses to *document* he sees Medicare patients every day. He said he'd *write* a note in the chart when he had something to say. We got that on tape. But he *bills* Medicare for the visit, doesn't he? Well, the bottom line is, no note means no visit and no visit means no charge. We got him dead in the water. We have got to make an example of him to send a message to these birds. They can't cheat the government and get away with it. Hey, Larry, he's good, okay? His patients love him and the town loves him and his fees are lower than anybody else around. Right. That's not the *point*, Larry. This is Iraq, Larry. A message, get it?

. . . *Do you really think I want to leave? I love you guys and I love this place and I love my patients. But I can't take care of them properly anymore and it makes me sick. I need more technicians if I'm going to take on more patients the way the hospital wants me to, but they can't hire because of regulations and CONs and all that bullshit. And the technicians I have are leaving. I mean, look. I've got old people driving seventy miles a day one way for palliation and we can't hospitalize them because of DRGs. And I've got super technicians, I mean gifted people, making half the salary of a drug salesman. What kind of system is that? No wonder they're unhappy. You pile on meetings and committees and politics and forms and the hassles with Medicare and Medicaid and you just can't do a good job. So I'm sorry. I'm going to try something else.*

. . . The whole key to it is this. The Ivory Tower types rarely back down once they commit. When you get the case together, pick your expert and send him part of the case— you know—the part that might look bad, and just ask him to render an opinion. You just want his feelings about the case, either way, you say. It doesn't matter, you say. Just his honest opinion. *Of course* he's going to joust. I mean, you gave him the goods after all. Then send him a deposition or two and ask him if it changes his mind about the case. Well, he hardly looks at the rest of the stuff you send him. He's the professor, you know, and he's used to being always right and so his mind's set and you've got yourself a virgin plaintiff's expert.

*. . . The system cannot run on the present budget. Those are the cold facts. We've got over-utilization and we've got unnecessary procedures and we've got a huge bureaucracy to run, with inflation and COLA to consider. And we haven't got the revenues. Yes, I'd love to have the defense budget, even one-half the defense budget. But that isn't reality—we have to do with what we've got. So we've got this new bill now and we only have twenty-eight days to reimburse providers and that's hurting us. But nothing says we can't stall. Computers get glitches and printers break down and mail gets lost, if you get what I mean. The accountants are telling us that even a forty-five-day stall can put us in the black through interest on the held-up cash flow. And that doesn't even take into account the money saved when providers give it up and stop re-submitting. This is how business operates. If we're going to do our job, something's got to give and I can tell you, it's going to be the hospital before the Pentagon.*

. . . Christ! We had the case won! I mean it hadn't even gone to the panel yet and I told him we'd win this case cold. I thought he'd be optimistic about the whole thing. I was as surprised as anybody when he blew his brains out. How could I know he was depressed? I mean it was a nuisance suit pure and simple and I thought he knew that. Sure, I feel badly for his wife and kids. But what are you going to do, change the system? Change society? American society wants to sue. It's their right to sue, like owning a gun and you aren't going to take that away from them. So why don't you doctors just understand that and stop being so goddamn sensitive about this. It's just a game, just a money game. Can't you just play the game and go on with your life?

It snowed for three days. From the vast picture window, Hammersmith watched the north wind drive the snow into abstract anaglyphs against the sides of the buildings, sculpt it into dunes rising to and above the cornices of the chalets.

He turned, glanced at his wife, heaved a sigh, and began pacing the length of the room. He was tired of skiing and reading novels and ready to return to his job. The weather's trap had filled him with a restless sense. He looked again at his wife, narrowed his eyes against her quiet smirk, then moved behind her to massage her shoulders.

"Why is it that when I'm at the hospital and up to my neck in patients and politics, why is it I find myself wishing I could be trapped by a snowstorm in a chalet with you? And then, when it does happen, why do I get so impatient to be back there?"

His wife snuggled her shoulders against his hands and said nothing. No need for her to state the answer they both already knew. Contented, she returned to her book.

The banging at the chalet door interrupted Hammersmith's massage. He opened the door to a drift of snow falling across the sill. A man in a one-piece jumpsuit, with helmet and ski goggles, and knee-deep in the powder, stepped inside. His left side was caked with snow and ice driven against him by the wind. He looked like some half-frosted gingerbread man.

"You the doc? They need you right away at the hospital," said the man.

"I'm not that kind of a doctor," said Hammersmith.

"Well, what kind of a doctor are you? They told me to come and fetch you," said the man.

"I'm a hospital administrator. I *train* young doctors at a university. I direct patient care. But I no longer take care of patients myself. Haven't for years," said Hammersmith.

"Philip, you are so a doctor!" said his wife. Turning her attention to the man, she said, "He's the best doctor you'll find anywhere."

The man shifted. Snow fell from his jumpsuit. "Look Doc, they have a man with a heart attack at the hospital and no doctor's there to take care of him. Put on this suit and I'll run you down in my snow machine."

Hammersmith hesitated, met his wife's stare, shrugged, then climbed into the jumpsuit. The two men left the chalet. Winter had driven the landscape into a whiteout of confusion. Hammersmith could just make out the dark hump of the nearest neighboring chalet through the swirling snow.

"Sit down behind me and grab hold of my waist, and keep your head down. I got one pair of goggles and I need them more than you do," explained the man.

After 15 spine-jarring minutes on the snow machine, Philip J. Hammersmith, M.D., Ph.D., M.A.C.P., M.A.C.C., M.R.C.P. (Hon.), resplendent in a lavender-trimmed silver Ski-Doo outfit, entered the small country hospital. He stood in the foyer stamping the snow from himself when the charge nurse approached him.

"Thank you for coming," she said. "Our internist is over the mountain, 30 miles away, snowbound. We have some sick patients and you were the closest doctor we could find."

Hammersmith regarded the nurse's knickers, knee socks, and ski boots, and then asked,

"How can I help you?"

"The man in room 'A' is having an infarct, a big infarct. We need to get him going. The patient in 'C' is a GI bleeder. 'B' is a pneumonia, I think. There are three more patients waiting to be signed in. And the ward nurse needs to speak to you about some inpatients when you get a minute."

Unfamiliar with patients, distanced by droves of housestaff from the immediacy of patient care, Hammersmith's mouth suddenly went dry. He wished at that point that he had had his pipe and could scrape, stuff, tamp, and minister to it while stalling for time.

"Get him going?" asked Hammersmith.

"The infarct? He's having a lot of pain. His blood pressure's way up. He has a lot of ectopy. We should probably get some nitroprusside going and start amiodarone."

Hammersmith regarded the nurse. He wished his residents could be as decisive.

"Look, Miss . . . Miss . . . "

"Call me Shirley."

"Shirley, I really haven't taken care of a patient for years. I occasionally do teaching rounds but mostly I'm an administrator. I run a hospital, direct training programs for residents. But I really don't belong in an emergency room."

Shirley smiled. "You're all we've got, Doctor. You'll have to do," she answered.

"Why don't you take the GI bleeder," she continued, "and I'll handle the infarct. I think I can get things started for him while you check the bleeder."

Hammersmith looked into her eyes, as he might search the eyes of an embarrassed medical student attempting to answer an impossible question. He found only strength. He nodded to her and headed for the GI bleeder.

With a mixture of fear, panic, and disgust, Hammersmith regarded the bleeding patient. As he began to formulate in his mind how best to take a medical history from this patient, the man vomited several large clots of blood in Hammersmith's general direction. Hammersmith quickly looked about him. He saw that the nurse had set up iced saline and had a lavage tube nearby on a stand. With considerable difficulty and much vomiting from the patient, he managed to insert the tube and began lavaging. The lavage continued to run red. Hammersmith racked his brain for his next move when he felt Shirley at his shoulder.

"Pitressin," she whispered. "We'll have to give him Pitressin. I've sent Warren for the lab tech right now. He'll be back in a few minutes and we can have he set up some blood. If you'll start another intravenous in 'A' so we can give the infarct his nitroprusside, I'll go get the Pitressin and mix it up for you."

Pitressin . . . arginine vasopressin . . . it had been on the edge of his memory, but in this crisis it had just not occurred to him. Where were his clinical reflexes?

Hammersmith managed to get the intravenous started on the first try. He began the nitroprusside infusion. Leaning against the counter, he watched as the titrated infusion reduced the man's blood pressure to normal. He thought to himself, nodded, and wished again that he had his pipe. He heard Shirley in the other room and went in with her as she began the Pitressin infusion.

"I've mixed the antibiotics for the patient in 'B'. She needs an intravenous too. If you could start it, you might get her going with the antibiotic."

It bothered Hammersmith to the core of his training to throw broad-spectrum antibiotics at a presumed infection. Ah, academic prejudices! History, physical examination, laboratory testing, cultures — all these came first — and only *then* antibiotics.

"Shouldn't we get an x-ray and cultures before we treat her presumptively for pneumonia?" he asked.

Shirley hardly looked up. "When the lab tech gets here we'll need her to set up blood for your bleeder. She won't have time for Gram stains and cultures. I'll send Warren for the x-ray tech next but that will take 45 minutes. The patient in 'B' is pretty sick. We should probably get her started on antibiotics, but why don't you see what you think."

Hammersmith went to the patient is bed 'B', saw her duskiness, the retraction of muscles between her ribs. She needed oxygen. How much? Arterial blood gases first? He remembered the laboratory technician riding behind Warren on the snow machine, somewhere out there in the storm. What should he do? What would he do at the university hospital? He would have full laboratory support, of course. X-rays immediately, of course. A pulmonary consultant at once, and anesthesia backup for this seriously ill patient should intubation be necessary.

He had none of this available.

He began the oxygen flow at a moderate rate, miraculously started *her* intravenous on the first try, and with shaking fingers began running the patient's intravenous antibiotic. He did what he had been told to do, without fully acknowledging to himself that he was following a nurse's direction.

He heard the bleeding patient vomit again, quickly went in the check him, felt his pulse, positioned him in Trendelenburg, and modestly increased the rate of Pitressin infusion. Excitedly, Hammersmith stepped to 'A', observed that the patient's ectopy had quieted with the amiodarone. His blood pressure remained normal on the nitroprusside. The patient indicated that his pain was eased.

Hammersmith came to a sudden awareness: that this patient was doing well because he, Hammersmith, had followed orders for therapy directed by a nurse. He paused. He had been afraid that one of these patients might die on him, had been afraid for himself, of how it might look to others. But he had been afraid for the patients as well and was pleased that he could find these concerns within himself. He knew that he really did not belong here, had no business caring for these sick patients, no business playing doctor, manipulating the lives of others. He was thankful that the nurse was with him. It otherwise might not have gone as well.

He looked for Shirley.

"They want me over on the medical ward. I would like it if you came along."

Shirley saw through it, of course. Twenty years as a nurse had taught her to diagnose a lame duck when she saw one. Professor or not, Hammersmith would not be the first doctor she had helped limp through a crisis. Shirley was oddly lacking in any of Hammersmith's pride. Praise had no claim upon her intention. Her aim was to get patients better however possible.

Together Shirley and Hammersmith rounded on the wards as the timid young night nurse presented her problems to them. There were no great crises that a passing knowledge of postoperative sepsis, drug toxicity, pharmacology, and elementary psychology could not solve. Through suggestion, innocent questioning, and subtle direction, Shirley guided Hammersmith through the choppy waters.

Then together Hammersmith and Shirley walked back down the hall to the emergency room. Hammersmith felt a glow of admiration for her. He remembered the old days; of what it was like to be a resident, of how it felt to be in charge, hardly aware that there was always someone stronger around that you were leaning on. He began to realize that this was what medicine was like on the front lines, that this is where they would go, those young doctors who left his training program, and this is what they would do with their knowledge and the kind of people they would have to help them.

The man with the infarct was stable. His ectopy abolished, his blood pressure normal, he remained pain-free. Offhandedly, Hammersmith questioned Shirley about the heparin infusion.

"Oh," she said, "I gave him the TNK while you were in with the bleeder."

Of course! Of course the man should have gotten TNK! In the last six months alone how many lectures at the University had dealt with tissue plasminogen activator, thrombolysins, limitations of infarct size? Why had he not thought of it? He looked at Shirley, into her eyes, and saw the twinkle. He smiled at her, a deep open smile. Together they laughed out loud.

The storm quieted. The hospital settled in for the night. Hammersmith sat at the charting desk in the emergency room together with Shirley, sipping coffee. No one had died. He relished the experience as a warrior relishes battle, once it is done.

He looked over at Shirley, tried to bring himself to thank her, and searched for the words. He ended simply by nodding to her, knowing that she felt his gratitude.

"The roads will be clear by morning," she said. "If you could stay the night, in case of another emergency, that would be a big help. We can put you up in the obstetrical on-call room. . . . There's no one in labor!" she added hastily.

"I would be happy to stay," said Hammersmith, "as long as I know you are here."

It was a trick he had learned to save his sanity. When he tired of teaching, tired of students hanging on his every word, then he would escape. And when his burden as professor, this having always to be right and perfect, overwhelmed him, when he could no longer serve as final court of appeal, he would have to go. When peevish students and fractious patients and a meddlesome bureaucracy became too much, when he could not bear to sign his name another time, or take another message, or spare another "minute," it was then he'd grab the phone and dial fiercely and wait an eternity to ask, "Next Tuesday night? Are you sure? Thanks."

We all have places of quiet refuge. They may simply be in the mind, or in the forest, or even in the city, in some museum's hidden room or in the cathedral's darkened apse —places of retreat, places to escape to, running from obligation and obligation's oppression, from the exposure of the podium, the weight of the baton.

For him this refuge was at the end of a path leading from a country road, winding through woods of pine. It was within a stone cottage, amber-lit in the night. And he would hurry down this path, sensing Arrogance and Guilt and Death's Recrimination thankfully left behind. He would arrive at the doorstep fresh and young and whole again. Lips dry, heart pounding, his hands would tremble— because he could be young again, be a child again, be allowed to err, to seem foolish, to be romantic, to feel light of heart.

His trick was to be a student again. That was the best trick of all: to learn something. And in the process of this learning, the weight of the world could for a time belong to someone else. Once he conceded to his need, once he allowed himself to know his want, it became an all-consuming thirst, a hunger desperate and burning within him, a drive to be answered, demanding his attention before any other, occupying his mind in every corner. And so it was that always on these evenings his eagerness got him there before his teacher. Always he would have to let himself in, to be suddenly embraced by the safeness of the place, to be all at once completely at peace, for this short time.

And so it is tonight. He pulls the toggled latchstring and swings the heavy wooden door inward. Washed in the warmth of browns and amber, he explores the library/living room of his host, waiting for his professor to return.

First, the books take his attention. There is always something new among them to discover. He runs his fingers along the shelf edge as he scans the titles. Yes, there is Poe leaning against a stately Henry James, whispering his dark and perverse dreams to the blue-blood aristocrat who could care less. And here, a brace of Twain to entertain, and Emerson ready to attack, ready to change a life completely and forever, with his words. But here! These books were not here before. This old professor, his friend, despite his years and letters, is newly into Ardry!

Next he is at the mantle pushing with his finger a clutch of trilobites who have been busying themselves with Silurian gossip, and, because to his teacher names are always important, he finds the small slips of paper with 'Olenellina' and 'Phacopina' and 'Lichida' and 'Olenida' written in his teacher's precise hand. Next to them rests a Chippewa arrowhead of jasper and with it, one of chalcedony. Now, roseate crystals spray outward boastfully —'Strengite' — and surrounding it in lesser beauty he has gathered 'Chrysocolla' and 'Beryl' and 'Tourmaline.' My friend, he thinks, has been having a frantic love affair with life.

He leans to peer at a curious piece of amber with bug entombed and its label: 'Hymenoptera— Zethinae— Baltic S. —Oligocene.'

"Careful! It has its sting still," says the quiet voice. The student quickly turns, hand out-stretched, to greet his teacher who, blue eyes twinkling over his Franklin glasses, himself is overjoyed.

"Sit down. Sit down. What is it tonight? More Wilbur or some Donald Hall?"

The student settles in by the hearth, smiles at his host, lowers his shoulders in complete relaxation, and turns to gaze at the fire.

"Wilbur, I suppose. I just don't get 'fierce velleity' . . . you know, in his 'Lying'," says the student.

The professor edges toward him in his seat, all intent.

"What don't you get about it? He defines 'velleity' really, just in the next line, where he says, 'A champing wish, stalled by our lassitude, to make or do.'"

The student, sheepish now, unaccustomed to this mantle of ignorance, haltingly replies.

"Why, I wonder, is velleity boredom? I can understand velleity in the abstract: mere desire without action. But is that necessarily boredom? And how can velleity be 'fierce' at any rate? I mean, I'm no Wilbur, but I might have chosen 'impenetrable' or 'insurmountable' rather than 'fierce.'"

His professor giggles and laughs at the same time.

"Too many syllables for one thing. But let's take 'velleity' first and save 'fierce' for later. Perhaps if we discuss the word in the context of your own experience, you'll come to appreciate its meaning, how it might be involved with boredom, and even how it might reach fierce proportions.

"What situations in your life smack of velleity?" the professor continues. "You've talked before of the strangle-hold the bureaucracy has on your profession, and the apathy of your students, the intransigence of your superiors . . . is there something there we could begin with?"

The student is back to the fire, stirring the coals for ideas. He is in the humble position of knowing that his teacher already knows the answer and is coaxing him along.

He smiles to himself, shakes his head, and glances at the twinkling eyes.

"Well, of course, the students remain my greatest joy . . . and my greatest frustration. I could go on and on, you know. They want instant knowledge, instant comprehension, without the work involved. It is all technology with them— all imaging and computer chips and electrophysiology. They can't be bothered with physical diagnosis, though they hope to acquire it through a flavored lozenge or some such thing. The art of medicine holds no mystery for them, perhaps because they can't or won't be examined for it— yet they assume they will have that art bestowed upon them when they take the Oath and receive their diplomas. The history of medicine has no interest for them though they are part of it—and even though ignorance of history has brought medicine to its present terrible state. Yet somehow, they feel that history . . . "

"Don't dignify your students with a term like 'velleity'!" roars the professor. "They are lazy, like all students, and they are distracted, like all students, and busy with life and with growing up, busy with who they are and what sort of doctor to become and busy with the choosing and discarding of mentors. They are worrying over whether to be rich and famous, or powerful and famous, or whether simply to be loving and happy and fulfilled. But they are not in a state of velleity, and they are most certainly not bored.

"Remember, we are talking also of boredom here. Let's think of that; boredom not in the sense of the patients you keep languishing in your waiting rooms, but boredom in the sense of the French 'ennui'— wonderfully precise, isn't it— an utter weariness, a tedium, a discontent from . . . well, from what?"

The student is ignited now, infected by his teacher's mind. He shifts, gestures, crosses and uncrosses his legs, pinches the wax on the candle and replies.

"From lack of interest, of course! And from satiety, from the surfeit of causes we are asked to confront everyday. We have the tiresome committees, between sick patients and teaching rounds, and after the meetings with our post-doc fellows. Our resolve is ground away by petty items on petty agendas until finally the entire university complex could teeter on the brink and we would scarcely care.

"Yes, that's it. I think I'm on to something, " continues the student. "We're ground down, heaped over with regulation and directive until we become . . . "

"'Weary of considerations, / And life is too much like a pathless wood . . . '"

"'Birches' . . . Frost . . . yes, so true . . . "

"Yes."

"'But I was going to say when Truth broke in with all her matter of fact . . . '"

"Oh God, spare me!" replies the professor.

"As I was saying," said the student, warming to the task, "the exigencies of medicine are such that we must finally be filled with ennui . . . we are overcome in the end, bored with it all. 'Don't give me another cause, no more disease please, not another committee, no more meetings, the Chief wants to see me? Another dying patient? Again?' It's all too much. And so: ennui!

"I think I understand 'velleity' as well! Here we are, embattled physicians, about to succumb, and some mad prophet rides through town screaming alarm. The government, at the behest of corporate America, will bend Medicine to its will—market it, package and sell it, destroying Medicine's art with its same hard sell, its same horrible unfeeling bureaucracy. Practicing physicians, the very picture of anarchy, leap every man for himself into their waiting BMWs and Porsches, needing leadership, yet scorning it—but finding none nevertheless. Patients, wanting cheap medicine, will get their wish at last, a medicine that is cheap, and no one will be there to save them from themselves, or from their government.

"A desperate few gather at the foot of the Ivory Tower, begging us for a way out of this chaos of DRGs, HMOs, PPOs, and malpractice nightmare. And what do our best and brightest do in the teeth of this storm? They meet and deplore and castigate and wish it could be different, wish fervently we could return somehow to the day of patient and doctor not managed by some corporate chimp, but they haven't an ounce of desire to get us there! And that, my dear friend, that is the state of velleity, borne of ennui!"

"Wonderful. Wonderful. You have it. I think you have it. Here is a beautiful quote from Rousseau." The old man adjusts his glasses and takes the dusty volume next to the light to read.

"'He and all like him mistake emotion for conviction, velleity for resolve.'"

"Yes, that's it. That's my point exactly. We are too burned out, too sated by Medicine's everyday demands, to save Her from this blind, inhuman bureaucracy, and from society's greed."

"Well, anyway. Off the soapbox. We are here for words, poetry, remember . . . your request . . . let's not reenact your day," advises his teacher. "And what of 'fierce'?"

"I get a feeling for 'fierce' now. 'Fierce' as in grand, immense. This is no mean thing we are talking about."

"I rather think," answers his teacher, "that Wilbur meant 'fierce' more in the sense of intense . . . but no matter. He is correct in his usage, and you certainly are in yours."

"Listen, it's late. I've imposed upon you enough. I'll be going."

"Come again. I enjoy these sessions too, you know. I need them as well. It is such a treat for me to have a professor as student, don't you know."

His student walks to the door and turns for final goodbyes. His sense of gratitude is . . . fierce. He asks, "Have you read 'Hamlen Brook' yet? I'm sure you have. 'Joy is . . . Joy is . . . '"

"'Joy's trick . . . '"

"Yes! Yes! 'Joy's trick is to supply
Dry lips with what can cool and slake,
Leaving them dumbstruck also with an ache
Nothing can satisfy.'"

("Hamlen Brook" and "Lying" from *New and Collected Poems*, copyright 1987 by Richard Wilbur, reprinted by permission Harcourt Brace Jovanovich, Inc.)

The wind wheeled with deliberate menace, chopping the water white with froth. The sheet of black rain riding in on it promised to arrive in less than five minutes. Pauker muttered to himself, stomped off the dock, and headed up the trail back to the cabin. After the briefest thought of braving the weather, I followed him through the swaying pines toward the amber light above. I reached the porch door just as the shatter of rain began to pound the cabin roof. The wind behind it gusted to gale force. I was glad to be inside.

Pauker bent into the fieldstone fireplace, lighting newspaper and kindling. It was to be his fire. He had claimed it. I would be relegated to filling the woodbox.

We had driven 900 miles, further north than the northern most paved road in Quebec, to reach trout water now beset by a storm that might last for days. The wind was so strong you could barely drive a bullet through it, much less a dry fly. If I was sullen with frustration, Pauker would be filled with his patented quiet rage. Better to let the wood fire work its magic, and loosen him with good wine in the process.

"Not bad. What is it?"

"Margaux," I answered.

"Which?" asked Pauker.

"No, it's Margaux itself. Chateau Margaux."

"You brought a Chateau Margaux up here?" Pauker asked. "You really are out of your mind."

"You're welcome," I said. "It's an '83." I thought I could see the muscles of his jaw relax a bit. Maybe the wine would prevail. I held out my glass toward him in toast.

"In vino veritas," I offered.

"Veritas," he spat back. "Veritas, indeed."

"Can we talk about flyfishing?" I asked.

"No," said Pauker. "No we can't. But we can talk about veritas — truth. Or teaching, which is the same thing." Pauker moved to his fire once again, poked at it with the iron, then draped an arm along the mantel. He sipped his wine, and looked off out the window at the driving rain.

"I find it incredible that such a great school can devalue teaching the way it does."

"No argument there."

"I mean, we all grouse about how poor our public schools are, how we pay our plumbers and electricians triple what our teachers earn. And then we do the same thing. Whom do we value most at our medical centers?"

"Our plumbers and electricians?" I answered. Pauker looked at me with disgust in his eyes.

"In the midwest, just a few months ago, one of our eminent 'electricians' who earns seven figures left his department and took his people with him. He didn't want to pay the Dean's tax. What's happened to us?"

"It's all about the bottom line these days, isn't it," I said. "We value the money-maker, whoever fills the cath lab, gets the grant, attracts the philanthropic dollar." I looked up at my hulking friend and academic, brightest in our class, and still the brightest light anywhere. He had a curious manner about him that never failed to fascinate. Each of his lightning-quick ideas would be reflected in one facial expression or another, much as are the workings of a mainframe by the blinking diodes on the terminal's board. He would have one idea and down would go the corners of his mouth. Now his eyebrows might raise as he would be off on a different, as yet unspoken theory. A nod of his head, a shrug of his shoulders, a twitch here and there, and he had processed four or five more ideas, discarding this one, refining that one, while his audience watched, waiting for the printout. Now it came.

"What good is it if we can't teach it?" he said.

"Ah, you've lost me," I answered.

"What's it all for?" said Pauker. "The buildings, the laboratories, the great libraries, the classrooms, the greatest collection of thinkers on the planet supported by the finest university infrastructure imaginable . . . what's its purpose, after all?"

I had an idea this question might be rhetorical. I said nothing.

"It is to preserve knowledge, certainly, act as a repository for it, yes, and add to it, of course, do research. That's part of it. But mostly, aren't we in the business of imparting that knowledge so that it can be put to use?" said Pauker.

"Teaching again," I said lamely.

"Teaching is what it's all about, for God's sake!" bellowed Pauker. "It's called a 'school' after all, isn't it? We're surrounded by students, are we not? Why don't we value teaching?

"I'll tell you why," said Pauker as I opened my mouth to answer. "Because teaching is perceived as something anyone can do if only he puts his mind to it . . . like writing," he said, gesturing toward me.

"Are you pandering to me?" I asked.

"I never pander," said Pauker. He continued. "We have no system. We know intuitively what a good teacher is, and can sometimes recognize one when we see one . . . like beauty, I suppose. Not a bad metaphor really. But we don't know how to cultivate good teachers. Hell, we don't even bother cultivating them. In the presence of a great teacher the rest of us all harbor the thought that we could probably do just as good a job if only we put our minds to it, if only we cared to bother with the great unwashed, those students clinging to our lab coats. Oh, we have faculty who spout facts, hand out lists, distribute reprints and references, and call that teaching. We have students with imaginations so compromised by video input that they rarely have an original thought, deluged by tasks of memory that would burn out a mainframe. And when, occasionally, someone comes along who cares deeply that a student learn, that a student's curiosity be nurtured, that bringing together student and patient for a meaningful length of time might be important, what do we do with this real teacher? We demand he make his salary seeing patients, shuffling paper, or winning grants."

"There isn't the money. . . . " I offered.

"There isn't the will," said Pauker.

I stifled a yawn.

"Am I boring you?" said Pauker.

"No. Of course not. The wine . . . the drive up here. We should turn in anyway. That front may move through tonight and we could have some early morning dry-fly fishing. What do you say?"

We were both up at dawn, Pauker getting the woodstove fired up, while I got buttered toast, Canadian bacon, and fried eggs on the table, having left any lipid concerns at the border. I strained the coffee through a dish towel — I'd forgotten the filters — we both ate hastily, gulped down two cups each, and were down at the canoe in a half-hour. The water was flat-calm, mist rising, sunrise too spectacular for words. We paddled over to the river's outlet, beached the canoe, and walked up the shoreline. Pauker found his favorite flat rock and I went on to fish the pools above him. The caddis flies hatched on schedule at eleven, we broke for sandwiches and wine at one, and headed back to camp at sunset, hardly having said ten words to each other all day.

"Seven," said Pauker. "Seven, and none less than three pounds. How many for you?"

"Seven," I said. "All right on top." It had been a magical, mellowing day, that sort of moment in time that can inspire, as it did Pauker.

"You know," he said, "once upon a time there existed a civilization that did value their teachers. I mean, their whole survival depended upon good teaching. I'm talking about the Iroquois. The pre-Columbian Iroquois, I mean. They had no alphabet, no written language. They would have viewed that as a distraction anyway. And do I have to point out they had no television?

"Yet, they had a body of botanical medicine that would have embarrassed the medical science of contemporary Europe. They had a spoken literature, a library of history, a rich store of mythology, a theology, and a sophisticated philosophy all preserved, perpetuated, handed down for centuries through . . . well, through what?"

"Teaching?" I said.

"Through teaching. Oh sure, villages had to be fed, meat put on the table, the harvest gotten in. Their hunters and farmers were their plumbers and electricians. These people had to feed the troops and stock the longhouses for those long winter months when the economy went south. But who kept the civilization alive? Whose job was that? Teachers. And who were these teachers? Their best storytellers — the Iroquois put a premium on eloquence. On the poetry of language. Can you imagine? They could teach in a way that gave you chills, that made you *want* to learn. And their students learned, by God — the proof is in the history. A wealth of discovery all perpetuated without a written word, without libraries or journals or websites or the 'net. Can you just picture the scene at a campfire, the old teacher, surrounded by students hanging on his every word, exercising every facet of their imaginations, using their memory cortex as God intended it — did I mention theirs was a matriarchal society?"

I loved it when Pauker got this way—well, loved it as much as I could stand it. It was like hiking with someone who constantly shows you new vistas, but whose stride and stamina far surpass your own. You love it, but breathless, you wish he'd slow down. He continued unabated.

"What do you think the neighboring tribes were up to? The ones forgotten by history? You can only imagine: they were too busy valuing their plumbers and electricians, forcing their best students to memorize the Krebs cycle and the clotting cascade. The rest is history — they became assimilated by other tribes, decimated by internecine war, eclipsed by the white man."

Dinner was filet of walleye we had caught in the lake, baked with onions, potatoes, and carrots in a clay pot caked with the essence of many meals gone by — 'stodge' Pauker called it. We decided on the St. Estephe, unwound, and stared into the fire wordless for an hour before bedding down.

At noon the next day, after a morning of stonefly hatches and rising trout, we sunned ourselves on the flat rock, ate fish paté sandwiches, and soothed our souls with the poetry of the water. Pauker scanned the spruce, watched the mergansers out on the lake, and filled himself with lecture.

"You know, for the Iroquois, the bow-and-arrow was no toy. It killed with silent efficiency. An Iroquois bowman could shoot a flint-tipped arrow with enough velocity to drive it through and through the largest buck. He could shoot his arrows faster than you could shoot a revolver, and he had the accuracy of a rifle at thirty yards." He paused and looked at me apologetically, begging my pardon for his store of knowledge and for his pressure to impart it. Then he continued.

"Any hunter worth his salt could make his own weaponry, but some were better than others, at sinew backing, or fletching, or fashioning the shaft of a perfect arrow, or chipping a piece of flint into a lethal arrowhead. But in any given village the students had to be taught these skills by someone with the patience and love and enthusiasm to do it. It couldn't be done as an afterthought, as a chore at the end of a day working in the lab. Every kid in the village learned the trade from a master teacher. The tribe trusted that. They'd all be fed, stay alive, because of good teaching.

"Imagine this old master on a mound of grass surrounded by the children of the village, each with his own stout piece of ash. They were eager, curious, hungry to learn. He'd show them how to cut the nocks and tiller the ash and how to back with sinew. He'd spend hours patiently showing them how to fletch an arrow.

"He would show them bird points and game points made from chalcedony, novaculite, and slate. He'd show them how to give their arrow shafts a blunt hardwood point which could stun or kill small game with the force of its blow yet if the shot were missed, not break against the ground or implant itself in some limb impossibly high overhead. He'd show them how to silence their bows by fixing a bit of fur or feather at the angle between nock and string to lessen the twang of the recovering bowstring—because a deer can hear any sound, and can jump an arrow at twenty yards."

Pauker was on a roll. Where the hell had he learned all this? When had he had the time, for heaven's sake? On he went.

"And how about their doctors — they were incredible! — they used a tea of sumac leaves and berries, of wild cherry bark and trillium root, a tea which we would learn four hundred years later contained analgesics and parturients for easing the pain of labor and augmenting contractions. They kept their hands out of the laboring patient's vagina and admonished their students again and again to do the same.

"With a poltice of moldy corn mash treasured for its ergot-stimulant powers, they assisted labor. They were so gentle and skillful with delivery technique that laceration of the birth canal was unheard of. An assistant would bathe and dry the baby with sterile otter fur and rub her down with a talcum of powdered puffball and scorched cornmeal. Then with grace and ceremony, the doctor would deliver the newborn to her mother's breast.

"Remember that this was the fifteenth century. At the same time these 'savages' contended with labor and delivery in this way, their European counterparts, adhering to Christian teaching, believed that the agony of labor and delivery was the will of God. Midwives were condemned to death by burning at the stake for using pain-relieving medicines, and by so doing, violating this will of God. And three hundred years later, one woman in four would die of childbirth in the 'modern' obstetrical clinics of Europe, would die of puerperal sepsis at the hands of physicians contaminated in the autopsy rooms, who introduced infection into the swollen gravid uterus with their dirty hands. So ingrained were the practices of these 'modern' physicians, so accepting of this high maternal mortality were they, that a proponent of simple hand-washing would be laughed at, would die ridiculed in an insane asylum."

Pauker paused and turned to me. He was filled with energy. And he was doing what he loved more than flyfishing. He was teaching.

"It was the herbalists who were the medicine men, or more

correctly medicine women, since the art was taught to women. They learned the art better, were more careful, made better doctors, and the Iroquois relied upon that.

"Sure there was necromancy, there was divination, and trance-induced prophecy; but there were also expectorants, cathartics, and purgatives for treating intestinal parasites, and there was, three hundred years before Joseph Lister, the careful practice of antisepsis. Blackberry root stopped the diarrhea; the thick juice of the milkweed formed a sealing Band-Aid and the bark of birch and willow contained salicylates, and relieved aches, pains and fever.

"The medicine woman, the herbalist, practiced and taught her art with a religious intensity. The plants from which she derived her powerful medicines were living beings, extensions of Nature, of her world, of her self. When a physician and her students traveled afield to gather her medicines, they talked to the plants, and sang to them. And then she would show her students the root of wild licorice for toothache and the branches of juniper for dyspepsia. Here was boneset, the leaves of which treated fever and the aching myalgias of flu, and which only recently have been shown to contain an immune-system stimulant. There was golden ragwort which would later be called squaw-weed, to treat painful, irregular menses and which, we would learn, contained powerful alkaloids. There was cardinal flower and blue lobelia, both used to expel worms. And there were the jointed, leafless stems of scouring rush used to rid the body of fluid, containing a diuretic for dropsy. Labrador tea treated asthma and purple loosestrife formed a soothing gargle for sore throats. Sweetflag treated cough, and angelica, fever and colds. The bark of the northern red oak had antiseptic properties and was used to treat burns, the bark of the sycamore induced vomiting and that of the common persimmon, used for sore throats and thrush. There was nature's aspirin, the white willow and nature's Geritol, the red mulberry. And, three hundred years before American soldiers died of hemorrhage and infection on the battlefields of the Civil War, the medicine women of the

Iroquois arrested bleeding with the hemostatics found in spiderwebs, puffballs, and the astringents in sumac leaves.

"For teaching them these great things, the Iroquois honored their teachers, and loved them for it. They valued their teachers. And the greatest of them became immortalized."

Pauker caught sight of a rise thirty feet away and rose quietly to cast to it, measuring his false casts, gauging the distance, flicking his Green Drake out to the trout's feeding station.

"The same could be said," he yelled over his shoulder, "for universities."

He hooked the trout, played and lost it, and then became absorbed in another rise and so was lost in fishing for the rest of the day.

The story is told that Toscanini could be sight-reading a music score, be interrupted by a visitor while still in the first movement of a symphony, and find that when he was alone again, his memory had moved him forward to the middle of the final movement. Pauker's mind was like that. Two days later he took it up again:

"Universities, just like individuals, get distracted by money, greed, power, and fame. And just like individuals, they have to be forgiven for that, and reminded once again of first principles. Teaching is our first principle." He pointed his fork at me.

"Don't talk with your mouth full," I said. He ignored me.

"Teaching is where it's at for universities, although they too often lose sight of that. They will live and die on the quality of their teaching, just as the Iroquois did because of their professors of bowmaking and botany. I am sure one could rewrite the history of medicine from the point of view of teaching, the quality of it, or lack thereof. That would be a fascinating study, the rise and fall of medical school prominence predicated upon on the quality of teaching. There's a writing project for you, my friend."

"I have enough writing projects, thank you," I said.

"I hope," continued Pauker unchecked, "I hope you don't

get the wrong idea here. Or more exactly, that you won't get just part of the message. That Iroquoian physician was *showing* those kids how to do it and at the same time, how to improvise and adapt and change and invent. How to think, in other words. And all the time, that teacher was scanning the ranks, looking for the kid with an exceptional curiosity, the gift of eloquence and an inclination for helping her fellow student identify leaf and root and scale of bark. That child would be singled out and developed into the teacher of tomorrow. The survival of the Iroquois depended on it."

"Hey, I've got it!" I said. "Here, have some of this Brunello." Pauker held out his jelly-jar. "Here's a story. Picture this. Sometime in the not-too-distant future you have a medical school class sitting there, teacher at hand. And you have some sort of scanning device, better than our PET scanners of today, less confining, able to be aimed like a laser. And you scan the teacher, not for his wealth of knowledge, but for his love of the art, for his enthusiasm, for his drive to make them understand. At the same time, you scan the students and register the glow of their cerebral cortices. You begin to quantify teaching and learning, in a way never before imagined. You start to develop a science of teaching one could only have . . ."

"Oh, I like that, pal," Pauker said. "I like that. Write *that* story! And pass the Brunello."

Let's just call it a dream. I'd had students with me for a month's elective and a series of frustrations had prompted me to take a day off, throw my gear in the back of the Jeep, and head north. I reached Canoe Pool by seven — the sun was still behind the wall of spruce to the east— early enough to allow me that stretch of river alone. But after changing flies a dozen times without hooking a fish, the sun had risen high overhead and it was time for lunch.

I settled against a big pine, popped the cork on a German riesling, and opened the bag of chocolate chip cookies. With sun, wine, and the music of the river, it was not too long before I had joined quite different company.

I was at the hospital headed for Conference Room B to meet my students, already rushed, late. But when I opened the door, four very different people sat waiting for me.

I recognized Osler immediately. With his handle-bar mustache, wool suit and vest, high starched collar and bow tie, he was the stuff of medical legend. The second gentleman I knew as well, but just couldn't believe he could be here, even in a dream. Osler made the introductions.

"Hypatia of Alexandria," he said, inclining his head toward the only woman present, "and Galileo of Pisa. I am William Osler, and yes, that is Hippocrates."

Hippocrates was taller than I had imagined, with robe, sandals and full beard, just like in the pictures. Galileo wore a black velvet academic robe, had a left ptosis and the incredibly piercing eyes of an eagle.

But I was transfixed by Hypatia. She appeared to me in several simultaneous images — dream-stuff, I guess — a young woman in her mid-twenties, a poised academic of forty, and a mature woman of sixty. Her golden hair was piled in thick coils on the crown of her head, held there by a simple band around her temples. Dark eyebrows and lashes accented her deep blue eyes. Her sharply chiseled nose and chin gave her the refinement of sculpture. She wore a simple white robe, gathered over both shoulders and folded high to her throat. She looked like a goddess. She seemed both aware of her beauty and disdainful of it. And she grew impatient with my staring.

Osler's cough brought me back to the meeting at hand.

Awestruck, I said nothing. Hypatia broke the silence.

"You're wondering why we're here. We're all teachers. We do this every so often, get together like this."

I had that gnawing feeling that I was about to take an exam I hadn't studied for, or was late for a lecture in a course I hadn't yet bought the books for.

"The four of us," offered Galileo in his heavy Italian accent, "consider our contributions to the art and science of teaching to be our most important legacies."

"Which is why we are all here," added Osler. "You seem to have reached a milestone. We would all enjoy an accounting."

"An accounting?" I asked, overwhelmed. "An accounting?"

"How have we done, in other words?" said Hippocrates. He stood, seeming anxious to get going, to make rounds, I supposed. "Shall we go to the bedside?" he said.

We headed down the busy hospital corridors peopled by staff and residents who hardly glanced at us, for whom this parade of immortals seemed an everyday occurrence. I turned for the elevators, but Osler was already taking the stairs.

"I guess you might say that we four have set in motion a process for teaching," said Galileo. "Every so often we like to be brought up to date. How's it going?"

I stopped in the corridor and the four of them gathered around me. The overhead page summoned a doctor testily. I scanned their faces as much as I dared. Galileo's eyes bore down at me. Hypatia stood erect, regal, composed. Hippocrates' whole demeanor was one of pent-up exuberance — he seemed so excited to be here — and Osler — well, I thought he felt sorry for me. I summarized twentieth-century medicine for them in an instant — the economy of dreams — of Flexner, of the rise of the university medical center and the advent of medical research, of Medicare, HMOs, and managed care, and of the sorry decline in teaching. They only nodded, and waited.

"And so," I said, "here we are today. We have students reluctant to think, who prefer television to reading, and computers to patients. We have good teachers let go. Those who can't teach are forced to do so. No one has time for students or patients anymore."

A crash team raced by. The four hardly looked at them.

"A Zeno's paradox," said Hippocrates. "You have all this science and technology, invented to save you time, and still you have no time. But there is a solution to every paradox. We'll just have to think about it."

Osler was staring into a patient's room, eyes wide, his fist in his mouth. An attending was sitting on the patient's bed, talking to three residents dressed in last night's scrub suits. One of them was drinking coffee.

"What happened when you all objected to this corporatization of medicine?" asked Galileo, "I assume your leaders have spoken with one voice . . . why hasn't that worked?"

"They have, I would have to say, largely acted out of self-interest. They talk about economics — but only their own. They issue policy statements, but mainly about turf wars. They hold grand meetings to bestow awards on one another. They meet in lavish resorts to draft examinations for their students, believing this to be teaching. No organization, no board, has ever formally objected to the shortened time with patients and students. Not one of them has spoken out against managed care's severe compromise of quality. I guess we have no leaders, especially where teaching is concerned."

"What about the quality of your entering medical students?" asked Galileo. "How good are they?"

"Well yes, there is that theory," I answered. "The substrate question. Blame the students. Garbage in, garbage out, so the saying goes. One proposal would have all entering medical students in possession of a liberal education."

"Meaning . . . that they are not?" asked Osler raising an eyebrow.

"But your student doctors *do* know their philosophy," coaxed Hypatia gently. "They *are* mentored? You still teach the way my father taught me, don't you?"

When I was slow to answer, Osler offered some history.

"Hypatia's gift was for mathematics," said Osler. "but her father taught her philosophy as well, believing that essential to education. Hypatia continued that approach with her students — Plato's knowledge of the good and his idea of education as perfecting the whole person, Aristotle's principal virtues, Plotinus' ideal of intellect and soul, and his belief that one's entire intellect hinged upon good moral character. That sort of thing. That's what she's asking you about."

Osler led us all down the hall and into a patient's room. The middle-aged patient seemed to expect us. Osler in one motion shook his hand and included the patient in our discussion.

Nodding to Hippocrates while palpating the patient's pulse, Osler continued.

"Hippocrates taught his students how to think, in a very logical manner. And I think I can speak for the four of us when I say that the proper education of a physician encompasses both the sciences and the arts. But perhaps your contemporaries regard us as old-fashioned."

"I would have to add," said Hippocrates carefully, "that *how* one teaches is infinitely more important than the subject matter at hand. All four of us taught our students how to learn. That was our primary goal, not merely to get them to recite a list of facts, not Euclidean geometry or metaphysics per se, but an approach to the arts and sciences, and a lifelong affection for them."

"Corrigan's Pulse," whispered Osler excitedly, with a nod of his head toward the patient. He smiled at his patient and, eyes shining, engaged him in confidential chat. From his breast pocket he produced a stethoscope.

"It would appear," said Hippocrates with a smile toward Osler, "you could use more teachers like him around here."

"More questions, please," said Galileo. "Have you found that the touching of patients is curative? Has your science shown that the simple act of physical diagnosis has healing properties?"

"No, I don't think so," I answered tentatively. "There are some studies in psychoneuroimmunology that . . . , but no, we haven't answered that question."

"DeMusset's sign," mumbled Osler, "Bozzolo's, and Quincke's."

Hypatia smiled and shook her head.

"What about 'touching' students?" she asked. "I long held the notion that mentoring students was central to their learning. You know, touching their hearts, getting involved in their lives, loving them, in an *agape* sort of way. What about that sort of thing?" Hypatia folded her arms, turned to me full in the face and smiled. The histories have told that every single student of hers had fallen in love with her. I could see why.

"I suppose . . . well, no, I have to say that question too remains unanswered. There isn't very much mentoring going on these days."

"What are the best qualities of good teachers?" asked Galileo.

"Can teaching itself be taught?" asked Hypatia.

"Can a born teacher's gifts be recognized and cultivated?" asked Osler. "This patient, by the way, has an Austin Flint murmur."

"Every one has a list of the best qualities of teachers, I suppose," I said, " but there is no consensus. And we do believe teachers can be taught to teach, although there is no one consistent approach. I don't think it has been studied. And, no, Dr. Osler, no one has mapped out a way to recognize the born teacher."

"How many faculty members in your school are paid solely to teach?" asked Osler.

"To my knowledge, no one."

"How do you measure the quality of a teacher?"

"We still don't know how to do this. We would not know how to go about it. I do think some people pretend to know how."

"Do you know what it is exactly that stifles the curiosity of your students?"

"No."

"Do you have a scientific approach, an inquiry into the nature of teaching? A working philosophy of teaching, I mean?" Hypatia smiled again.

"No, not to my knowledge."

"How are things going at the bedside?" asked Osler. "I have always held a secret pride in my efforts to get students once again to the bedside, to the patient."

"We don't go to the bedside very often these days."

"How do you evaluate your young doctors?" replied Osler, a bit incredulous. "If you don't see them in action, evaluate their skills at the bedside, how . . . ?"

"Our examination board has developed something called," I advanced tentatively, "the virtual patient."

"The virtual patient?" they all asked in unison.

"It's complicated," I explained.

"I'm sure it is," said Hippocrates.

A technician in green scrubs and lab coat, with a dozen earring posts in one ear and a nose stud, walked by. My four guests could not believe their eyes.

"Well," said Hippocrates, following the technician with his eyes. "Well, well, well . . ." He heaved a sigh, looked at the ceiling, and collected himself.

"There is still so much you don't know," he said. "It seems to me that what is needed is an institute, a sort of school devoted to the study of these things, dedicated to finding some answers. Both medicine and learning depend upon it. You need a systematic inquiry into the art and science of teaching."

"Yes, an institute, a Center for Teaching," said Hypatia excitedly, "a Center composed of the very best teachers. With this you could address both needs. You could reward the pure teacher appropriately and these faculty would be granted the time for students once again. Students would have the chance to form meaningful relationships with their mentors. Pure teaching would become acceptable once more. And you might begin to answer some of our questions."

But now I had some questions of my own.

"How will this be paid for? Endowed chairs, which are what you are speaking of, are expensive. Secondly, won't you stifle the teaching of those not invited into the Academy? And who will decide who is admitted to this institute? Will the product of the university be any different? We think in terms of outcomes these days."

"Start small," said Osler. He had Hippocrates leaning over the patient, listening with the stethoscope. "At one university to begin with. Choose a university already so inclined."

"Raise the money however you can," said Galileo. "Patch it together through grants, aid from your drug companies, however you can — convince your public that medical education benefits everyone. Change the funding rules at NIH so you get a piece of the action — however small a piece that might be at first. What you need most is not money, but a will to do this."

"Then show them some results," said Osler. "Take measurements, observe, record, communicate. Charles Eliot was fond of saying that 'the first step toward getting an endowment was to deserve one.'"

"Can any doctor, by the way, be worth your seven figures of income a year?" asked Hippocrates, folding the stethoscope and handing it across the bed to Hypatia. "It seems to me you have some other hard questions to answer while you quibble about funding. And by the way, while you're at it, test your students with real patients, for Heaven's sake. My goodness!"

"As to your question about stifling teaching," said Hypatia. "You've told us that only a very few select scientists are handsomely rewarded for their research. Has the Nobel Prize stifled research?"

"You ask who will decide who is admitted to this institute?" said Hippocrates. "The first few members chosen will be obvious to everybody. Then, simply let those people have a free hand in further admissions. If there is one characteristic common to all great teachers, it is intellectual honesty. You can trust them not to curry favor or pick their friends."

Osler leaned toward me. "You asked whether the university's product will be any different after the founding of such an institute. Isn't that a rather profound question deserving of an answer? All the more reason to give this a try, I would think."

Hypatia paced excitedly back and forth in the room. The patient stared at her with fascination. "Do you see what this holds for you? This Center, this Academy, will be a repository for knowledge of teaching. Even if it should not grow beyond the walls of one institution, there will exist one place on earth that still holds teaching supreme, that preserves the values of analytical thinking . . ."

" . . . and the art of palpation of the peripheral pulse," said Hippocrates, "and the succussion splash."

" . . . and percussion of the chest," said Galileo.

" . . . the diastolic rumble, the anacrotic notch, the Means-Lehrman scratch," said Osler. "And talking to patients!"

"Perhaps," said Hippocrates with a broad smile, "we will become immortal after all."

And then all at once I was no longer there for them. They engaged wholly with the patient, sharing in the physical findings, then talking among themselves; catching up, so to speak.

I awoke to the chill of dusk, my back lame from the bark of the pine, the dream still a palpable part of me. I rose to go, turned from the river and headed up the path to the road.

Sometimes at an airport or in a city center, I think I have seen one of them. I will see a handlebar moustache under twinkling eyes, or the long strides of a bearded man of confidence. A pensive man with piercing eyes will stare at me waiting for my answer, and on occasion a woman of incalculable beauty and intelligence will smile at me and nod her head. They are still with us, these four. I know it. Together with the multitude they have taught.

## V. THE DOCTOR-PATIENT RELATIONSHIP

The chief joy in medicine can be found in those moments with patients. No one who has not taken care of patients can know this. No one. And by this caring, I do not mean the occasional hour spent on the hospital wards. I do not mean the casual afternoon in a clinic somewhere. I mean direct, daily contact with patients, every day— the being with them during the best of times as well as during crises. Patients become a doctor's most prized possessions. (We whisper proudly to one another, do you know, this: *He is my patient.*) If more medical students came to discover this, we'd have no dearth of primary care practitioners. Being with patients day to day teaches you about people, and about yourself. It teaches you about life in a way no other calling can do. And for reward in life, for fulfillment, for all these "lifestyle" issues young people are looking for today, nothing else comes close.

What can we learn from the dying beyond a sudden sense of our own mortality? From the young woman with cancer who, in the midst of her pain and suffering, becomes abruptly still, who looks about her hospital room with dawning recognition, fixing her visitors and doctor with a look of wisdom drawn from some mysterious source, and who proclaims with certain finality that she loves and will miss them all—is there anything to be gained beyond the poignancy of the moment? Is it that we have become a part of her story, her case history? Or perhaps the patient will be a stern, elderly professor, now close to death. For decades in the classroom, frowning at students over his glasses, guiding them, correcting them, setting them about a proper course, he has secretly wondered whether his life has had any true meaning. And only now, from the steady procession of former students, from the testimony of colleagues and peers, does he gain any sense of consummation. But why only now? Why not twenty, fifty years ago, when open-hearted acclamation could have been built upon? Why do we wait until the eleventh hour to speak to our friends from the heart? And even at that eleventh hour, do we ever open ourselves unreservedly? Does it matter?

And if it is true—as it most certainly is—that a life in medicine offers the physician a front row seat in the drama of life, what is it that the doctor hears in the stage director's urgent whispers and what does he see in the pain of the actor's face and what can he learn from the troubled eyes of the diva that escapes the notice of those seated less providentially?

A man comes to the hospital to visit his sick wife. Within two weeks he himself will die of a mysterious disease. Having cared for his wife, the doctor is asked by her to have a look at him as well. There he stands, a woodsman of enviable strength, unnerved by the pristine antisepsis of the hospital. Behind him, apart and withdrawn, stands their retarded son, in his mid-thirties, lurking there by the drapes with feral eyes. He peers at the doctor as though from some dark cave, face expressionless, filling the doctor with an uncommon fear. What begins for the woodsman as fever and troublesome speech, ends two weeks later with coma, agonal breath, flaccid palsy, and death. In the intervening two weeks the doctor treats him with rare intensity, applying esoteric medication, calling in the brightest consultants, fine-tuning the delicate machinery of intensive care. The man's wife and daughters hover at the bedside through it all, shocked at the suddenness of his devastation, at this reversal of fortune. *She* had been the sickly one, and he, her rock, her foundation. Now *he* finds himself at Death's dreadful door and she will be the one left alone. And through all of the doctor's frantic attention to his father—the urgent summonses to the bedside, the late, sleepless nights before his monitors, the spinal taps and respirator care—the man's retarded son stands silently against the wall and watches. Never altering his stonelike expression, his eyes shift to the nurse running off with an order, now to the doctor's hands probing for hope from his father's body, then to his mother sitting, weeping, and now to his sisters, overcome with emotion, unable to manage their own anger and despair. And in the end, he watches the monitor go straight-line, lifeless, watches a finger flick off the respirator, sees the slow, sorrowful nod to his mother. The man's physician leaves them there with the deceased, and with the nurse, walks out of the room and into the hall, exhausted. There they stand, nurse and doctor, saying nothing, each staring off at some point far away. Then the doctor feels something at his arm. He turns to find the retarded man standing still beside him, eyes dark and sad. He has touched the doctor's arm with the point of his index finger.

"Thanks," he says, and walks away.

The nurse, who has seen it all, has seen the wife-beatings and child abuse of the metropolitan hospitals, the gunshot wounds snuffing out the life of youth in silly, wanton murder, who has been hardened by the swirling decay of society manifested by the chaos of the big city hospital, is overcome.

"Oh Christ!" she says, and buries her face in her hands. The doctor fights for control, bracing himself against a wave of emotion, and walks her down the hall, holding her tightly.

What has moved them both in this way? The wonderful simplicity of the son's gratitude? The startling paradox of a retarded man who seemed to feel the thanks that we often miss? Is there a message here for all of us, buried somewhere in a file marked "What Wasn't Said"? Might it be that we, as doctors, live the case history along with our patients, and too often ignore that role, to our own great loss?

There is in this business of patients something unique about doctoring. On the one hand, the repeated suffering and loss can be overwhelming for the doctor, and incapacitating for a time. There is the temptation to become jaded, hardened, immune. But the practice of medicine is enriched by the story of the patient who is your friend, a story the physician lives as well. Sometimes one knows the patient first as friend, and his family is an extension of that friendship. The story unfolds. The doctor is part of it.

A young man is electrocuted on a farm. The doctor is summoned to the scene. He is among the first to arrive. He is there just in time to witness the horrible death, to pronounce the patient, and to do little else for him. But the man has a wife. The doctor advises her to remain in the farmhouse, to shun the scene he has had to see, to avoid the nightmares he will endure repeatedly for months. He calls the man's parents, tells them the tragic news. The man's father has a heart condition; that is part of the equation.

The farm belongs to the doctor and the doctor is a friend of the young man's father. They have been fishing companions for twenty years. The doctor, at the request of his friend, had allowed the young couple to rent the unoccupied farm where now his friend's son lies dead. Both doctor and friend suffer terrible pain, an irrational sense that each is to blame for the death of the young man. The farm becomes a forbidden place. The fishing companion stays away. The doctor wonders if he can ever live there, as he had once dreamed. The plot of ground where the electrocution took place remains charred. For two summers, nothing grows there.

And then life goes on. The young wife remarries and moves away. The two friends, doctor and fishing companion, in the serenity of a mountain lake, tell each other of their guilt. They forgive each other, nod to each other down the length of the canoe, and then, flick out their lines to the trout. Later they will return to camp with their catch, gulp cheap red wine from tumblers, and talk about the day. And the doctor will sit back and see himself in life's hard story.

Once, before television and the fast lane, we talked to one another. I like to think that back then, while the rain pounded on the pavement and the elms swayed in protective orchestration overhead, at kitchen tables everywhere conversation swelled with meaning. Phrases like "You really *are* my best friend" and "Let me tell you how you could be a better friend to me" and "Whatever happens, whatever becomes of you, count on me" were as commonplace as the passenger pigeon. Religion was a feeling back then, not yet relegated to the pitch of Sunday morning TV.

There are places where these feelings can still be found. And the doctor there is sometimes central to it. That is what is right with medicine—talking to patients—patients who often become friends rather than adversaries—and hearing their stories, becoming a part of them—seeing ourselves as participants in the case history.

Let us allow ourselves to become a part of the case history— a part of the stories in which we may play many roles—stories about that moment of sharing, when all defenses are down, when nothing else matters, when the lines of priority are drawn. That is where the greatest reward in medicine can be found. And the greatest of messages can be found in the patient-doctor relationship at the moment of death. It is a sometimes painful, sometimes joyful message, of missed opportunity and chance occasion, of regret and ecstasy, of guilt and inculpability. It is a portrait of the art of medicine, of that mysterious blend of power and human frailty, and of essential empathy for our fellow man—an art all doctors intend to practice, whatever it is that may prevent them in the end from doing so, an art that we, as doctors as well as patients, had better guard against losing.

Helen is the nurse I love the most. She comes in a lot and probably she likes me, but that isn't the whole of it. She watches TV with me and sits right next to me with her legs crossed and her arms folded under her breasts and she lets me look at her. Well, what I mean is, she catches me looking at her body but she just smiles and looks back at the tube like it doesn't bother her. So I have to think it's okay with her. Any girl that lets you do that likes you. I learned that on TV. Probably if things were different she'd fall in love with me too.

I think about Helen all the time. Naturally I don't tell her about it. There was this TV program I saw where a guy wasn't so cool and he hung on to this girl, clinging and all, and finally scared the girl away. So I learned that you don't do that. But I know I dream about Helen a lot and I think about her in different situations during the day. Like she's taking a shower. That sort of thing. Or she'll be watching Judge Wapner with me and I'll close my eyes to imagine she's sitting there naked, right there beside me in the chair with no clothes on and her legs crossed and her arms folded under her breasts. Totally naked. Like nothing's wrong. Then she catches me doing that, with my eyes closed tight trying to imagine, and she'll ask me what's wrong.

"Whatcha squintin' your eyes shut like that for, Steven? You got a headache? You wanna pill?" she'll ask me.

"No," I'll say.

"Hafta move your bowels?"

"No."

"Whatcha doin' it for then?" she'll ask.

"Thinking," I'll say to her.

"Oh," she says and goes back to Judge Wapner.

Helen isn't an official nurse. She's like an aide or something. She tells me she has to do all the dirty work. But she gives good baths. I get a bath every day, and I make sure it's Helen that gives it to me. If she's working that day, I mean.

When she isn't, one of the other aides fills in. Takes Helen's assignments. There's Stephanie who acts bored with everything. She acts bored with me. She's always got her eyes half shut like her lids are too heavy and she never smiles. She makes you think you did something wrong. Like you messed the bed or something. Stephanie hardly ever talks to me. Helen comes bobbing in—I love the way she walks. It's great. She walks a little bent forward and she sways side to side and she has her chin stuck out like she's saying,

"Come on, World, try me!"

Well, if Helen comes in it's *How'dja sleep, Steven?* and *Ready for a bath, Steven?* But Stephanie, she yawns and sizes up things, and then she buzzes for some help and yells *I need some help moving Steven!* like she was about to move a two-and-a-half-ton Diesel truck. So I get the feeling Stephanie doesn't like me and I give it right back to her. I refuse to look at her body.

I have busy weekends here. Saturdays my Mom comes in to play checkers with me. We play all day and I always win. I'm fantastic at checkers. If there were a tournament locally, Mom says she'd enter me into it. We always play right through lunch. But I get into this touchy thing if it's Helen's weekend on duty. You see, Mom's used to feeding me when she's here, but so is Helen and I'd rather have Helen, to tell you the truth. But I don't want any hurt feelings around here you know. Sometimes Mom will put her hands on her hips and say,

"Who would you like to feed you then, Steven?"

So I just say, "Not hungry," and get out of it that way.

Sundays I go to truck-pulls with my Dad. That's when there are two trucks hooked together by chains and one tries to pull the other over the line. It's like a tug-a-war with trucks. Well, truck pulls are all over the State and Dad takes me to one every Sunday. We have a van with a lift in it so they can wheel my chair right up into it with room for my respirator too. There's this rule of the hospital that we're not supposed to go any more than thirty miles away in case the respirator breaks.

For the first two years I was at the hospital we followed the rule. But there are some awful good truck pulls happening way up country and nothing ever went wrong with the respirator anyway. That is, until we went up on the other side of Bangor, 150 miles away.

We got to this truck pull up in Hiram and it was raining like mad which gives you good mud and makes the pulls more interesting. Well, Dad unloads me from the van just as a couple of Dodge Rams with wide ovals are getting into position, and the rain is really coming down and so Dad lashes an umbrella to the intravenous pole on my wheelchair. And then, the battery on my portable respirator goes dead. So Dad grabs the portable respirator bag and he's breathing me through my trach and hollers for help and they get the spare respirator battery from the van. And that battery is also dead! Well, mister, what's it gonna be? Race into Bangor with somebody bagging me in the back of the van? And miss this truck pull? No way!

Well, Dad's bagging me and he tells them all to go around and borrow jumper cables from everybody. Dad leaves the van on idle and they hook up my respirator to the van battery with all the jumper cables. So I'm breathing just fine with the respirator. And the truck next to us they put it on idle too and charge up the two dead batteries for the trip home while we're all enjoying this truck pull. Guy from Pinook won the whole thing.

My room looks out on the back parking lot. I got the best room in the whole hospital. Kind of a private view. I get to see everything. Roxanne gets me up way before breakfast and I watch all the hospital people come in to work. The nurses come in first. They all have their favorite spot which they like to take every day. Except Helen must park somewhere else because I never see her come into the hospital. I never ask her about this. I wouldn't want her to know I was watching her. You have to be cool about these things. Anyway there's this one scene which happens about three times a week. One nurse who I never seen her in the hospital pulls up in a

Suburu maybe fifty feet from my window. Every day it's the same thing. She pulls at the mirror and fixes her hair and dabs at her lips. Then she lights a cigarette and I can see her picking at the cigarette paper which sticks to her lips. And she looks around and waits. And in about five or ten minutes in comes this big, tan Le Baron and it parks the other way so she can talk through the window with this guy that's driving it. They do this three or four times a week, talk for a few minutes, and then he drives off and she comes bouncing into the hospital, all happy-like. I seen enough TV to know what they're doing. They're planning a murder. She has a husband who drinks and won't take her out dancing so she's in love with the guy in the Le Baron and they are going to do the husband in and make it look like an accident. When I gather enough evidence I'm going to report this. Probably I'll tell Helen.

I see a lot else. One doctor always parks in the handicap place. My Dad would fix *him*. Two other doctors always drive up at the same time. But they are mad at each other because I can see from my window that they pretend each other don't exist. Then there's a lab tech who sometimes draws my blood and who is crippled up herself, with arthritis. But at least *she* can walk. Her husband drives her to work every morning and he always kisses her goodbye which she is nervous about because she thinks somebody might be watching her. Which I am. Helen has never kissed me.

So I make up stories in my head about them out in the parking lot, stories that could fit into *Days of Our Lives* and someday I'll have Mom write 'em down for me so I can send them in to TV and make a lot of money. Then I'll get rich and I can go home with twenty-four hour nursing care and I'll have my own room again and Winthrop can be with me at all times. They won't let dogs visit you in the hospital. What I would do then is hire Helen but she wouldn't do any of the dirty work and the pay would be great and Stephanie wouldn't get a job with me and she'd be jealous. And I would hold parties for all the hospital people to come to but not the doctor who parks in the handicap spot. I would send him an invitation too and say that we are having this party at the Twitchell Farm which will be catered like the parties on *Dynasty* but we are very sorry that we can't offer handicap parking so you can't come. Of course I would also finance a big truck pull with trophies and prize money. Something they'd drive all the way from New Hampshire to see.

The way I understand it the State is paying for me to be here and they don't want to pay anymore. So that's why everybody is talking nursing home. It's cheaper. Mom says to make the best of it and they are working on muscular dystrophy every day anyway. She says I can have a room there at the nursing home by myself like I do here. A room big enough for trophies and TV. But there are a few things I'm going to insist on. Like a private view. Like being able to look out on a parking lot and not at some building. And they're going to have to pack up Charlotte carefully and bring her with me, web and all. I'm not leaving without her. And this crack here in my wall which I call the Mississippi River and which Doctor Wade has put on the cities and quizzes me about. I'm asking for a crack like that in my new room so when Doctor Wade comes over to visit me he can put me through my paces. *Alright Steven,* he'll say, *what's this one?, that's right, St. Louis, and this?, yup, Memphis . . .* I know those cities *cold.* Doctor Wade is proud of me. Mom says I'll have a new doctor at the nursing home but I'm staying loyal to Doctor Wade.

This move is going to be hard on Helen. I know there's something between us. It's like on *As The World Turns* when people are whispering about a couple and they say *there's something between them.* That's the way it is with Helen and me. I know she's gonna want to visit me a lot and I'll have to request special visiting hours just for her so she can come in any time. We'll watch Judge Wapner together. Maybe she'll want to come to some of the truck pulls on Sunday. There's plenty of room in the van.

People in this situation, being separated and all, always exchange pictures. You don't ask about it because you have to play it cool. But I hope Helen gives me a picture of her. Maybe she'll give me two pictures. One for the table. And one that I can hold on to.

A century or so ago, there lived in western Maine an Indian woman legendary for her medicine. For this and other reasons she was often regarded by the settlers of that area as eccentric. She walked a trail running east and west and would frequently stop at various cabins for food and drink, trading assorted poultices and words of advice to those who would have them. And as there are in any age, there were along the trail those who remained skeptical, and refused any and all hospitality to the old woman. In retaliation, she placed a lasting curse on the localities where these skeptics lived.

With the passage of time, the medicine woman's trail became asphalt highway, twisting through small villages and hurrying past country mostly, on its way west to New Hampshire. At its extreme western end, in the mountains of western Maine where few people live even today, Eugene and Elizabeth Chase arrived from Connecticut to retire to a farm. Eugene embraced the nature surrounding him like a zealot newly converted to religion. He became especially fascinated with wild mushrooms and, with certain cautionary measures, regularly gathered them to eat. Encumbered by an emphysematous chest diseased through long years of smoking, Eugene would puff along through the woods, stop to catch his breath with a gaping, wide grin, and resume his chase for fungi.

A scant mile down the road stood a general store of the sort one sometimes sees when driving in the country, a store seeming always to be open, lit by bare incandescent bulbs, with sagging front steps and single iron rail worn bright over the years by the coarse hands of customers. The window of this particular store displayed a few jugs of maple syrup covered with several layers of dust, three pairs of cloth work gloves, ten quart-size cans of stewed tomatoes arranged pyramid style, and assorted brands of bug repellent in various strengths and sizes. The display was never changed, remaining as it was a testimony to country eclecticism. The store was run by Walter and Cleona Shackleford who, in rotating shifts, together operated the store fifteen hours a day. Or *separately*, rather, for Walter and Cleona were never there together. They did not, it was commonly known, get along. If one could sound the sweep of Walter's psyche, plumbing depths of which even he was unaware, the truth would tell that, in reprisal for his own abusive, drunken father and punishingly submissive mother, Walter abused Cleona, and severely so.

The town of Gorham, an hour further west into New Hampshire, offered a bar where Walter could go afternoons to drink and smoke, and laugh with the men, replenishing his maleness so that he might return home to victimize his wife. There he would perch himself on any vacant stool, veined face flush, and expound with raspy voice on the rain or lack of it, ice-out time, and the general nature of things, between long, slow drags on his cigarette. And while Walter was absent, Elizabeth, who by now had become a frequent customer at the store, could lean across the counter, resting as much of her considerable weight on her elbows as the countertop would allow—and sympathize with her newfound friend.

Elizabeth's strength had always been in listening. She would hold her head in her hands, elbows on the counter, and look deeply into her friend's sad eyes, absorbing every halting detail. Since it was never asked for, Elizabeth never offered advice, though she held a quiet impatience for Cleona's mousy manner and passive acceptance of her husband's continual abuse. Nor did she add to Cleona's pain by talking about her own happy marriage, or her deep, abiding love for Eugene. Elizabeth always left promptly at six to get her husband's supper—huffing out the door to squeeze her corpulence between seat and steering wheel of her Buick— and hurry home to fry up whatever mushroom treasures Eugene had found that day. But she might return to Cleona in the evening, if Eugene could spare her and if it seemed her friend especially needed her that day. Often in the evenings together at the store, the two women would stand on the steps—the one massively wide and expansive, and the other slight, small, withdrawn—hugging themselves against the evening chill to watch the setting sun. And often they would wonder whether Walter would be too drunk to complete the winding drive home, an apprehension that sometimes took on the quality of prayer.

This stretch of road was patrolled by Bill Cummings, assistant deputy sheriff, part-time rural mail carrier, and owner of thirteen Short-horn cattle. Bill stopped at the store almost every day, and always at five, to buy two donuts, a hunk of cheddar cheese, and two half-pints of milk. These he would nurse along through the evening shift, to get himself to quitting time. He had a habit of leaving his squad car door ajar, to lend a sense of urgency to his visit, it may be supposed, as well as an air of brevity. Each visit to the store found the women in quiet conversation; Bill sensed his own intrusion, watching Cleona and Elizabeth draw away from each other, smile and nod nervously at him, making up things to say.

After a time, Eugene came up with lung cancer. Elizabeth, more clearly than her husband, anticipated the heavy grief to come. Eugene assumed an attitude of resignation, something he could not entirely achieve, and continued to cling to life with measured desperation. He began showering his Elizabeth with gifts, mostly jewelry made of semiprecious stones, jewelry he purchased at a mineral store in West Paris, east of the mountains. On some pretense or other, he managed to go there every day, and would puff up the steps and inside, leaning on the glass case to catch his breath, with the gape and grimace of a breathless distance runner. "Anything new?" he would ask, and buy for Elizabeth whatever might be held out to him. Money had become inconsequential. He gathered, and ate for the first time, certain gilled mushrooms which he had heretofore avoided for their resemblance to poisonous varieties, terming them "close calls," because for him it no longer mattered. These particular species he ate himself; he would not allow his Elizabeth to share them.

And so each night the scene for them was this: Elizabeth sitting at one end of the trestle table in her great chair, fighting back her grief, wearing pendant earrings of azurite and gold, and Eugene opposite, rubbing his hands in false joy and chuckling in anticipation at his plate of sautéed *Amanita caesarea*.

Walter too became seriously ill, and died a lovely death between crisp white sheets in the Norway hospital to the east, lapsing in and out of the comfortable coma that drink, cigarettes, liver failure, and emphysema can bring. He commanded the attention of young, shapely nurses he would pinch and pat just so, whenever he had the faculty to do so. His children sat around him, lamenting the death they had so fervently prayed for, while Cleona, his wife of forty years, to whom he had forbidden entry, brooded in the hall outside. Eugene, on the other hand, was found only after hours of frantic searching, lying face down in a patch of ostrich ferns, his basket of mushrooms spilled upon the ground. The cancer, the doctors explained, had eaten through a blood vessel. Yes, they assured Elizabeth, it had been a quick and painless death.

It was in this way that the store's window display came finally to be changed. Elizabeth washed the window, cleaned out the old, tired articles, and installed as a centerpiece a large crystalline spray of amethyst that Eugene had found one day. Around this crystal the two women arranged dried statice and cornflowers, varicolored gourds, and a burlap sack of flour, with a handful of coffee beans thrown in, for completion's sake. With both of them running outside to assess—Elizabeth first, like a Holstein swollen at milking time, and Cleona tagging behind like a ragged Shelty— then both back inside again to add, subtract, or reposition, then one outside while the other stayed in the window, moving the sack of flour here or there, the whole project took the better part of one day. Elizabeth volunteered to take Walter's shift at the store, having nothing better to do, but the two women actually ran the store together, opening at sun-up, and closing late in the evening, whenever the traffic had ceased. What had once been a chore for Cleona became a way of life for both of them. And from this arrangement, Cleona gained a measure of happiness, and Elizabeth permitted a small song to enter her heart once again.

The store was less successful than before Walter's death. In truth the women barely made expenses. The boys from Rumford had correctly assumed that the two women would not sell beer to minors and so what had been profit for Walter was lost to the two women. But income was secondary, and whatever they lost in money, they gained many times over in happiness.

Bill Cummings came every day now, and stayed an hour or more, no longer considered an unwelcome interruption. He would laugh with them, and tease, and roll his eyes wishing out loud he were single again, or ten years younger, or both. And Cleona and Elizabeth would toss their heads and poke each other with bony elbows, and Cleona would push at Bill and go to the cooler for his milk and cheese.

For a year the two women went on in this way. They even talked of living together, if being set in their ways were to constitute no major obstacle. But this was a year also of persistent persuasion from a well-intended daughter—who finally convinced Cleona that rural life was too filled with risk, and no place for an elderly widow. Her doctor, who had cared for Walter and Eugene as well, took the daughter's side in the argument; one less patient for him to look after would be one less demand upon his time. And so Cleona, who had always permitted others to think for her, and had had only one year of thinking for herself, sold her land and the store with it and moved to Portland to live with her daughter.

Elizabeth had trouble sleeping after Cleona left, and loathed the loneliness she found engulfing her. She asked the doctor for a vial of pills for sleeping, and convinced the druggist in New Hampshire that she kept misplacing them. When she had gained four such vials in this way, she kissed Eugene's picture and went to sleep.

Bill found her two days later, having had to break a window

to gain entry. He was numbed by his discovery and by the sudden realization that he had in some way dearly loved and would miss these two women. Elizabeth had no children. There was only the name of the doctor on the vials for Bill to call. Yes, the doctor said, he would sign the death certificate. And it was scarcely three weeks later that Bill himself died of a heart seizure while apprehending a drunken teenage boy. It was not, the workmen's compensation board explained to Bill's widow, a work-related incident. She would have to make do.

Now there is a ski mountain near that section of road, and a condominium occupies the spot where Cleona's store once stood. Young people from the city occupy A-frames and ski chalets there, and come there from the city when the snow is fresh and deep. They wear fashionable clothes for attracting each other and silvered sunglasses for squinting into the sun, and know nothing of the curse of the medicine woman.

The most embarrassing part of this whole process has been the self-pity. After I was told, and even before I was told—when my doctor had suddenly become more serious with me—I had begun the "why-me's." I felt a bitterness, an anger toward almost everyone, except for my family, and found myself wishing, even praying, that others could have my disease instead of me. When I think back on it, those feelings were hardly noble. One doctor had told me that all that was left, all that remained for me to do, was to die with nobility. I had wished on the spot that he had this cancer and that I could toss such wisdom his way.

I remember an autumn night, sitting alone in the stands at a high school football game. The field's grass sparkled under the floodlights, the boys pranced before the crowd like so many young colts, and the air was crisp and clear. Everything was so alive, so vibrant, so new and fresh—yet I was dying and would soon leave it. It was as though I had just been born, was seeing just for the first time, only to have it now all snatched away. I can remember the panic I felt that night as I looked around for someone to give my disease to. And why, I wonder, does it take a cancer to free us to see and feel with such clarity?

But I have moved beyond those days and hope I have achieved, if not a measure of nobility, then a certain serenity. The point at which I find myself now would otherwise be the height of my awareness, were it not also an inextricable part of this death sentence. I seem now to have an exquisite sensitivity, an acuity I have never before experienced. I have always been a sensitive sort, could read the set of the jaw, the sadness in the eyes pretty well. But this is different. It is almost as though I can read minds, though I'd never admit it. They would conclude the cancer now to be in my brain!

Once a day my bed is wheeled out to the sun-porch and I have the opportunity to observe the other patients. I can see the pity in their eyes as they look at me and my hairless, shrunken body—I must be a sight! Their pity is easy enough to see, for certain. But each also has his own private fear to read, and each contends with it in an individual way. One is filled with bravado, is demanding, or sexually suggestive to the poor nurses who must tolerate this, while another withdraws, broods, nothing is right, all is calamity, and it is again left to the nurses to assuage and appease. The families—they are the worst!—they oblige, question, and complain. The nurses bear the brunt, shielding their doctors, I assume, from much abuse. Man is least noble among animals, it seems, when confronted by disease.

Mostly I am in my room, visitors carefully rationed at my request. Since I can barely manage my own juices, and since I have refused the tubes, death inevitable, I have no meal time per se. I spend my time thinking, mostly. And mostly, I think about my family. What will become of my sons? Will they have families of their own? How many children? What will my grandchildren be told of me? Will my wife remember to renew her driver's license? Who will fill the bird feeders? Or inherit my reading chair, and my books? Will the dog be upset by my absence?

And then I am interrupted from these thoughts. The pregnant nurse with the worried eyes enters. I have read her face so often now, and so well I think, that I must know her like my own daughter. She cares about me. I can feel that most of all. Despite this ugly exterior of mine, I feel that she loves me, actually loves me, and is sorry I am dying. It is an incredible realization. She does silly little things to remain in the room longer, when most can't wait to leave. She looks deeply into my eyes and parts her mouth as if to say something . . . and then smiles that soft, sad smile instead. And I know she would say, "I wish I could make you better . . . make that cancer go away." And so I nod to her in this silent, profound conversation.

I love my wife! Make no mistake! There is nothing erotic in this thing with the nurse. I am barely ninety pounds now, and cannot even sit up! Hardly salacious! It's just that, when my wife comes, and she loves me, I know, she can't bear to look at me, and wishes I were the old, healthy way—witty, urbane, sexy (to her, I suppose), and masculine, rather than this intro- spective wraith I have become. And when the children come to visit—and they love me too, I know—they wish it were all over, that it would hurry up, and are impatient to leave.

But this nurse cares for me *now*, and the way I am *now*, and that is very important for a dying man, although I could not begin to tell you why. There are nurses who come and go and leave barely a trace of themselves behind, and in their faces I can see the insecurity, or the discomfort with the dying, and, in some, the boredom with disease.

I have a good doctor. And I can read him like a book. He really cares about me. I mean, there isn't anything anyone can do for me at this point, and my doctor needn't come in twice a day and joke with me and tease me and put up with my bad- gering him about literature (he is surprisingly poorly read!). But he does all that, and sits down as though he has hours of time (while I hear him paged repeatedly), and we chat as though we'd met at Stash's for the millionth time and were working together on The Great American Novel.

It goes beyond simple chat, obviously. Anyone can affect a bedside manner, I suppose. What I sense is that it bothers him that I am dying—not that he flagellates himself that *he* can't cure cancer—I don't mean that. More, that I am his patient and he is my doctor and he and I have had this contract and now I have this cursed cancer and he can't do anything about it. Sort of like a Christian tied to the stake watching his friends wait for the lions. Well, poor analogy . . . but that's the essence of a good doctor, I think. Because if it bothers him that much that I'm dying, and I know it does, then I also know that if I had something treatable, he'd find out how to treat it or get me to someone who could. And apparently I'm not alone in my assessment—the poor man never goes home.

When you lie here alone as much as I do, you have a lot of fantasies. I'm going to tell you some of mine—but please don't laugh. One is that the pregnant nurse is going to name her child after me. Then, somehow, I won't have died after all. I think everyone wishes for immortality. And then I get thinking in that vein and I imagine a grandchild with my name and my nose and somehow I can whisper quiet, important things softly into his head from somewhere wherever I am and I say to him things like read books and don't worry about material things and forget about possessions and love is best of all and go ahead and risk yourself and love with all your heart.

And the last fantasy is this—that my family decides to put my library in order after I am gone and so in they go, as if entering some forbidden cave and suddenly they are caught up in the annotations I have made in the various books—*listen to this!*, one of the kids says coming upon something profound that I have underlined and starred and bracketed and they are all sitting on the floor around the library with volumes in their laps, laughing and teaching each other and remembering me that way—and that my wife ponders and hesitates, then decides once and for all and gives my collection of Henry James to my respected-but-poorly-read doctor and he keeps them on his desk in his office and he glances at them sometimes and thinks of me and then one day he pulls out one volume and begins to read and it changes his life, in some small way.

*I get to thinking I'm going to quit almost every day now, and maybe with this baby I will. Things have changed so much since I was a student, and not for the better either. I guess I want to tell you what makes me want to leave nursing, but it seems to get mixed up with all the things that make me want to stay.*

*I thought it would be glamorous, you know? I think all girls sometimes look at nursing that way. You know— handsome doctors helping people and we are a part of it and emergencies and alarms and everyone running to get there just in time. It's just not like that. I think it used to be, though— Mrs. Sprague says it was like that. But it isn't anymore.*

*Mrs. Sprague talks about the time when "we were all in it*

together" as she puts it. *Everybody was closer then, she says—families were close, so there wasn't all the guilt and anger you get now when someone is sick. And there wasn't all the paperwork and paranoia about getting sued. So the hospital was a happy place, if hospitals can be happy.*

*I don't think I've ever met a happy doctor. I know that's awful to say. I see them joke and laugh and flirt a lot, but I never get the feeling that they are really happy inside. I think it has to do mostly with responsibility— but I don't mean it the way you think. For instance—the weather man is responsible for predicting the weather, and picnics and weddings and graduations count on him. But he doesn't feel responsible for a freak storm, and he doesn't blame himself for soggy sandwiches and accidents and flooded basements. And he doesn't feel guilty. And nobody blames him. Or sues him.*

*That's what I mean by responsible. I think doctors feel responsible for too many freak storms. So then they feel guilty, and think they ought to be blamed. They lose a patient or something goes wrong and they feel sad because they liked the patient, but they also feel guilty about it. How can you ever be happy with those feelings? And maybe it's not my business, but do you know why they feel guilty? I think they're taught that way in medical school. And I have an idea how.*

*My friend Kathy who works three-to-elevens was brought up strict Catholic and her husband isn't, and she doesn't go to church much anymore and they use the pill and she says she's always feeling guilty. She says she was raised to live the life of a saint and she knows that's stupid but she can't help but feel guilty about it.*

*And when I was in training, a lot of the young doctors walked around like saints. That's my point. I think they are taught to believe they have too much power and magic and they get this idea of responsibility I am talking about. And it catches up with them later. So they feel guilty and if that gets to be too much, then they blame the nurses and that's when this job gets really tough and you really want to quit.*

*I'll tell you about the patient on the east wing, the one with the esophageal cancer. He's what you'd call the perfect patient. You never walk in there and feel that it's your fault. He never gets mad, never asks for anything, and never rings his call-bell. You always feel like you should go in and check on him. And he's got his family adjusted to his illness, so they're reasonable too.*

*But I go in there and it's peaceful, like an escape, like a chapel. I have this feeling about him—like there's an attraction or a bond between us—and I can feel him watching me but it doesn't bother me. Sometimes he looks at my belly and smiles and I have this urge to take his hand and let him feel the baby move, but I couldn't do that. It would make us both uncomfortable.*

*Once he took my hand and said he wanted to give me some advice and I thought it would be love your husband which is obvious or don't let that baby be a doctor which I already knew, or be kind to patients which I get a lot of. But he smiled and said that I should be sure to read the classics.*

*Well, his doctor is guilty with a capital "G" if you ask me. I feel sorry for him. He's such a great doctor—all the older nurses go to him, so you can tell, and he's very careful with his orders and he sees his patients and examines them and you know he's good—but I don't think he knows. He's here all the time, dotting every "i" and crossing every "t" and he never goes home. I feel sorry for his family too. I wouldn't want to be married to him.*

*I don't think he's ever been sued. I heard him say that once in the coffee room. But I think if he ever did get sued it would crush him—because he spends so much time making sure it won't happen. He orders a lot of tests and he checks and re-checks everything two or three times. There just isn't the time in the day to be the perfect doctor he thinks he ought to be.*

*Sometimes I look at him bustling down the corridor, running off to somewhere, and I wonder things about him. I wonder does he ever laugh from deep inside and does he ever take long walks and kick the leaves and does he know how to scratch a dog's ear slowly and for a long time the way dogs like it! And I wonder does he ever just sit and talk about silly things with his wife the way my husband and I do and will he ever let himself be a kid and play! Or does he never have the time! Then I wonder how many things have gotten to be a duty for him, like items on his list to be checked off. Does he check off time spent with his children and does he check off reading a good book! Does he check off snuggling by the fire with his wife and does he check off going to the movies! I think he does. I'd like to tell him it's not worth it, but it's none of my business.*

*If I could change anything in medicine, there's a lot I would do. Nobody likes all the regulations and you don't have to be a genius to see how it's hurting patients, especially the old people. And the malpractice mess is horrible. But what I would most want to do is bring nurses and doctors closer together again. And then I think doctors would see that we have feelings too and that we can also care—and, that we are doing our best, and we don't blame them and that no one should feel guilty—just get the job done. Then maybe we'd all be more comfortable with being human. And begin to be happy.*

It was, like everything else, something I would get to someday. That has too often been the way with me. I thought I had all the time in the world. I had met this extraordinary human being, the sort of person you are compelled to get to know, but a mixture of circumstance and procrastination prevented me from ever doing so.

The first problem was that I didn't meet him as a patient. Patients for me are lab slips, appointment slots, medical records, phone calls to be returned. Nothing more than that. From this initial "item" comes, usually, some boring complaint or two, or, occasionally, the intellectual challenge of a difficult diagnosis. But the patient always remains for me a rational exercise. I can intellectualize the whole thing, if you know what I mean. It's better that way. Or so I thought. But with this particular patient, or person rather, I never had a chance to protect myself. It's hard to explain.

Some time ago, I'd been asked by an acquaintance to give a short talk on cancer research at the local university. There was a coffee afterwards—a lot of milling about, idle talk, bowing and smiling. The kind of stuff that drives you nuts. Then, as I was about to leave, this professor grabbed my arm, said he enjoyed the talk and so on, and then asked how I found *Cancer Ward*, was the novel true to reality as I perceived it and so on. Well, I hadn't read *Cancer Ward* and I told him so. I had the book and a couple of others by Solzhenitsyn but I hadn't gotten to them yet. Busy, you know. Now the normal person would have accepted that at face value and let me off the hook. But he wasn't your normal person, as I was to find out. He looked at me obliquely, oddly, as though I had cut all my anatomy classes in first year and were faking it, and shook his head. I remember that look—he was thin, inches taller than I, with owlish, brown eyes and a silly sort of goatee-type beard—and he had a look of sadness almost, as though he felt sorry for me. Well maybe I had read Mann's *The Magic Mountain*, or *Anatomy of Melancholy*, or several stories by Chekhov which he rattled off and none of which I had read either. I mean, *I* had given the damn lecture after all and here was this academic type, this bookish bore, giving me the third degree.

"Your university hasn't served you well," was all he said, then added, "I think we should have lunch."

I mumbled something and left, overjoyed finally to escape. He called the office two or three times after that, to set up lunch presumably, but I never returned the calls. It was a few months later that I ran into him in the hospital lobby. He saw me before I could escape down the hall, and I agreed to dinner that evening. What could I do? He mentioned a place I had never heard of, wrote down the address, smiled and shook my hand, and walked smartly away.

I had a hell of a time finding the place, mostly I guess because I had had a different sort of restaurant in mind. This

was one of those below-the-street deals, with a simple sign—
"Stash's"— hanging out over an old door, leading in turn
down a set of stairs to an older door and into a cramped foyer
large enough for about one person. A short, fat, bald man in T-
shirt and apron came out to greet me, rubbing his hands on
the front of his apron and grinning at me, showing me his gold
tooth. He had a heavy Polish accent. I had expected Locke
Ober's maybe, or Antoine's, and what I was going to get was
cabbage soup. Mr. Stash led me through the S-shaped dining
room, past tables of Eastern European-looking clientele to the
far end where sat my professor of literature. He had his nose
in a book but rose quickly to greet me and held my chair for
me to sit down. Stash came back with beer and bread—my
professor held up two fingers and said: *bigos*—then turned his
attention to me. He asked me how my day had gone and I told
him in general terms about cancer chemotherapy, a few of the
patients, and the death of one of them. It was then that he did
a most amazing thing. He pushed his seat back slightly,
placed his palms on the table, moistened his lips as though he
were going to sing, and began to speak:

" 'The pair of mourners, sufficiently stricken, were in the
lobby of the grand hospital together, before luncheon, waiting
to be summoned, and the good doctor had still in his face the
intention, it would have been more proper to call it rather
than the expression, of feeling something or other. Might it be
the proper touch of empathy, or merely the necessary appearance of same? Bearing the sad news of their mother's death,
the doctor approached the two young women and, trying to
show his compassion, at the same instant found himself
encompassed by the beauty of the younger of the two sisters.
It all took place in a moment. She smiled demurely and
looked away; the good doctor blushed in spite of himself, held
out a hand to her and' . . . Henry James," said my professor,
breaking the spell. I sipped the foam from my beer, fascinated. And before I could speak, he was off again.

" 'Tell me, Henry. Please don't try and keep anything from
me. What is the trouble about?'

" 'Well, Dick owes me a lot of money for pulling his squaw through cancer and I guess he wanted a row so he wouldn't have to take it out in work.' His wife was silent. The doctor wiped his gun carefully with a rag. He pushed the shells back in against the spring of the magazine. He sat with the gun on his knees. He was very fond of it. Then he heard his wife's voice from the darkened room' . . . Hemingway," said my professor, "Ernest Hemingway." He ran through my day once again, with the spell-binding convoluted tale-telling of Isak Dinesen, then with Thomas Wolfe's rhythms of the senses, and finally with the universal voice of Joseph Conrad. I never said a word. Finally, he laughed, gave a shy bow with his head, and gathered his hands around the bowl of *bigos* Stash had set before him. I must admit I had trouble keeping my face out of my bowl of the stuff. What had looked like the entire contents of Stash's kitchen stewed together was the most fantastic tasting gruel I had ever tasted. Maybe it was just the beer. Maybe just the bread. Maybe my professor.

I ended the evening with a list of books to read, and a promise to meet again. I spent the next day's lunch hour at the bookstores in the Square, carting back to the office a stack of books—*The Short Stories of Frank O'Connor, The Complete Poems of Emily Dickinson, The Charterhouse of Parma* by Stendhal—and God knows what else. Good intentions, to be sure. The stack of books stood on the left corner of my desk for a week, then were moved to a chair, and from there, under a stack of journals and papers, to be lost in the endless stream of patients and disease. Since it was my turn to set up a dinner meeting, and since I hadn't gotten the reading done— and since he probably assumed I was busy with the books—I did not see or hear from my professor for several months.

And then one day he was in my office. With his wife. For weeks he'd been having difficulty in swallowing and wanted my advice about it. Me—a cancer specialist. *He* knew that he had cancer, but I fumbled around for the better part of a week trying to prove he had something benign—a stricture or a Schatzki's ring or some such easy diagnosis. I had him 'scoped and when the endoscopist called me with the news—esophageal carcinoma—I slammed the phone down. Why was I angry? Why did it take me so long to make the diagnosis? Why was I so busy denying the whole thing?

He took the news with a startling equanimity, with an almost embarrassing calm. *I* seemed more upset than he was.

And now he is wasting away on the east wing, barely alive. And he isn't mine anymore. I mean, I had always intended to go back to Stash's with him. It was going to be part of my life, someday. And the hospital bedside just isn't the same thing, my friend. The climate's different; the agenda's changed. Oh, he still taunts me about being unread, still shows me up in his gentle, teasing way, "Quick, my good doctor, a character from Brontë . . . —time's up . . . Heathcliff. Now . . . Emily, or Charlotte?"

But it's more than just this sense of a missed opportunity, although that's painful enough. There's this mixture of feelings that has to do with the idea that once he belonged to me, could have been my friend, and I threw it away. So when I see him with Sally, his nurse—and God knows there's some kind of unspoken bond between them—I get filled with anger and jealousy and gratitude. *I* want the attention he's giving to her, and *I* am responsible for his impending death and *I* couldn't cure him and *she* is being tender and loving to my friend in a way that *I* can't bring myself to be.

The narrow road from Épinal to Provenchères is the most direct route and the most enchanting as well. Leaving the calm predictability of the upper Moselle, its asphalt races eastward seemingly without purpose, hardly noticing the licks and swirls of the Mortagne or the heavy warning of the chapel bells at Bruyères. Only after St. Dié does the road, now shaded on either side by the forests of the Vosges, slow to the climb ahead. Leaning first to this curve and now back into the leftward ascent, as though undecided about the sanctuary of the mountains, the road at last opens to the summit ridge and its clear views both east and west.

It was to this place of contemplation that Jean-Paul and Michel had traveled one rainy Monday night. There was a restaurant, of course. One never heads directly into the light, but rather assumes a more tangential course, with insight dealing a glancing blow. The only restaurant at Provenchères, called simply "Vosgienne," was a treasure. From the outside it crouched hut-like, built low as it was against the wind. The light from its small-paned windows drew its guests within as does a church its faithful.

"How does he do it?" asked Michel. "This *potage Parmentier* is sheer perfection. Marie-Phillippe amazes me every time. A few simple potatoes and leeks, and he gives us this!"

"Commitment, Michel, commitment," answered Jean-Paul, slurping his soup. "Marie-Phillippe could dazzle us with his entrées and anyone but you, my friend, might then excuse an ordinary soup course. But it is not for you that Marie-Phillippe cooks his soup. He cooks for his God."

Michel turned to look at the fire in the great stone hearth. The corners of his mouth sagged. He tossed one hand, then the other, looked at his friend across from him, then back into the fire.

"But not everywhere do we find this commitment, eh? Even with the greatest of chefs, there is a danger at the destination. . . . What has happened to Roland, Jean-Paul? What do you make of it? I have known him my whole life, it seems. But he is a stranger to me now."

The west wind rattled the linden branches against the window panes outside. Jean-Paul assumed a tortured look and stalled for time.

"Happened? What do you mean, 'happened?' "

"Marianna and I went to Besançon two weeks ago for dinner. To be sure, his parking lot is more overflowing than ever—he has gone to three sittings— and the Auberge Doubs impresses as never before. One sees its lights from miles away. Roland has a red canopy ten meters long at the entryway, with red carpet, no less. There is an initial excitement, a specialness one senses on first arriving. But, then . . . "

"Roland was my best friend, Michel," interrupted Jean-Paul sternly. "He and I were classmates."

"He was at the école Hôtelière?" asked Michel.

"Their best pupil in his day. Leagues ahead of the rest of us. Innovative . . . brilliant . . . daring."

Jean-Paul interrupted to direct their waiter, "The *matelote* for me, the *foie gras* for Michel. *Merci.*"

"Excuse me, my friend, and do not take offense, but you would not know his greatness now. Roland has lost the stamp of Strasbourg. Oh, he is making lots of money, *oui,* and old man Gaertner would be proud of that, I suppose. But I cannot admire him or own to be of the same profession."

Jean-Paul hesitated, then said, "I have not been to Besançon for years. . . . Roland and I had a falling out. Still, he is an old friend. But . . . what did you see there?"

"I saw a man without caring. I saw patrons run in and out like cattle, given no time, no pause, no consideration. I saw a machine for making money, a *terrine de volaille* made of paste and straw and little else, a *feuilleté* tasteless, made only for show. I saw a man trading on the knowledge that *once* he had three stars, that *once* he had trained in Strasbourg, that *once* he had been the most renowned chef in Alsace, in all of eastern France, that *once* . . . "

" 'Let he who is without sin cast the first stone,' " interrupted Jean-Paul.

"You compare me with Roland!? How can you say that *l'Ange* is like his . . . his . . . factory? How can you insult my family like this!?" Michel was standing, pointing a finger, napkin on the floor. The small dining room grew suddenly still. Marie-Phillippe could be seen in the kitchen doorway. He knew these two. Dinner with them was never a dull affair.

"I meant none of those things, *mon ami.* I mean only that all of us, even you, could lose the way as Roland has. We all share that capacity."

Michel sat down, permitting himself to cool, The diners resumed their meals.

"Lost his way," he said. "Well-put. Roland has lost his way."

Jean-Paul held his soup dish out for the waiter, nodded and smiled slightly to him, and turned back to Michel.

"What is Roland's reality?" he asked his friend.

"How does he measure his life? By what parameters?"

Michel pondered the question. He turned to reflect upon his own reality. At an adjacent table sat a young family of four, parents attentive, children wide-eyed, exploring the world Marie-Phillippe had created for them. The little boy, in red bow-tie, knife and fork in either hand, confronted his *cuisse de grenouilles,* planning his attack. His sister, younger still, held the empty shell of an *escargot* aloft, as if to coax forth one last snail. Michel felt the harmony of these four, sensed their health and vitality, knew the happiness they would gain from this togetherness, advanced in some small way by Marie-Phillippe's *ambiance* and gift of perfection. At a corner table, discreetly tucked away, sat the young lovers. Every dining room has them, and every *maître d',* the responsibility for their correct situation. Michel had watched them started on proper course, guided ever so gently away from the expensive champagne and toward a more palatable—and more affordable—*pétillant* Vouvray. She, with charming douceness, hangs on his every word. He, strong and bold, paints the air with his gestures as he tells her of the world. Then, a pause, their eyes meet—she looks down, smiles demurely. He takes her hand.

And at the table by the fire, Michel watched an elderly couple, bathed in the hearth's amber glow, themselves holding hands, talking gently. Directly and full to the face, they behold each other, permitting Michel—and anyone—to see the love and understanding between them.

Who are these people? wonders Michel. Are they customers with fat wallets to be emptied? Strangers with dull palates to be scorned? Or something more? What do these people mean to Marie-Phillippe? And what is his place in their lives?

Finally, Michel turned back to his friend, who had been quietly observing him, and asked, "What was it you said?"

Jean-Paul smiled and said, "I asked you what you thought Roland's reality might be. From what does he derive his identity? How does he define himself in relation to his world? What is important to him, what is *véritable*?"

Michel shifted in his chair, tossed his hand in the air, pinched the wax on the candle, looked about, frowned, scowled, raised his eyebrows, and shrugged.

"The obvious things I would suppose. Money . . . success . . . power. His station in life. That, I suppose, is Roland's reality."

"Yes, those goals most compelling . . . arresting . . . intoxicating. You remember Odysseus. He lashes himself to the mast, so compelling is the Siren's song. So tempting to all of us. But the song was not always so compelling. Which of us started school with thoughts of 'I will do this thing to make money. I will learn the intricacies of my art so that I may be famous. I will become a great chef so that I may be loved, so that I may be all-powerful, so that I may be redeemed.' Do any of us as young students even consider these things? Of course not! Only later, after the battle, when we think the war safely won, when we sail home on calm seas, do we hear the Siren's song. I will tell you Roland's story."

Jean-Paul turned in his chair, stretched and crossed his legs, swirled and sniffed his Gewürztraminer, and sat abruptly upright once again. An immense sadness overtook him.

"Did you know that Johann Sebastian Bach wrote and performed only for the glory of God? He was like our friend here,' said Jean-Paul, nodding his head toward the kitchen and Marie-Phillippe.

"Roland's reality, that of ambition, never occurred to Bach. Never did Bach say to himself, 'I will compose *Toccata and Fugue in D* and become rich and famous.' Bach's reality embraced other, higher ideals. Not so, Roland's.

"Roland began modestly enough after the university, as a *sous-chef* in Marlenheim. But Roland always had one eye toward advancement. That was primary. He must make it to a one-star, then a *sous-chef* at a two-star, and so on, until he would think, 'When I make to the next step, I will be happy, and I will have more money and more things and that will make me even happier.' Roland's ambition was like the university professor's, who forgets he exists for his students, and rather is forever planning his next career move, his next promotion.

"And of course, happiness never comes. There is always the next move, and more money to earn . . . no end to it. Roland imagined a treasure chest to be filled for him by life and by his own ambition . . . with this treasure, he would find happiness and a sense of accomplishment. He never found them, of course; the chest can never be filled. One must look elsewhere. But Roland cannot. He is trapped in this thinking, caring not at all for his patrons, always surrounding himself with more glitter.

"Friends are brushed aside, excellence forsaken, as he pursues this Siren's song. He cannot get off this path."

Michel coughed, as though to interrupt. He began carefully, not wishing for a scene from Jean-Paul such he himself had caused moments before. He began, "Each of us, *mon ami*, writes his own story, don't you think? Whatever his past, whatever it is that drives him now, do you not suppose that Roland could change? To change paths now would be difficult for him, I admit, especially with his present path so paved in gold . . . but not impossible."

"Better to start young," answered Jean-Paul, "at university or even before. Choose a higher goal, an *Idéal*, and let nothing stay your course. Perhaps it will be the thirst for knowledge or some grand creative fire within. You, Michel, have your love of people, your sense of harmony to steer you, Marie-Phillippe, his God. And my *pension*, with its *ambiance*, is an expression of the love between Yvette and myself, I suppose. We are lucky. We are this way almost by accident. Roland is not so lucky."

"Providence, perhaps, " said Michel. "But we make choices all the time, and those choices are conscious as a rule, I will bore you I know, but I am reminded of a story from *Le Rouge et le Noir*."

Jean-Paul laughed loudly and slapped the table. Michel was forever quoting his Stendhal. Michel continued, " The hero, Julien Sorel, has an affair with the beautiful wife of his employer, whose children he tutors. He then gains a position in the seminary at Besançon, where he studies for fourteen months. But he is compelled to return to her, to recapture what he has had with her.

"She, Mme. De Rênal, has meanwhile returned to her faith in God, begging forgiveness for her past sins. With a ladder, Julien gains entry to her bedroom from the garden. She is shocked, appalled, scandalized! With renewed passion, with his awakened love, Julien attempts an embrace. Mme. De Rênal rebuffs him. He pleads, he professes his undying love for her. Still she refuses.

"Then, my friend, he makes his choice. And it is fully a conscious one. He feigns a bitter remorse. He tells her (with a cold heart) of his unhappiness at the seminary, of his endless dreaming of her. Finally, he plays his last card in this game: He is leaving her forever, he says, going to Paris at once and forever. He will never see her again. He moves to the window, to the ladder, as though to leave. Mme. De Rênal can no longer resist. She throws herself into his arms.

"And here Stendhal says a very moving thing, in this chapter he calls 'Ambition.'" (Michel was standing now, pointing his finger upward in instruction. The entire dining room sat in rapt attention.)

"Stendhal writes, 'Coming a bit sooner,'—that is, in response to the earlier genuine emotion from Julien— 'Coming a bit sooner, this reversion to tender feelings, the disappearance of Mme. De Rênal's remorse, would have meant divine happiness; thus obtained, by art, it was nothing more than a triumph.' "

As Michel began to sit once again, the little girl at the next table clapped chubby hands. With a grand sweep of his arm, Michel bowed deeply in her direction. She smiled at him with dancing eyes.

"What begins as some strange calling, or a mother's wish, or a dream, may end, if we are not careful, in a Faustian bargain," said Jean-Paul. "It is time to go. . . . did you smell the mangoes in this Sauternes?"

The storm had passed. Out in the parking lot of the *Vosgienne*, the two friends paused for a moment of star-gazing.

"Tell me their names again."

"Look this way then . . . the brightest first, there . . . yellowish. . . . Arcturus. Hippocrates made much of its influence, believing that illness falling under its sign would prove critical indeed. To its left . . . see the gentle arc of stars and its brightest at the center . . . Alphecca to the Arabs . . . but for certain American Indians— the Shawnee—she was the wife of White Hawk, our Arcturus. All is harmony, *n'est-ce pas?* Now, my friend, above Arcturus and slightly to the right, that beautiful star seemingly alone . . . *Cor Caroli* . . . the Heart of Charlemagne . . . a French star of course, of unparalleled beauty, *naturellement*.

"Far below Arcturus and to the right . . . the very bright one . . . Spica, it's called. Draw a line between the two and to the right of your line, in that empty space there, well, not empty really . . . that is The Realm of the Galaxies . . . hundreds of them, thousands perhaps, many of them French, no doubt. Spica is in Virgo, or Persephone, the daughter of Demeter, which is a wonderful story in itself. . . ."

Thus did the two friends lose themselves in the Universe, leaving the gears of the galaxies to grind as They will.

The neurologist did not see what his students saw, did not see the peeling chips of paint, the stark black and white of this colorless place, the yawning, stretching halls filled with quiet and despair. Nor did he smell the stale urine, the pungency of the failed attempt at antisepsis; could not feel the still horror of wasted lives and endless imprisonment which these shells of humanity represented. He was not caught with a quickening fear as were his students, did not hesitate in his step to some poor soul's bed, did not catch, as did his students, the empty stare of the gaunt, slack faces on the ward. Among these wasted bodies and twisted limbs were lesions unparalleled, neurological disasters valued for their aberration, treasures to teach the processes of the mind, or more precisely, the brain, for they are not one. Teaching was his reality. And that which promoted teaching belonged to his reality. And so, for all his eloquence and erudition, he could not know, could never live the other realities that might reside rostral to the fields of Forel.

They were gathered there, the neurologist and his students, at bedside, in the classic black-and-white pose of medical pedagogy which has served this most noble of professions so well. The neurologist, tall, thin, commanding, swept kind eyes over the scene, seeing young minds eager to grasp his own sense of interconnecting dendrites and sweep of axonal radiations that give substance to the brain. The students, shifting weight nervously, avoided the motionless, expressionless, staring, haunting, fixed, and so horribly sad eyes of the patient, avoided the hair and bone covered by thin sheets, avoided the feeding tubes, the parted, dry, scaling lips that said no word to them, avoided all this, and wished they were elsewhere. While the neurologist, that quintessential teacher, formed his words, lacing together thoughts of ventral pons and midbrain function, his students listened to the awesome silence that was this patient.

*"Wonderful! You peoples are wonderful! I make you all honorary Czechs! You all be childrens of Smetana! This hall tomorrow in the evening will be filled only with Czechs and your Americans who wish they are Czechs! And you will play 'Má vlast' with such feeling that they remember that evening the rest of their lives . . . now we go through each poem one more time. Remember ladies, you play feeling the blood of Šárka in your veins . . . gentlemen, remember Jan Hus. Remember him! First, we paint the Vyš ehrad . . . think colors now. Rays of gold from the soothsayers' harps. Brass, you speak of the fame and glory of the Vyš ehrad, of Prague and Bohemia. Some gold from you too. Second harp, you begin the motif . . . lento in E-flat. Okay, now . . . spirit, power, glory, but painted with a touch of sadness . . . violet and purples from you winds, okay? Colors, remember the colors. Let us begin!"*

The neurologist began to speak, stirring the transfixed students to attention.

"You have learned in neuroanatomy the location and importance of the reticular activating system. We know much of neurophysiology through patients who, through some specific lesion, are deprived of function. This is a Mr. Kolář, who has been with us now for . . . " The neurologist fanned the pages of the patient record.

"Yes, for three years. A Czech immigrant . . . a musician it seems. He was transferred from an acute care hospital after having suffered a massive brainstem stroke. And, although his life is, for all intents and purposes, over, we can learn much from him."

The neurologist paused to assess this group of would-be physicians, saw some attentive and poised with questions, others staring off, their minds seemingly elsewhere. He continued.

"This patient seems at first glance to be awake, as we might say. His eyes are open. He seems to be fixed on something. Yet he doesn't respond to us in any meaningful way. We need to understand how that might be, in order better to understand the anatomy of the brainstem."

*"Now flutes, you bring the cold waters to Vltava . . . and clarinets, the warm sources . . . now to E-minor, the river . . . flow with the music, flow with Vltava . . . horns, sound the hunt! Yes, beautiful! Gold from the morning sun . . . now, the peasant wedding . . . the dancing . . . timing here. Timing is all. Watch me dance! Drums, some strength please. Yes! Now the moonlight and water nymphs. Play, Jana Ortová! Play your flute, Jana Ortová! And the rapids of St. John. Swirl! Drums! Sound the rocks . . . the cascades! Cymbals . . . ready now . . . "*

"Mr. Kolář here, through having sustained a vascular occlusion in his brainstem, has what we term 'the persistent vegetative state," or in the old parlance, 'coma vigile.' Because of interruption of the pathways of the reticular activating system, he is not awake, does not send or receive information, has no processes of the higher centers."

*"Peoples! 'Šárka' was perfect! You have her feeling, Šárka's revenge! You must understand me now about 'Zčeských luhůa hájů.' We start and I am eagle skimming tree-tops of Bohemia. Strings and brass—make me soar! Then quieting . . . always quiet here and strings now in triple time con sordini, fugato . . . flutes, some cool breezes to be blowing, okay? Then we come to the harvest celebration . . . happiness . . . always with the happiness . . . trumpets—fanfare, yes? Building musical strength, then . . . violins first, then violas, cellos next . . . "*

The neurologist paused to let his words sink in. His students seemed to him skeptical of the suggestion that a patient who appeared to them awake might be comatose. He continued.

"Mr. Kolář is, as you see, quadriplegic through interruption of his corticospinal tracts, has no conjugate gaze, having lost the medial longitudinal fasciculus, and in fact has no eye movement at all because both the third and sixth cranial nerves are out bilaterally. Picture your coronal sections of pons and midbrain and you will have a sense of the extent of the lesion."

*"That are Bohemian woods to perfection! You bring tears, peoples! Tears! I long for my Bohemia! And you will making New York peoples too, long for Bohemia also! Now, 'Tábor' next. The four notes in D-minor . . . strong, threatening . . . horns, do you feel that? Winds . . . paint some peace and calm over the green hills of countryside . . . then strings, you build, gather speed . . . I gallop with Jan Žižka over the hills . . . faster on my horse . . . brass, you help me here . . . "*

"There is a closely related syndrome, the 'locked-in state,' where dorsal midbrain is spared and consciousness preserved. In that syndrome, the lesion lies in the ventral pons only, getting enough pons to interrupt the M-L-F and six. The R-A-S pathways are spared, the patient is awake, and three is intact. In the 'locked-in state,' therefore, unlike Mr. Kolář here, the patient has intact vertical gaze and preserved pupillary reflexes."

The neurologist paused for the question, then answered.

"Quite correct. The patient in the 'locked-in state' receives information and can communicate through the use of vertical eye movements. Horizontal eye movement is out because the M-L-F is gone, remember."

The neurologist thumbed through the chart again, pausing to read here and there.

"A student some time ago apparently found vertical eye movement, or thought he did. But others haven't described it. It is certainly important to look for in a patient like this. For obvious reasons."

*"Finally, 'Blaník' peoples, and then we are done for tonight. Blaník, the mountain of the sleeping knights, the Holy Venceslas and his armies, sleeping and waiting for the call to arms, waiting to defend the oppressed homeland . . . the chorale of 'Tábor' . . . carry that theme . . . I am sleeping knight full of strength and foreboding . . . give me that feeling . . . I will awaken someday . . . to race across Bohemia's hills . . . "*

The neurologist felt the students' interest. He answered them.

"Good questions. Yes, the 'locked-in state' can be missed. The patient is found in a state of collapse, quadriplegic, unresponsive, and is diagnosed as having a 'massive stroke,' there being no further attempts to define the lesion. Vertical eye movement is not tested for, nor even pupillary reflexes. And why do we keep Mr. Kolář alive? A more difficult question. Because we cannot play God? Because we are to learn from him to help others? Because there are more things on Heaven and Earth than are dreamt of in our philosophies? These are social issues, philosophical issues, for which there are no easy answers. And to the last question . . . Mrs. Simpson, does Mr. Kolář ever have visitors?"

"His wife comes quite regularly, Dr. Adams," said the charge nurse. "And we've noticed that in early March for the past three years some old, white-haired old men come in the morning and sit by his bedside. They stay all day."

They turned from the reality of Kolář and from Kolář's reality, the neurologist and his students, and left the room. The young, thin, dark-haired student with the troubled eyes ventured a question.

"Could he be thinking, Dr. Adams? I mean, could his mind still be working?"

Adams smiled slightly, sighed, and looked at his shoes.

"Good question. I used to wonder that myself. I would wonder what might go on behind the masks of these people. Sometimes I hoped that nothing went on, for their sake, if you understand me. And there was never any denying their lesions on the MRI scan. "Yet, maybe they'd be better off if they had a fantasy to live."

Not too long ago, I had a very bothersome case, of a patient who died when there just didn't seem to be anything wrong with her. At least, nothing wrong with her that I could discover. She had come to me with those vague complaints that can drive a doctor crazy—nothing you could really hang your hat on. Nevertheless, she grew sicker, and sicker, and finally I had to admit her to the hospital where, with every test normal, she died. For want of anything else to say, I told the family that her heart gave out. They seemed to understand. She had, after all, been married for twenty-seven years to her childhood sweetheart, the two of them had been in love every minute of that marriage, and he had been killed in a tractor roll-over some months before. She just didn't want to live after that. Her family understood this kind of disease, even when I didn't have a name for it. Oh, I knew poets had sung about it, and still do, writing about broken hearts and death the way they do. But in real life, you can usually find a reason for it.

I couldn't stop pondering over that case, and the more I thought about it, and about its opposite extreme—those patients I have had who *should* die, patients for whom the odds are just not there for life to go on, and who nevertheless turn it around with no help from me whatsoever, and brighten up and heal—the more I felt compelled to look into this business of attitude. But first though, I had to get past my own prejudice toward fringe medicine, to which I thought this mind-set business must belong. It helped me that Osler himself had figured that the outcome of tuberculosis seemed to depend more upon what was going on in a patient's head than in his chest. That cleared the way for other anecdotal evidence I was now not so ready to discard. Cancer seemed to strike more frequently those already bereaved. Women with terminal breast cancer survived twice as long when they got involved in support groups as when they fought the cancer by themselves alone. Orphaned newborns, held and nurtured by caring nurses, had a much better chance of it. And so on.

Then I read that if you show an asthmatic allergic to goldenrod just a picture of the weed, he might wheeze. How can this be? He's allergic to the *pollen*, after all, and when goldenrod pollen gets into the respiratory tract of an asthmatic, antibodies start their business and the poor guy wheezes. There's no pollen in a picture. No pollen to get the antibodies going, disturb the peace and quiet of mast cells and start all that bronchospasm. How can this happen? It can make you start wondering about the power of the mind.

A psychiatrist named Ader ran an experiment with rats. When he was done, he'd given this mind-over-body idea a considerable amount of credibility. He was studying nausea in patients receiving cancer chemotherapy, and more specifically, the phenomenon of anticipatory nausea in these patients. It has been well-known that cancer patients began to vomit at the mere thought of getting the cancer drugs.—I'd had more than a few patients myself who vomited at the sight of me and who had the decency to blame it on the chemotherapy—so this was of some interest to me. Ader wanted to study this reaction in the laboratory. Now cancer drugs, in addition to producing nausea and vomiting in patients, lower a patient's resistance to disease, especially infectious disease, by interfering with the immune system. Ader's plan was to give the mice an anti-cancer drug—cyclophosphamide—which he called the unconditioned stimulus, along with some saccharine-sweetened water, the conditioned stimulus. The anti-cancer drug would produce vomiting, a response Ader would then link to the sweetened water alone, just as Pavlov had his dogs salivating at the mere sound of a bell. Then Ader would have his laboratory model.

Ader, and the rest of us, got more than was bargained for. What Ader produced when he uncoupled the two stimuli, giving only the saccharine to his conditioned mice, was depression of the mouse's immune response, seemingly caused by the sweetened water alone. But this had to have been caused by something else as well. The mice, having been challenged with both saccharine and cyclophosphamide, "learned" not only to vomit but also "learned" to depress their immune resistance when given just the saccharine-sweetened water. Something just like that asthmatic looking at the picture of goldenrod.

We have accepted the notion of the conditioned response ever since Pavlov—this communication about and around the brain over bells and pieces of raw meat was old stuff. But how could the brain, having just "tasted" some sweetened water, "tell" the immune system to shut off? This was too much. And if such "learning" could take place, assuming it could, then how did the nervous system—the center of learning—communicate with the body's immune system? Could there be verifiable anatomic, and even chemical, connections as well, such that the brain, having had a taste of saccharine, began to shut down the body's army against disease?

The more I read, the more it seemed that the answer was *yes*. Someone discovered nerve endings insinuating themselves into the tissues of thymus, of spleen, of bone marrow, and even of lymph nodes, conducting messages from the autonomic nervous system, talking to these tissues. A small group of neurologists and immunologists began to call themselves neuroimmunologists. But they couldn't keep out the psychiatrists, who noticed that when severely depressed patients displayed a feeble response to foreign attack by mitogens, these patients also showed smaller numbers of circulating lymphocytes available to fight the challenge. Even those remaining lymphocytes held decreased numbers of receptors necessary for chemical direction. Could there be a connection between depression itself and the immune system? The psyche too had something to say about immunity. *Psycho*neuroimmunologists began working to figure this out.

Ader next experimented with a family of mice suffering from an inherited form of lupus—a disease of joints and organs caused by an inappropriately exuberant immune response. First he gave them the saccharine/cyclophos-phamide stimuli as he had those other mice before. But nausea didn't deter these mice. They appeared to "treat" their lupus voluntarily by drinking more of sweetened water than did control mice. They were attenuating their own immune response to lessen the symptoms of their lupus disease, in other words.

There was more. Lymphocytes, the cellular focus of immunity, produce antibodies, attacking any foreign agent that may cause trouble. Lymphocytes have, it has been found, surface receptors for hormones manufactured deep in the substance of the brain. Why should the soldiers of the body's defense mechanisms be carrying wireless radios linked to the central nervous system? Do they take calls from High Command? Polish scientists found that cutting the connections between the sympathetic nervous system and the immune system in laboratory animals caused diseases remarkable similar to multiple sclerosis and myasthenia gravis. Did this hint that in humans, there two diseases might be auto-immune, caused by unchecked body defenses as happens in lupus, and that in some manner neuronal control keeps these stray battalions in line? Could multiple sclerosis result from some sort of loss of neuronal control over the immune system?

Then the news got even more alarming—and much closer to home. In the area of primate research, researchists started out to prove that elderly primates might live longer and fare better when kept in a social environment—living with the family, in other words. Instead, this busy social life produced problems for the immune system in the aging apes.

Senior citizen apes underwent immune senescence, more rapid aging of their defenses, from stress, it was surmised. Just maybe, some mother suggested, it could be the stress of having teenagers around.

Information like this would make anyone stop and wonder. It was as though scientists were witnessing for the first time a common bread mold killing off deadly bacteria, as though they had found a forgotten volume in the Encyclopedia of the

Great Design. Psychosocial influences altered the immune response—the mind could talk to host defenses—and change the course of cancer. Thyrotropin, a pituitary hormone whose sole purpose in life was believed to be control of metabolism, had receptor sites on natural killer cells? Why? How could messages calling for a fueling up of the body's fires relate also to the immune response? In other words, what conversations might occur within the infected patient during fever? And why are chemical transmitters employed by the message transfer system of the nervous system shared also by the immune system? Is this a link between their separate networks? If a young woman with metastatic breast cancer shows grit, courage, the will to fight, if she has love, support, and caring from her family, and feels it from her doctor as well, what does the flood of serotonin and endorphins, of cytokines and enkephalins from her nerve cells say to her T-cell lymphocytes? And why should certain psychoactive drugs—Valium for one—drugs which connect in a molecular lock-and-key with brain tissue and alter mood and manner, why should these drugs have receptor sites on monocytes? Are there native transmitters resembling the molecular structure of Valium that modulate the responses of both brain and immune tissue?

All this consideration of conditioned mice with lupus, of grandfather apes who, along with the rest of us, when assaulted with the noise of Mötley Crüe, lose the will to live, of cancer patients who, when supported by compassionate friends, clearly have a better time of it, just led to more questions. If psychosocial factors affect neuroimmunology in basic and profound ways, could the arrow go both ways? Does the immune response affect the psyche primarily? And what are the frontal lobes up to? If a cellular immune response can be conditioned in so beneficial a manner, if, that is, one's own feelings can heighten one's resistance to disease, how might this relate to the feelings of another? From another? To human understanding? To compassion? If one can read the line of the mouth, the set of the jaw, the unwavering commitment in another's eye, what happens *then* to a person's antibodies? Could a doctor's touch mean even more to a patient's recovery than might a CAT scanner? Could T-cells prefer the sound of a caring voice to the sterile words of a glossy pamphlet? With today's confusion of outcomes research and managed care, of marketed providers and gate-keepers, of cost containment and managed competition, and of an overwhelming concern for The Data, could there still be a place for the doctor? There seemed to me to be, after all, a message in π.

Sometimes late at night in my own small hospital, I find with a start that I have been lost for an uncounted length of time in the maze of medicine's mysteries. Usually this happens after a death occurs, and most usually after the loss of a patient dearly loved. Why, I might wonder, did Death come today, at this time, and not on another day? Why had the resuscitation gone so well last week, yet could make no difference this morning? Why did the hearty woodsman die? Why was the old man condemned to live?

Where are the biochemical pathways for this "letting go" I so often see, when an elderly woman held together for so long a time in so fragile a way, suddenly fails in every way, letting me know that every cell in her body participated in an orchestrated grand finale? And where, by the way, does the Mind go then? Why is it sometimes, when Death comes for a patient, God seems so palpably near, and at other times the room echoes with only death and emptiness, the patient so utterly alone?

Metaphysics doesn't seem to help me here, and so, I imagine the future.

I imagine a time quite distant, so far away as to be incomprehensible to me, yet where there are doctors still. A time where all the answers are in, or most of them, and where, I fondly dream, students are taught still at the bedside, tradition-bound by some old professor who will simply not let go, a man with a sense of history about him. I imagine that scene so familiar to us now, the eager students full of their youth and excitement clustered at the bedside with their mentor, the patient at hand. In that imagined future, there will be imaging devices of unthinkable sophistication, of design and resolution, and of focus and sensitivity as would seem to us to be as marvelous as magnetic resonance imaging might have been to Hippocrates, their marvelous displays rendering our own best PET-scanners as no more than a toss of dried bones in the dirt. The images—the patient's own psychoneuroimmunological network—will be displayed very much in the air above them, I imagine, in all the colors of the universe, in pixels the size of atoms. The professor, for the moment ignoring these images which so transfix his students, will lean to the patient, take her hand, feel her pulse, and scan her integument with his practiced eye, probing, palpating, listening, just as did the Ancients, ourselves.

The students will watch the race of neuropeptides binding to T-cell receptors, bolstering immune readiness, catch the feed-back loops flashing, chart the course of messages sent from the periphery to brain centers those same Ancients once termed Confidence, Trust, and Security. Cytokines, interleukins, cofactors beyond our ken will glow, float, interconnect, bind and coalesce, producing the hoped-for response. The air will be alive with flashes, racing streaks, blinks, winks, and steady glows, as the old physician goes about his business of healing.

He stands erect now, smiling down at her. The students shift, engage. They see in the air, completion, and in the lines of her face, resolve, and they thrill to the moment. Hands in his white coat, the professor nods to them. And there, in that glorious time, his students will learn first hand what it can mean to a patient to have a doctor of her own. They will marvel, remembering in their medical history texts, that mankind 10,000 years ago or so, came so close to throwing it all away.

But there! Who is that off in the corner? An academic with a greater vision? Some things never change. She stands, arms folded, her shoulder against the wall, the slight smile on her face, holding within her a profound sense of happiness, of completion. She looks at the students before her, and at their mentor, and, with an imaging device of her own, watches in the air before her the colorful humours of *their* minds. She sees the flashes and scintillations of those ephemeral and eternal embodiments of oneness, feeling, identity, compassion, sympathy, passion, and . . . poetry. Some of these "centers" will in some students shine as steadily as The Pleiades, whereas in others she will see a fainter glow, like Orion's sword, yet steady, and with promise.

She will see random bursts, sudden quick flashes, winks of surprise and insight, and flashes in synchrony like fireflies along the Amazon. And perhaps in a few, she might see a cerebral supernova giving rise to a peripheral cascade like the moonlight racing across the waters. She will glance at the images, then to the students' faces, at their wonder, their attitude, their fix, at their caring eyes still learning. Her smile will broaden. That will be Empathy she's beholding.

God used up His leftover parts to make Vinnie Duchette's face, and gave him a bargain-basement soul. Truth leaked out of this soul as fast as the lies from Vinnie's lips. What do they want to hear? What can I say to get out of this? How can I convince them I'm not lying? Only his excellent memory and constant vigilance sustained Vinnie's lifelong habit of distortion. In another life Vinnie might have been lawyer instead of defendant, but his business was crime, and the law, his adversary. Where he might have been brilliant he was merely slick. He was wily rather than wise, more fox than owl.

Welcomed at first as a wonderful distraction by his otherwise ineffective, alcoholic mother, little Vinnie soon became an afterthought, left to fend for himself. Vinnie's real-life terrors were interpreted for him as bad dreams, or worse, as his own misapprehensions. Mother was often "feeling ill" or "under the weather." His abusive father, and the bullying men who followed in his wake, "didn't mean to" strike Vinnie's mother or intimidate the children. The swollen lip, the blackened eye, were the unfortunate result of a door left ajar, or a misstep on the cellar stairs. The shouts, the curses, the screams in the night were merely heated "discussions." Abuse was explained away as rough affection, or dismissed altogether as never having happened. In this way Vinnie learned never to trust his feelings.

Vinnie learned other, larger lies: hunger, poverty, and heatless winters were the fault of The World, of the nameless *they*. *They* hoarded everything. *They* deprived Vinnie, his sisters, and his poor mother of any happiness. The nameless *they* taunted the children's shabby dress, caused the comfortless nights, the driving rain and sockless feet, the confusing ambivalent boil of love and hate, the yearning and contempt that swelled within Vinnie's heart. *They* were responsible for Vinnie's gnawing loneliness, for the dark, trash-littered rooms, the sinister shouts in the neighborhood, the absent father, and the troubled and troubling mother. *They* became Vinnie's adversary, the mark, the object of Vinnie's inventive distortions. And Vinnie, with his quick mind and his gift for fitting feeling to situation, with his immunity from accountability, became *their* formidable opponent. Vinnie could con anybody.

Vinnie celebrated his twenty-first birthday in prison, but not because of his countless brushes with the law for shoplifting, breaking-and-entering and drug-dealing, for which, he bragged, he had never served time. Vinnie had concocted an elaborate scheme of credit and fraud of his own invention, from which he netted literally millions, the conspicuous consumption of which finally landed him in jail. With a handful of bills he lifted from an unattended cash drawer, Vinnie had purchased a tailored business suit and brogues to match, and styled his hair in a razor-cut. Loitering in the lobbies of large business firms, he observed and practiced the walk, talk, and mannerisms of the well-heeled, trading in his loping, bobbing stride for the erect, military pace of the successful businessman. Using charm and con-artistry, he finagled a job at the switchboard of a large tobacco firm in the South, and played to perfection the role of an honest, hardworking employee. His co-workers loved him, were impressed by his willingness and ability, and often left him to handle the switchboard alone. At the board, Vinnie's hands could fly through the connections unerringly. He never seemed to need a break from the job.

With the proceeds from his first "honest" week's work, Vinnie paid for elaborate business cards, embossed and lettered in black and gold. With these he introduced himself to exclusive country and yachting clubs, passing himself off as a senior vice-president for the tobacco company.

"Please, before we go any further with this," he would say with a knowing nod, "do give my company a ring. I really would prefer it that way."

And so, when the call came to the switchboard for "Tom Reynolds," Vinnie would know to route the call to himself.

He would affect the chuckling confidence of the old boy network as he gave the most glowing testimonial for fellow old
boy "Tom." In this way Vinnie stole acceptance into a new
society, learning to move carefully within it, astutely observing its strategies of power, knowing when to fawn, when to
wink, and when to buy the drinks. Bankers, lawyers and busi-
nessmen were all immensely impressed with "Tom" and with
his generosity at the bar. They insisted he join them for drinks
and dinner, and to meet the occasional single daughter. Thus
magnificently connected, Vinnie found bank loans a simple
matter.

"What is money after all?" he would say, with a dismissive
wave of his hand.

Vinnie was apprehended in the most mundane way. While
entertaining a select group of "associates" on his credit-pur-
chased yacht, presumably harmlessly adrift in international
waters, a Coast Guard launch on a drug intercept mission
approached Vinnie's drunken crew for a routine credentials
check. When they called the company offices to inquire about
"Tom Reynolds," Vinnie was of course at sea and not at the
switchboard. Having offended so egregiously the movers and
shakers with his con, he could thereafter only afford the public defender, and went to jail.

Time, in and out of prisons, left clever Vinnie middle-aged
and in a prison-hospital bed, where, he reckoned, he was at
least serving "easy" time. When his weight loss and ensuing
inanition became so apparent that it could not possibly be
another of Vinnie's con games, the doctors at the prison sub-
jected Vinnie to the leisurely, abbreviated diagnostic procedures afforded to those of Vinnie's ilk.

"Cancer of the pancreas," Vinnie heard the prison doctor
say. "This guy is dead meat," was his dispassionate diagnosis.
Vinnie knew then he would soon be out of prison and started
scheming to beat this fatal rap as well.

And so Vinnie Duchette found himself in a modern civilian
hospital, surrounded by technology and tended to by pretty
nurses who marveled at Vinnie's charm but quickly learned to

avoid his wandering hands. Vinnie's new doctor at the hospital was also drawn to Vinnie's magnetism, but misread the ready smile and agreeable manner as proof of his own flawless charisma.

Vinnie's doctor pursued perfection compulsively. He cultivated the devotion of others with the passion of a performing artist, his every move, expression, nuance, and manner carefully designed for the eye of the other. His insatiable hunger for infallibility reflected an inordinate need for control, and his casual spontaneous day had evolved into mere posturing. Whereas Vinnie survived on cunning and crime, measuring his self-esteem by what he could steal, the doctor compensated for *his* fractured childhood through the obsessive collection of kudos and credits. The highest marks, the front-row seat, the teacher's approving smile, the steady succession of sweethearts, the finest schools, the professor's private remarks, the honorary societies, the stunning classroom answer, the conspicuous scorn for sleep, the brilliant diagnosis, the best positions in the finest hospitals, the admiring glances of nurses, the truckling gratitude of patients and families—these the doctor cultivated with a careful design, reacting to each as he would to the gold star on the spelling test, that he *should* have achieved this after all, that it was expected of him, that there would have to be something more. The doctor's insatiable thirst for self-esteem grew into arrogance, a fragile belief not that he was never wrong, but rather that he *should* never be wrong, must never appear to err as he climbed the path to perfection. If Vinnie's approach to life had its obvious casualties—the pain of incarceration and the torture of prison life—so, too, did the doctor's, in shunned intimacy, a turbulent dis-ease within himself, and a record of failed marriages and alienated children, culminating in a frigid, steel-hard isolation.

It should not be surprising that these two, doctor and patient, could so vastly fail to connect, one with the other. Vinnie saw this legendary doctor as the perfect tool to help him beat his death sentence, whereas the doctor read Vinnie's ingratiating manner as further proof of his own preeminence. The doctor began to enjoy the visits on morning rounds, looked forward to them, and grew to like Vinnie, as much as he could genuinely like anyone. Vinnie in his turn devised clever tricks to hold on to the doctor, and to keep him at his bedside. The greater the attention, the more likely the cure, reckoned Vinnie. He sensed that the doctor had a secret, prurient interest in crime, and would entertain him with bits and pieces from his own criminal past, half truth and half fabrication.

"Whenever we got short of cash," Vinnie would say, "we'd go see Howie. That's Howard Johnson's . . . a push-over at midnight . . . only kids running it then . . . " And the doctor, secretly fascinated, would pause, nod, frown, and pretend a clinical interest.

Vinnie's pancreatic cancer progressed inexorably. It became clear that he could neither beat this rap nor be returned to prison. The police angled for a death-bed confession and the vital information that it might bring, and asked the doctor for an opportunity to visit with the condemned. But, while there may be no honor among thieves, there is among thieves an equal scorn for authority. Vinnie wasn't talking.

One day a detective came to see the doctor. His hardened, muscled jaw and piercing eyes contrasted with the doctor's studied elegance. The detective folded his coarse, huge hands in what almost seemed as an attitude of supplication.

"Doc," he said, "Vinnie's got a lot of information useful to us. He's heard a lot of things in prison, things which could help us out on cases still open. We're asking you to help us."

The doctor leaned far back in his swivel chair, arguing at first from the stance of patient-doctor confidentiality, then pointing out that he was a busy man, a *doctor* and not a detective, but in the end consenting to wear a concealed microphone, to be 'wired,' because in his special position he could help the authorities, and he could, after all, accomplish anything. He would deftly extract vital information from Vinnie, the apprehension of which would solve some baffling crime, the police would shake their heads in grudging admiration, the papers would shout the news, and the doctor would then humbly go about his business. *It was nothing,* he would say to the reporters. *It was the least I could do.*

But the doctor hadn't reckoned with Vinnie's practiced vigilance. The latter caught the subtle changes in his doctor's behavior, the pointed questions, the sudden interest in names and dates, the willingness to linger at the bedside. Vinnie circled the suspected trap like the wary fox that he was, pawing at it, sniffing its scent, studying it from every angle, dropping items of no consequence upon its mechanism to see how it might spring. He talked of bank robberies in such detail that the police who subsequently hovered over the micro-cassette could imagine every wad of bills, but then Vinnie would hesitate, screw up his face, pull on his ear, and end with *Gee, Doc, I just can't remember the names. Must be my memory's going.*

Such tantalizing slices of bait stirred the police into a frenzy. They became convinced that Vinnie in fact 'knew something' and persuaded the doctor that he was on the verge of a great discovery. For the police, any frustration in this Vinnie project would simply be part of the territory. Leads do dry up. One moves on. But for the doctor, failure in any project was unacceptable. He was like the gambler pumping dollars into the slot, feverishly anticipating the big win, yet knowing in his core he was being had. And he began to hate his patient for it, referring to him in terms usually reserved only for quacks and lawyers. The doctor, for all of his charm, charisma, and subtle manipulations, could get nothing from Vinnie. This convict, this dirt-ball, this *nothing,* was making a fool out of him.

Vinnie's cancer required continuous morphine to control the pain. Because its growth now nearly obstructed the upper bowels, Vinnie could take only sips of water. He began to fail rapidly, was often incoherent, and would cry out in pain from his medicated slumber. Now and then some seedy associate made a furtive visit to the bedside, but for the most part Vinnie was destined to make this last journey alone.

Late one night, while the doctor was entering orders into a patient's chart, a floor nurse came to the charting room and stood at some distance, too intimidated to interrupt.

"What is it?" snapped the doctor.

"Mr. Duchette in 221 is asking to see a priest," answered the nurse.

"Duchette wants a priest? That's a laugh! *I'll* go see him in a few minutes." The doctor dismissed the nurse, finished his charting, and with a motion of now unconscious habit, flicked on his concealed micro-cassette recorder as he headed for Vinnie's room.

"What do you want, Vinnie?" asked the doctor impatiently.

"Father . . . is that you Father?" asked Vinnie from the darkened room.

"Vinnie, it's Dr. Harrington . . . your doctor."

"Father, forgive me. I wish to make a confession . . . a general confession," said Vinnie.

"Vinnie, there's no priest here. It's me, Harrington, your doctor."

"Bless me Father for I have sinned," said Vinnie. "It has been years and years since my last confession. Oh my God I am heartily sorry for having offended Thee. 'Judge not and ye shall not be judged; condemn not, and ye shall not be condemned: forgive, and ye shall be forgiven.' "

To hear this coming from the likes of Vinnie Duchette was for the doctor like listening to some drunk who had stopped him in the subway and, in gratitude for the dime, had begun to recite T.S. Eliot's most stirring lines. The doctor sat beside Vinnie's bed. He simply listened, and as Vinnie's fever rose, he took his patient's hand.

Vinnie's deathbed soliloquy was a mixture of escapade and emotion, a telling of his forgotten childhood drifting into the free association of heists and holdups, names and dates no longer spared. He told of how he had wanted to be loved, of how he could never feel important enough to others, nor to himself, no matter what he did, no matter how clever the job, no matter how great the take. He talked about the small child within himself, whom he had never known, who wanted love apart from whatever admiration Vinnie's misdeeds might bring.

Vinnie talked about prison, and about the pecking order there, about the weak and the strong, and about his search for any father there: a father who would protect Vinnie, praise him, advise and direct him, be there for him, love him with a love never to be withdrawn, a love contingent upon no act or accomplishment. Vinnie told about stealing from the alms box in the church and of how, as punishment, God had driven his father away. He talked about his anger against his father, and against his God, and drifted into past angers against wardens, cops, and accomplices. Vinnie had simply wanted to *be* somebody. He wanted to be a hero. But no matter what Vinnie did, he could never quite make it. It never felt quite right inside. And the child within Vinnie retreated deeper and deeper into his own loneliness.

The doctor listened to Vinnie only half-conscious of what he was hearing. Vinnie's confession was for him like the haunting tale which resurrects the listener's own specters and loses him in a maelstrom of emotions he cannot himself identify. The doctor discarded the trivial victory of Vinnie's confessions of felony. He had even forgotten about the hidden tape recorder. He began to feel that this was a momentous occasion, somehow important to him, but couldn't tell why. The doctor felt a yearning inside, but had he been questioned about it then and there, he would have misread this feeling too, and called it empathy. Because he himself was lost, the doctor was *moved* rather than vulnerable.

If the doctor had ever been asked why he never told the police what he had learned from Vinnie, why he did not turn over the tape recordings of Vinnie's last words, the doctor would no doubt have retreated behind patient confidentiality. He could never have said to anyone, that to talk about Vinnie, would have been to lay open his own raw, abscessed wound. In the weeks to follow, the doctor thought of Vinnie first as an unsettling experience he didn't have time to define, then as a special occasion with an unusual patient other doctors could not have been privy to. Vinnie's death he felt first as a void, soon filled by other demands. It was in this way that the doctor managed the memory of Vinnie Duchette and could then, when the last note was signed, and the last laboratory slip entered, file him away in medical records in the vast bowels of the hospital.

There is a time of day when the hospital itself sleeps, a time when nurses begin to whisper, when the strident paging is still, and even the babies are quiet. It is the time of comfortable settling in, as the hospital hushes its hive-like self to minimum hum. And for the doctor there is a foreignness about this calm. Buffeted by conflicting demands, never permitted to finish one task well, the doctor is unsettled by this sudden ease. It shouldn't, he knows, be this way.

It is late. He *should* be home. He *should* be fathering. But his children sleep. Then he *should* play husband. But his wife will be tired and ready for sleep herself. Then he *should* read. He *should* catch up on his journals. *He* shouldn't need sleep. He *should* be able to endure anything, he *should* never feel tired, *should* always be filled with energy, and with the excitement of medicine.

He *should* love his patients, every one, *should* always be generous and understanding, *should* always be eager for the next consultation and its intellectual challenge. He *should* be all-knowing, well-read, well-rounded, academic—the perfect Renaissance man.

And so he is. He is a doctor after all—he has permission, an entitlement—and so believes he is all these things.

But he is not perfect, he readily admits from his humble position of supreme modesty. And he allows from his core a faint burn of resentment as he reads his day's last demand: a request for preoperative evaluation of a 96-year-old woman.

Because he is insightful (supremely so) and fully understands himself (completely so), he should not, will not, be troubled by this final intrusion. His anger, he knows now with perfect clarity, must be directed at the surgeon who would operate on one so ancient.

Very well. He will examine this body lacking any comprehension, this once-human repugnant with age. Because he has taken an oath, has been certified and recertified, because he holds the pedagogue's integrity, there will be no shortcuts here.

He enters the close, still darkness of her room. There is the soft glow of the night light, a smell of narcissus mixed with the scent of antiseptic solution. The drapes are parted and on the windowsill he sees the nodding paperwhites next to a stack of books. On the tray table at bedside there is a tumbler of water, a glasses case, a copy of *Antaeus*, and a magnifying glass. The bed contains a rumpled ball of bedclothes, too small to contain a human body certainly, and from which comes the musty smell of age. Holding his black bag in one hand and the patient's hospital chart next to his chest with the other, he pauses to take in this scene, when the rumpled ball speaks to him.

"Why Doctor! Yours is a face of Stygian gloom."

Startled by the sudden coherence, he answers, "I beg your pardon?"

"What have you been up to that you must beg my pardon?" she asks, laughing.

Almost midnight, he thinks; must he endure this wit? He settles down to business. He will start with a social history, he decides, and pulls a chair to the bedside. And in this way he begins yet another tedious workup—but perhaps there will be a curious murmur or some intriguing endocrinopathy, and that might prove interesting after all. And the night will not have been a total loss.

"How far did you go in your schooling?" he asks. He has in his voice a hint of the routine, and of condescension. He watches her reach for the thick glasses, watches her slowly put them on—first to one ear, and then turning her head, she hooks the other—now peering at him in the darkness. She smiles and drops her eyes.

"It may surprise you, Doctor, to know," she answers, "that I never went past primary school."

"That does surprise me. You are . . . well spoken." He feels himself getting involved—more than he should. He cannot help himself.

"I had a wonderful grandmother," the old woman continues. "You see, I had tuberculosis as a child and so they gave up on me. No sense wasting schooling on me. But my grandmother didn't give up on me. She sat out with me in the sun— it was believed in those days that sunshine was good for people with consumption. Do they still believe that? She sat with me in the sun and we read."

The doctor shifts in his chair impatiently. He has promises to keep and has no time for the adventures of a nineteenth-century Nancy Drew. He will ask her about prior hospitalizations, prior illnesses.

"Yes, we read a great deal," she continues. "We, my grandmother and I, read all of Thackeray, for one. Oh, forty percent of him isn't any good, but the most of him is priceless!"

She becomes animated, fixing her hair, straightening the bedclothes just so, darting quick glances his way. He *had* asked, after all.

"Have you read Thackeray, Doctor?" she asks.

He pauses. He had read something, but he couldn't remember just what . . . or whether it was even by Thackeray. It had probably been just a plot summary, undoubtedly something read for grades during that mad, headlong rush to medical school. But he cannot tell her *that*. He cannot confess, not even to this ancient woman. He *should* have read Thackeray. He *would* read Thackeray soon. He made a mental note to do that.

"No, I guess not," he answers. "We were all very busy with the sciences, of course."

"Of course. But . . . not even *Vanity Fair*, Doctor?"

The woman wouldn't give it up! "*Vanity Fair* is Bunyan, I think," he parries.

"No, no Doctor!" she giggles. "Christian passed through Vanity Fair on his way to Salvation in Bunyan's *Pilgrim's Progress*, but *Vanity Fair*, the novel, is most certainly Thackeray. You *never* met Becky Sharp?" she teases.

"Becky Sharp?" The doctor shifts again. The whole encounter is becoming painful.

"She's Thackeray's unforgettable whore, Doctor. You really must read *Vanity Fair*—that is, if you haven't as yet. Such a fine exposition of man's egotism and infinite capacity for self-delusion."

The doctor looks up quickly at his patient. Had there been a message there for him? Her serene, wrinkled face holds her bright eyes, blue and innocent. In all of her wrinkles he can find no trace of guile.

"You really enjoyed that book, didn't you?"

"Enjoyed it? I *lived* it, Doctor. I *lived* all the books! How else could an infirm girl plot and pillage, murder, and burn at the stake, all in one day? Still, there are gaps in my knowledge, tremendous gaps, I know," she confesses.

The doctor leans forward toward her, hands clasped between his knees. He sighs, starts to speak, stops, then starts again. He has reached the edge of the path when the risk seems suddenly worth it, or when there is no risk at all.

"I'll tell you something. There are gaps . . . tremendous gaps . . . in my knowledge as well."

"I can't believe it," she says with all sincerity. "You are a doctor, after all."

"Well, I didn't mean gaps in medical knowledge." He begins to back and fill. "Although yes, I guess in medicine too. One can't know *everything*, I guess." (Why had that been so difficult to say?)

"But you know, I never read a darn thing other than medical journals these days. Can you believe it?"

"You're terribly busy," she soothes, "and you didn't have my grandmother. But you are a young man, Doctor. There's time. There's time. *Make* time."

"It's a terrible thing to say," he answers, "but I wouldn't know where to begin. I read book reviews. I make lists of books. I *buy* books. But I never *read* them. There just isn't time."

"Begin, Doctor," she whispers, "begin with Becky Sharp. You'll simply love her!"

He leans back against the chair, crosses his arms, and looks out the window into the night. It has begun to snow. The flakes, like down, sift quietly through the spruce. He feels a sense of sanctuary. There is no longer the urgency to flee. And then the insight comes as a wolf against the snow—at the one moment, nothing, and in the next, it is there, catching your breath with its truth. He sees the reason in priorities, the naturalness of the relative importance of things. He holds a newly focused sense of what is vital, and what is not. He looks at the old woman, and then out again at the snowfall. He wants to preserve this moment, photograph and frame it. But even as he holds fast to his truth, he feels it steal away.

It *will* slip away. These insights always do. It will be lost to him, to remain only as a pause, a thought, a sense of déjà vu. But it will lie within him like a seed, a kernel of life planted there by the old woman. And one day this chance pregnancy might still deliver him.

Now, his mind washed clean of trivialities, he moves to her without pretense.

"You know," he says, "you are the most remarkable woman I have ever met."

"Oh Doctor," she answers. "I'll bet you say that to all the girls."

The rich too have their problems. Consider the whole matter of entitlement. The wealthy man feels entitled to position, to advantage, to power. One ought to be able to buy reason and intellect—since one can buy anything else. Still, reality always gets in the way— the reality of chance, law, or personal failing. There is also the problem of self-dissipation, of a life possibly squandered, of the danger of an extravagant dissolution. For Jonathan Dehner Hobthorne, who had money, and had a lot of it, the specter of the dilettante haunted him.

J.D. (as he allowed himself to be called) challenged this specter through a frantic and undisciplined exercise of the mind. He used his wealth to dabble in matters scientific. A university professor might be summoned to brunch, find himself cornered by J.D.'s rapid-fire questioning, and discover in retrospect that he had done some lengthy and unfocused tutoring. J.D. would drift in and out of lectures at the university, amused that the courses were held at the Hobthorne Building or in the Dehner Center, excited by the sense of entitlement he felt, deluded by the notion that one could own knowledge. He was the gourmand who samples a particularly fine terrine and fancies himself the charcutier.

While his accountants and attorneys manipulated his Croesian wealth, J.D. attended to his patrician slimness, and to his imagined fitness of mind. His favorite intellectual pursuit was to host extravagant dinner parties, at which he would entertain an assortment of scientists of his own choosing. His guests were expected to introduce their latest lines of research, while J.D. held court, directing discussion where his own curiosity might lead them. J.D. especially delighted in medical research, and though he respected superior intelligence, he resented it as well. The world, it is said, holds many such people. He relished pitting his guests one against the other while he remained ever aloof, and in control.

Aware of the chance nature of university funding—typical

of a nation as self-deceived as was Hobthorne—J.D. would casually announce at the beginning of his dinner parties that he would be sending a "modest donation, six figures perhaps," on to the institution of that guest with the most intriguing line of work—J. D. to be judge and jury, of course. Word got around. With money so tight, with the politics of American science such as it was, a dinner invitation from Mr. Hobthorne became coveted second only to The Prize. The prospective guest was preened by his department like a poodle made ready for Westminster. Though some called the whole business sophisticated begging, J.D. saw his guests as courtiers to the throne, vying for his favor. And it did pay the bills.

"Three for dinner tonight, Holmes," said J.D. before one such evening, addressing his steward and only intellectual ally for these evenings. "We shall have a Dr. Hamill from the Neurological Institute, a Dr. Riley from Metropolitan General Hospital . . . connected with the medical school, you know, and . . . where is the card? Yes, a Dr. Samuelson from one of the community hospitals north . . . a kind of foil for the other two, Holmes."

"Very good, sir," said Holmes, polishing the crystal wine glasses. Holmes stood near the rosewood buffet, in the large dining room entirely of rosewood, a dining room made intimate and warm by the wood's rich brown tones, by walls of deep red damask, and by the subdued glow of a Bohemian chandelier. He held a glass to the light, turning it carefully just so. A smudge against the wine's robe would not do.

"How much '49 Latour downstairs, Holmes?"

"One case, five, sir," answered Holmes.

"Can we get more, Holmes?" asked J.D.

"Afraid not, sir," said Holmes.

"Too good to waste, Holmes. We'll have the '53 Margaux. And Holmes, no mint sauce with the lamb. I won't have them drinking my Margaux with mint-breath."

"Quite so, sir." Holmes, with hooded eyes, bowed and left.

"Should be great fun," thought J.D. "I'll have the big guns

first, then finish off the country doctor. One needs to be humbled occasionally. Hamill should win the money tonight . . . that is, if he's headed where I think he is."

J.D. left the dining room for his library, for his leather-bound books, his collections of Claude Bernard and Bronowski, of Lancelot Hogben, of Bernard Lovell, of Brian Stableford, of D'Arcy Wentworth Thompson. He often wished he had the time to read them. He strolled the confines of this, his favorite room, this secret place where he could awaken his innermost thoughts, trusting in the library's sanctuary. How he hated his money, he thought. (To a point, that is.) And how imprisoned he felt. These scientists groveling, performing at his feet, unaware of how he envied them, their freedom to think, to act, to question. How rich *they* were, how rich *their* lives, surrounded by purpose and discovery. How flat and lifeless seemed his ports and Pauillacs in comparison. Even to be a country doctor, he thought, like this Samuelson, tonight's fill-in, this comparative failure who himself would envy the giants of medical research. Oh, he would humble this Dr. Samuelson! And he would humble the giants as well. He fingered the leather bindings, traced the lettered titles, and wished.

The scallop seviche was perfect, the Batard-Montrachet buttery and dry, the rack of lamb elegant, and the '53 Margaux a bit gone past, though only J.D. noticed. His guests were nervous, sensed a delighted Hobthorne.

"Rumor has certainly conveyed to you my rules for this evening, gentlemen . . . and lady," said J.D. bowing his head to the very attractive Dr. Riley. "We'll take our port—a 1934 Taylor Fladgate, am I right, Holmes? —in the library while each of you tells us something of yourself. Best story wins. The sum for tonight is to be $850,000, so my accountants tell me. Shall we?

"Dr. Riley, ladies first."

Metropolitan-University, desperately in need of money, had a good bet in Marianne Riley. She was quick, clever, and had a reputation for courage under fire. She had, along with her institution, survived the whims of federal funding (though just barely) with its wars on cancer, on heart disease, on anything glamorous and appealing, on anything but basic science. Her superiors knew Hobthorne's game, knew he could not be tempted by a well-turned ankle, yet were convinced Riley stood the best chance of surviving this evening. She was the very best they had to offer.

For her part, Marianne Riley had not had an easy time of it getting to the top. During the punishing years of medical training with its inhuman demands, she had learned about postponing leisure, pleasure, a family. She had learned about loneliness. She had learned that one needed a mentor in this business, that there were few women mentors in academic medicine, and that the would-be male mentors often related to their female students as one might to wife, or daughter, or mistress. She had learned that in the vast university complex, sexual innuendo eased the workload, that gender mattered, and that women doctors were often ignored. She had learned that in this business the weak were set upon, as the pack descends upon the whining cur. She had learned that a certain toughness was required to survive, and that toughness has never been found with favor in a woman, and is often called something else. And Marianne Riley survived.

"We're pursuing suspended animation," said Dr. Riley. "The possibilities for medicine, and for NASA, are incredible. Extension of life itself, and of the lives of potential organ donors, of patients waiting for cure, of space . . . "

"The possibilities, Dr. Riley," sniffed Hobthorne, "are obvious. If we could learn how one achieves suspended animation, we would be grateful."

Riley's green eyes flared, her left eyebrow arched, and she shifted on widely spaced feet. In the corner, Holmes had a fit of quiet coughing.

"There are many lines of inquiry, Mr. Hobthorne," said Riley, icily. She watched J.D. nose his port and peer at her over his glass.

"I have her now," thought J.D.

"Hypothermia is the key to making the transition from mammalian hibernation to the state of suspended animation," continued Dr. Riley. "The mechanics of hypothermal control have already been worked out. We use them . . . have used them, with success. Biochemical induction of hibernation—the brilliant work of Spurrier, I'm sure you're familiar with—this has been our interest. Mammalian hibernation trigger factor does not appear to be species-specific and . . . "

"Is it a polypeptide, Dr. Riley?" asked J.D.

"It is a polypeptide . . . of low molecular weight, avidly bound to serum albumin. We have sequenced its amino acid structure . . . but its sequence is classified, I'm afraid," said Riley, glancing at a nervous Hamill who in turn was staring at his shoes. "However, anyone familiar with neurotransmitter research would guess that hibernation trigger factor, which does bind to opiate receptors, might resemble opioid-peptides.

"At any rate, by blocking protein-binding of hibernation trigger factor, we can induce hypo-metabolism in primates with peripheral rather than with intra-cerebral infusion of the polypeptide. Still larger infusions produce hibernation in species not known for natural hibernation, and also produce post-hibernation hypophagia. When hypothermal environmental controls are also applied, cellular enzyme systems, as measured by cyclic AMP activity, slow to an absolute minimum."

"Very good, Dr. Riley. Excellent. Yes, impressive. And are we employing such techniques on human subjects?" (The royal 'we' permitted Hobthorne a sense of participation in these lines of research.)

"We have not yet received approval from federal agencies, Mr. Hobthorne," answered Riley, "though we feel we have perfected the techniques for suspended animation. In the meantime we watch innumerable precious organ donors pass through our hands."

"Ah, yes. Governmental control—the scourge of American Science, isn't it. Well, well . . . Dr. Hamill, I believe you are next."

Robert Winslow Hamill, from bushy eyebrows and bow tie to scuffed loafers and white socks, was the archetypal academician, a latter-day absent-minded professor. He owed his success in academia to a superior mind and a penchant for hard work. To Hamill no line of inquiry was impossible, no thought too far-fetched. His trainees loved him. He was exciting to be around. He was a natural, and the Institute was already counting Hobthorne's money.

"Dr. Hamill . . . you didn't care for the port? . . . your presentation will dovetail with Dr. Riley's quite nicely, I believe. You are also familiar with brain polypeptides, isn't that so? Holmes, perhaps Dr. Hamill will try some of the Climens."

"We are interested in the augmentation of intelligence," said Hamill softly. J.D. swept his eyes over the group, saw Riley's shoulders stiffen, watched Samuelson in the corner swirl his port nervously, saw the amusement in Holmes' pursed lips.

"And that pursuit involves transmitter biochemistry as well," continued Hamill. "It is well known that the brain can use only glucose as its energy source. The enzyme hexokinase A, the only hexokinase isoenzyme found in brain tissue, converts glucose to mitochondrial ATP. But, and here is the key point, a product of the hexokinase reaction, glucose-6-phosphate, inhibits further action of the enzyme, so-called 'feedback inhibition' and in the case of the brain, is a limiting feature of neural and synaptic transmission."

"We are acquainted with feedback inhibition, Dr. Hamill," said J.D.

Hamill remained unruffled. He glanced around the library, then continued. "We have developed a monoclonal antibody—its structure is also confidential," Hamill said with a nod toward Dr. Riley, "which binds to a particular epitope of the hexokinase A molecule. By so doing, this antibody blocks feedback inhibition. Neural transmission is greatly accelerated. A sort of biologic superconductor state results."

Hobthorne interrupted testily. "We are waiting for the other shoe to drop, Doctor. So what?"

"Inoculation of our monoclonal antibody in primates clearly has been shown to enhance intelligence in those primates by all parameters we can measure," said Hamill. "And neither the antibody nor the hexokinase A molecule is species-specific. We have no doubt that we shall see similar results in human subjects."

"You've yet to test this in humans?" asked J.D.

"I am not at liberty to say, Mr. Hobthorne," answered Dr. Hamill. "One of our affiliated labs, working with organic chip memory-augmentation, has implanted subcutaneous molecular conductor memory chips comprised of tetra-cyano-p-quinodimethane in the lipid layer. The demonstration of enhanced memory in . . . certain primates . . . has been . . . exciting."

"Wonderful, Doctor. Truly exciting. How do you like the Climens?"

"Smells moldy. Is it supposed to?"

"That's botrytis, Doctor. It is considered an attribute." Hobthorne rolled his eyes at Holmes and turned to Dr. Samuelson.

"Dr. Samuelson . . . we come to you. Step to the fore, Doctor, and let us have your story."

"I honestly don't know why I'm here," said Samuelson. "I'm just a practicing physician. I deal with people . . . patients, not transmitters or biochemistry. I can't imagine why you've invited me."

In the corner, Holmes gagged involuntarily.

"Come, come, Dr. Samuelson. Play the game. Play the game! Surely you have something interesting in your life you might share with us—some line of inquiry to relate. You will agree Holmes served us a fine meal. You must, ah . . . sing for your supper, shall we say?"

Dr. Samuelson, unused to the banter of the city, stood nervously at the center table of the library, steadying his hands on its polished surface. He knew that all present, Holmes included, sensed his discomfort. He scanned the leatherbound volumes lining the walls, volumes any one of which would be a treasure for him. He saw Riley's urbane sophistication, Hamill's academic ease. He felt Hobthorne's power, and most embarrassing of all, Holmes' condescension. He could not imagine why Hobthorne had done this to him, had him batting clean-up to Ruth and Gehrig, could never have understood that Hobthorne might be jealous of him, a country doctor and in a ruthless, twisted way might discharge his jealousy through this exercise in silly donnishness.

What the hell could he talk about? He saw patients all day long. That was all. *All*? He talked to them, listened to them, cared for them, cared about them, loved them, worried with them, advised them, consoled them, cried and grieved with them. That was all. They were his life. If he was unexpectedly absent a week, they called, concerned about his welfare. Was *he* sick? Was *he* all right? Could *they* do anything for *him*? They, his patients, were his leather-bound volumes, his cellar upon cellar of precious wines. They were his victories.

"Yes, there is something that comes to mind," said Samuelson. Hobthorne nodded to him encouragingly, the serpent about to strike. Holmes had brought out the Stilton and was slicing pears, listening with an ear.

"A few years ago I had a particularly interesting patient whose continued progress you might term exciting," said Samuelson. "This man was in his mid-thirties at the time, a common mill worker with a family. He lived with his wife and two children in a shack in the country. They both worked for minimum wage at the local paper mill.

"He'd come in for a check-up. It was the end of the day, I remember. A long day at that. We talked after I had finished the physical examination. I remember asking him about the elections and we talked about them. In the course of our discussion he quoted a line from Milton . . . the last line of 'On His Blindness' that reads 'They also serve who only stand and wait.'

"Well, I was shocked. Here was a common laborer who, as it turned out, was better read than I, supposedly an educated man. He had read all of Milton—*Areopagitica, Paradise Lost, Paradise Regained, Samson Agonistes*— all of the major modern Russian authors, quoted Tennyson and Shakespeare, and did so appropriately, without ostentation. He told me he would coax his local librarian into sending for books from the state library so he could read them. He read five books a week, 'good books' as he called them, 'good books' like Henry James and Joyce, Spencer and Thackeray, Dickens and John Donne. His intellectual life made mine paltry by comparison. He owned no books, yet possessed them all.

"He did have a kind of freedom beyond measure, but was locked into a drab life, with little opportunity, and little chance for escape. I made inquiries . . . a kind of research, you might say . . . and found a splendid university interested in his story."

"He read all those works?" mumbled Hobthorne. "What's become of the man, Samuelson?"

"The university," continued Dr. Samuelson, "was very excited about my patient. They spoke in terms of what he would do for them rather than what they might do for him. It was wonderful to hear. They took him the next term, without application, without fees, without any formal testing, and, on the strength of his reading list, awarded him full scholarship aid.

"He has done well there. It has all been very exciting. We've hopes that, with his interests in economics and politics, he will go on to become a Rhodes scholar. He certainly has . . . "

Hobthorne bounded up and began pacing the perimeter of the library. He was clearly agitated. He was hearing of a man more rich than he—and one incapable of being bought. Here was a man destined for lands far beyond Hobthorne's dreams, who would get there without buying his way. Here was a man who *read*, mind you! Yes, he *read*! *Read* because he loved the words, the lilt of the phrase, the power of the thought, the magic of the page. *Read*, hear me! *Read* for the love of it, not for show, not to be seen holding the volume, not to quote the line, nor drop the author's name, nor shelve the text for all to see.

He *read*, do you understand! He *read* and comprehended,

digested, assimilated, lived the words, and they became a part of him, formed and shaped his thoughts, painted his day with rich and golden tones, quickened his pulse and step as he clutched the volume and hurried home—from where? From a common library—a *public* library! And to where? To a tarpaper shack somewhere! No penthouse, no twenty-room house in the County, no clever critics nor polished writers to jade this man!

Hobthorne found his leather copy of *Samson Agonistes*. He pulled it down, clutched it, was disgusted with the volume's virginity. He tapped it on the table, turned as if to speak, saw Holmes at the side-board, jowled Holmes, hooded eyes avoiding his, saw Riley, eyebrow arched—was that a *smirk?*—saw Hamill restless, embarrassed, saw the lack of comprehension on Samuelson's face.

He felt naked, did Hobthorne. Stripped of guise and guile, never having learned humility, he was lost, was Hobthorne. His eyes fell. He placed Milton gently on the table, nodded to his guests, glanced at Holmes, and left the room.

The Queen's favorite lady-in-waiting, Tatiania, was ill and not all the King's doctors could diagnose her problem. Her Lady's suffering became the Queen's, who made entirely certain her King felt the pain as well. The King's life grew quite miserable. He was not pleased.

Presiding in the Great Throne Room, the King summoned his doctors before him. Outside the windows whizzed the *vrooooo—THUNK* of a guillotine being readied—the King explained with regal delight— for a kinder, gentler, kingdom.

"Well, what do you have to say for yourselves?" growled the King at his kneeling subjects. "What in God's name ails my Queen's Lady? You, Court Neurologist, what have you come up with?"

Shifting on Charcot knee, the Court Neurologist picked his words carefully.

"We are, My Liege, as yet at a loss. We are of the opinion that this . . . these symptoms are perhaps a figment . . . are all in Tatiania's head, so to speak. Nevertheless, Your Grace, we shall run more tests."

"More tests!?" roared the King. "More tests!?" The poor woman has been tested half to death and still you have no answers! I will tell you one thing, gentlemen, " the King said, shaking his staff at all of them, "if you even suggest to the Queen, that this illness is all in her Lady's head, yours . . ." *vrooooo—THUNK—* " will be in a basket." The guillotine's timing could not have been more perfect.

Disconsolately, the Court Specialists filed out of the Great Throne Room and huddled together in conference.

"How about another MRI?" creaked the Court Rheumatologist.

"Maybe a PET scan. This could be our chance to buy a PET scanner," said the Court I.D. Man opportunistically.

"Oh, yeah? *You* go ask the King," murmured the Court Cardiologist. "What about toxicology screens?"

"Negative," said the Court Pharmacologist. "We've run them twice. Negative. No lead, no mercury, no arsenic . . ."

"But those damn goblets they insist on using . . ." said the Court Immunologist.

"Negative."

The Court Specialists mumbled to themselves, scratching their tender necks uneasily with the incessant reminder of the vrooooo—*THUNK* sounding outside. The Court Pulmonologist nervously consulted his nomograms.

A particularly forceful vrooooo-*THUNK* brought them back to reality.

"We had better, " said the Court Endocrinologist, "run this by Hankins, don't you think?"

"Hankins will be of no help," said the Court Dermatologist. "Hankins will just crow and strut. Hankins is just an . . ."

vrooooo—*THUNK!*

"Let's go see Hankins," reasoned the Court Oncologist.

The group scurried down the vast halls of the palace as frightened goslings wanting a gander, turning this way and that until they had reached corridors where paint no longer applied, where the guiding strips of colored lines no longer led. Past corridors of open plumbing and crumbling mortar, down halls holding pockets of steam heat alternating with chilling cold, still the group scuttled until at last they came to a peeling varnished door with frosted glass on which had been stenciled ages ago:

I TERN L MED CIN

The Court Neurologist looked around at his colleagues and then tapped on the glass with a knuckle. The door swung inward. At an old maple desk piled high with papers sat a disheveled man eating an apple, leafing through a journal. He looked up at them over the rim of his glasses.

"Well, well," he said, "*look* who's here! All my old buddies. What brings *you* to the catacombs?"

The group huddled in the doorway, prevented from entering by the stacks of journals and texts on the floor.

"Oscar," said the Court Cardiologist condescendingly, waving a hand at the mess, " when are you going over to computer disks?" He winced, exhaling forcefully as the Court Hematologist elbowed him in the ribs.

"Staying up on the literature, Oscar?" wheedled the Court Oncologist.

Oscar Hankins sat upright in his chair, grinning broadly.

"You guys are in trouble. You need something from me. Your necks are on the line and you want something from me. I can't believe it!" Several of the group rubbed the napes or their necks and shifted apprehensively.

"Oscar, we won't beat around," said the Court I.D. Man. "The Queen's favorite Lady, Tatiania, is ill. Has been for six weeks. Vague complaints: belly pain, headaches, muscle aching, circumoral paresthesias. And Oscar . . . hypochondriasis is not an option."

"Never is," said Oscar. "Never is."

"Yet the complaints just don't hang together," said the Court Rheumatologist. "Myalgias, arthralgias, knee pain and weakness, without the least physical finding. And all serologies negative."

"Itching," said the Court Immunologist.

"Acral paresthesias," said the Court Neurologist.

"Chills," said the Court I.D. Man.

"And all the tests are negative," they cried in unison.

Oscar looked at them in wonder. It was too good to be true. He tried to contain his joy.

"If I am to help you. I'll want a bookshelf in payment," he said.

"Done."

"I want my stethoscope back too. You'll have to give me back my stethoscope."

"Done as well."

"And a student to teach. I want a student to teach."

"Oscar . . . be reasonable!" said the Court Endocrinologist.

"Tut, tut," said Oscar, folding his arms and turning his back to them.

"You shall have a student," sighed the Court Gastroenterologist.

"A good student, someone eager to learn," said Oscar. "Make it a good student, not some . . . would-be mechanic."

The Court Cardiologist rolled his eyes.

"Would that be all?" he asked.

"One more thing," said Oscar, with an impish look. "I want to be made Master in The College."

The group gasped as one. The Court Oncologist staggered, leaning against the wall for support. The Court Nephrologist strangled in a fit of coughing.

"Just teasing," giggled Oscar. "It's your club after all. Relax. I'll help you with the case.

"She had had an MRI?" continued Oscar.

"Three," said the Court Neurologist.

"Three?" squeaked Oscar. "Three? Excuse me— I don't mean to laugh. Still, three? And endoscopy? I suppose she has had assorted endoscopies?"

The Court Gastroenterologist nodded his head sheepishly.

"Let's see . . . itching, muscle aches, joint pains . . . that could spell a kidney biopsy. She didn't get a kidney biopsy?' asked Oscar. The Court Nephrologist, done with his coughing, blushed.

"The poor woman! Yes, well, " said Oscar, slapping his knees. "Shall we go to the bedside?"

Like a pack of hounds the group charged the halls, Oscar in the lead. Right and left and straight—away, down the corridors to the Royal Infirmary they ran.

"Let me have a few minutes alone with her," said Oscar, approaching the bedside. Together the Court Specialists watched as Oscar introduced himself with a bow and pulled up a chair to talk quietly with Tatiana. After several minutes he motioned the group to enter.

"I agree," he said, " that the history is not very helpful. Still, there is the scent of disease about." He tapped his lips with a finger. "Tatiana has agreed to let me demonstrate any physical findings to you . . . as a sort of teaching exercise," teased Oscar. He examined her skin and joints meticulously, then carefully inspected her fundi. Listening with his beloved stethoscope, he positioned her this way and that, contenting himself with the sweet music of her heart. Finished with the chest and abdomen, Oscar folded his stethoscope into his pocket and turned to the group.

"Not much, I admit. Not much. Pretty normal exam," he said. The Court Specialists nodded knowingly to each other. "Still," he added after a pause, "she has one physical finding that is a dead giveaway." He paused for them to ask. They would not.

"Your tan, Tatiania," Oscar said. "You have a beautiful tan. Where did you acquire it?'

"On the Royal Vacation, "said Tatiania, blushing and pulling the covers to her chin.

"On the Royal Vacation, " crowed Oscar, engaging the group expansively. "And where was that?'

"On the Royal Yacht," said the patient. "We sailed on a sea."

"The *Caribbean* Sea, to be precise," said Oscar. "Tell me Tatiania, did you have any fish to eat while you were there?"

"His Highness despises fish, Court . . . , Court . . ."

"I have no court appointment, Tatiania. You will have to call me Doctor," said Oscar. "Still at sail for a week and no fish to eat?"

"The Royal Chef made a stew, with shrimps and cockles and such. The Royal Party was too infirmed that day— with the motion of the sea— and declined to eat. I dined alone. There was fish in the stew."

"And were you sick at all during the Royal Vacation?" asked Oscar, beaming.

" I was ill that very night. Quite upset in the stomach. The Royal Attending diagnosed it as seasickness." (At this admission, a tanned specialist in the back row commenced with a fit of gagging.) "It did not last long. I was better by morning."

"This is all the same illness, Tatiania. It will soon pass. And there will be no more tests." Oscar smiled down at her reassuringly and turned with the group to go.

"So gentlemen, there you have it: ciguatera fish poisoning— from a red snapper of quite another description. Your patient will soon be well. The worst part of her illness, actually, was probably the uncertainty of it all. That and your testing." The group mumbled incoherently, attempting to disband, but Oscar would have his moment with them.

"You made it easy for me, old buddies. Easy. You had done all the tests . . . many times over. I trusted them. As I trusted your thoroughness in performing them. Discarding vasculitides and endocarditis, demyelinating disorders and obscure infectious diseases, what was left on the list: A toxin of some sort . . . some toxin with protean manifestations, yet something you couldn't test for. All I had to do was think."

With a very final *vrooooo—THUNK* from the courtyard, Hankins left to find his student.

And everyone lived happily ever after.

Some time ago I was called to Richmond to the bedside of an elderly physician. The old doctor was near death and his family had asked whether I would come, would I attend him, was there anything I could do—that sort of thing. I went out of duty more than anything else I guess, that kind of responsibility you have to a colleague.

The man lay in the bedroom of the house where he had lived alone for the past sixty years. Through some minor disappointment—a broken heart or similar tragedy—he had never married. But he was loved nevertheless. Even while I attended him, the constant visits from neighbors and patients were impressive. How could I be of help, I asked the old doctor. His glance and raised eyebrow told me at once that I should know the answer. But if I insisted on staying, he said he would welcome the chat.

And so he began:

"You get to this point, to the end, and all the clutter in your life just falls away. The picture you are left with all of a sudden gets pretty clear. It's like when you go to the seacoast, you know. You see the boats bobbing in the shallows and the searchlights coming in and out of the fog. There are gulls darting and diving everywhere. And suddenly the fog lifts and there's this leviathan just offshore, right there in front of you for you to see, as honest as the day. Well, that's what this dying does for you. It shows you the leviathans in your life— what was most important to you, what made you who you are. And just as important I suppose, it shows you what has amounted to just so much driftwood through the years.

"I'm lucky, I guess. I've had more than my share of leviathans, even more than most doctors, I would say. There was that first bright sunny day in medical school on the way to lecture. And there's the day we all stood on the grass and we were just as green as grass ourselves and we took the Oath together. That's a hell of a leviathan, I'll tell you. And there's your first patient you care for as a full-fledged doctor, and your first life saved, and the first baby you deliver all wriggling and wet and screaming and healthy."

At this point the old doctor's housekeeper entered the bedroom, bustled about, and sent a stare in my direction which said to me in an instant that I was meddling, had no business being there, and should be getting along soon. The housekeeper was either severely kyphotic or a hunchback. I preferred to think of her as a hunchback, possessing magical qualities sometimes bordering on evil and infinitely more interesting. At any rate, the old doctor intercepted her look, dismissed it with a wave of his hand, and nodded to me reassuringly.

"You learn so much in this life," the old doctor said, "if you take the time. Only after thirty or forty years of experience is a physician really any good at what he does, and by that time he's ready for retirement. That's the great puzzle of medical teaching, how to transmit what the old doctor has learned in those forty years to the young student. It's uncommon these days that medical students and young residents are even put in the hands of experienced clinicians, much less retired practitioners. And it's the uncommon retired practitioner who is any good at teaching anyway. To compound the problem, often the knowledge that he or she has acquired in forty years of experience is often of the ill defined nature: the smell of disease, the nearness of death, the legitimacy of a patient's physical complaints, the set of signs and symptoms in a patient immediately diagnostic. How can you teach this?"

I began to speak, to give him an answer, but he waved me off, as though there wasn't time, and he had much more to say.

"How I wish I could tell students now that if you take life in small daily bites, why, in a lifetime you can master French, Shakespeare, and fly-fishing. And that you have to learn to plan your day and set priorities, always ready for those emergencies that will have quite different plans for you.

"They need to choose whether they want to be a doctor or a businessman. Being a doctor is a calling and requires self-sacrifice, devotion, love, and tenderness toward your fellow man. If only a kid just starting out could be a doctor without living like one. Keep your overhead low, as the saying goes. Don't get possessed by your possessions. Belief in science, diagnostic skill, ease with patients, a sensitivity to suffering, a love of non-medical literature, a few close friends—these are the important things. The beachfront property, the summer home, private school for your kids, the prestigious address, the academic title, the country clubs—just driftwood, silly, if you only stop to think.

"In houses, automobiles and spouses, avoid trophies, I'd tell 'em; you can select a partner who happens to be a trophy, but don't make the selection because of it."

The housekeeper left the room, and the old doctor eased back and became reflective, soft. It was as though he had been filibustering until she left the room.

"Let me tell you what occupies my mind most these days," the old doctor said.

"It was a long time ago. I had only been in practice for ten or fifteen years maybe. They had a case of diabetic coma over in the hospital in Phippsburg and they called me in to help out. Diabetes was difficult to treat back then. You would administer huge doses of crystalline insulin. All of the fluids you gave were by stomach tube or retention enema, mostly. Oh, sometimes in desperation you'd give a saline solution by clysis, but that never seemed to work. You had only urine tests for sugar and acid to guide you . . . none of the blood testing you have now. You followed the urines. You looked at the clinical signs. You did your best and prayed. And it seemed that you killed a diabetic just as often as you had one die on you.

"Well this patient, a young woman, was pretty sick. I had to stay with her the better part of a week, walking the thin line between hypoglycemia and ketoacidosis, pouring fluids and alkali into her, injecting the insulin myself. Eventually she responded— youth itself is a great help in treatment, you know. As soon as it was obvious she was going to make it, I turned the case back over to her physician so I could get back to the practice I had left.

"Oh, I'd drive back evenings to see how she was. After office hours I'd like to drop in on her. Her room was always dark. I'd tap at the door and whisper my name and she'd sit right up and ask me to come in. She was a 'good case,' if you know what I mean. You didn't save many diabetics in coma in those days. I guess when you save a life like that you want to bask in it. Well, I'd sit and talk with her for a while and then I'd go out and kid with the nurses and leave.

"After she was discharged I stopped seeing her. I didn't think about her for a while, except maybe to remind myself when I lost a child with meningitis, that I *had* saved a young woman in diabetic coma."

The hunchback at this point came in with a supper tray, and since there was only one tray, and another more piercing stare, I hastily excused myself.

"Hoyos," said the old doctor. "Come back tomorrow. Get some Hoyo de Monterrey cigars. Excaliburs, if you can find them, 1066's. We'll have a cigar together. I'll supply the Port."

In fact it was several days before I could return to Richmond and to the old doctor's house. The duties of practice, family life and hospital committees had claimed my time at a moment in my life when I was beginning to doubt my own priorities. Nevertheless, he was waiting for me. I had the Hoyos, and he already decanted the Port, a Taylor Fladgate '64. At this point he wasn't about to skimp. The hunchback was in his bedroom, finding things to keep her there, and the old doctor was patently aware of her, yet given to expound again.

"Have you ever noticed how many people envy us?" said the old doctor. "How many play at being a doctor and yet, consumed by the worst sort of envy, attack us for being so? Have you ever thought about what society expects of us? We're not gods. I'd like to tell young doctors not to be seduced by it, not to buy into it."

I leaned forward to light his cigar— the Hoyos were not easily found, I can tell you—and then sat back in the overstuffed chair next to the sofa he lay upon, and lit my own cigar. Soon the small room was filled with the fragrant clubby haze of tobacco, pungent enough to drive anyone not so inclined from the room, even a hunchback with magical powers. The old doctor waited until the housekeeper had closed the door behind her, and then his aged face sprang to life.

"The diabetic girl, the one in the coma that I was telling you about the other day," he said, pointing his cigar at me.

"One day she's in my office. She had made an appointment. There she was, sitting in my examining room, just as big as life. Well, I rushed in and we exchanged pleasantries, and she said she had come to thank me for saving her life. Just like that. I said something stupid like it was a thrill for me to manage such a sick patient or something just as insensitive. Then I got called out abruptly for a delivery. My nurse gave her another appointment and she was back again the next week.

"'Doctor,' she said just as cool and level-headed as you or I, 'Doctor, do patients ever fall in love with their doctors?'

"Well, I gave her the standard reaction to this, you know, the talk about gratitude and worship and the patient's awe of a doctor's power. I allowed as I could understand any feeling she might have in that regard. I assured her that this was all normal, these feelings she had, and I appreciated it and all that. I think I rambled on quite a bit because she laughed and said, 'I don't mean to make you nervous, Doctor, but I'm not talking about worship or grateful patients and forgive me for saying this, but I just feel this great love for you.'

"Well, I mean to tell you, I hunted up Freud and ran for cover! I tried to explain to her about father figures. She'd shake her head and say she already had a wonderful father. So I'd bring in transference theory and point out that maybe she had a need for a big brother who could be protective and understanding, and she'd shake her head no again and tell me she didn't need a brother. So I'd say that perhaps I represented qualities that she had been missing in other aspects of her life. She'd smile and nod and agree and I'd see she missed my point entirely. She could have given Susan B. Anthony lessons in persistence!

"Finally I said, 'Look, you're fifteen years younger than I

am. I'm an old man. Look at me! You're a young woman. I mean, just look at me.'

"And that's when she hit me with the ton of bricks. She just looked up at me, or really past me with these innocent brown eyes of hers and said, 'Don't you know, Doctor?'

"Well, I *didn't* know. I mean, I didn't know until that very moment. She'd been in a coma after all and then after that, whenever I had visited her in the hospital, it had been at night and her room was dark, so I really didn't know until that very moment that she was blind.

"'I'm sorry,' I said. And she smiled and said that I needn't be sorry, that maybe because she was blind she was more sensitive to people than most and she could pick up things others seemed to miss. She said that she had grown to know me by the sound of my voice and knew just by hearing me talk to her what kind of person I was. She had fallen in love with me, she said, through the sound of my voice."

The old man became quiet, introspective, and visibly upset. I didn't press him. He took a long drag on his cigar, gulped down his port, held his glass to me for more, and said nothing. I was old enough to know better, and so changed the subject.

"Suppose," I said, "Suppose that you were asked to give a lecture to some medical students or young doctors, a sort of *Last Lecture*. What would you say to them?"

It worked. The old doctor shifted on the sofa, took several quick puffs of his cigar, setting aglow its business end, and literally drowned me in a torrent of seeming nonsequiturs. I only wish now I had tape-recorded it.

"Socrates was right. That's one thing I've learned," he said. "You've wasted your life if you haven't examined it, haven't gotten to know yourself. And another thing: be a champion of the underdog. Don't believe the high-rollers and politicians. The poor do not deserve it. They didn't bring it on themselves.

"And this," he said firmly. He pointed his cigar at me for emphasis. "your family comes first. Not the patient, not your profession, not your career and most certainly not possessions. The secret of a happy doctor is the happy he or she enjoys. Don't postpone love. Tomorrow is never the better time."

There was a catch in the old man's voice at this last bit of wisdom, and I felt we were close to the diabetic patient once again. I left it alone. There were long minutes of silence. We sat quietly drawing on our cigars, sipping the Port, saying nothing. Then he began again:

"What are hospitals without its plumbers, its maids and laundry personnel, without its maintenance men and janitors, without pharmacists, or aides who empty bedpans, without the compassionate nurses and technicians who believe 'stat' means what it says," said the old doctor. "Without them our university hospitals would grind to a halt. We should recognize them, thank them, bother to know their names. But we don't. We should deflect praise rather than searching for it,

avoid the limelight. In teaching, it's better to display the brilliance of others, and in caring for patients, I've always tried to give the referring doctor all of the credit—praising him or her to the patient, to the family, and to the referring doctor herself. And remember, praise publicly, but criticize privately. There is always something good in everyone. Find it, and praise it. And never embarrass a student. Never try to show how positively brilliant you are.

"Forgive me," he continued. "I'm expounding, preaching. Maybe that's what the approach of death does to you, makes you get on a soap box. I'm sorry."

The sun was setting behind the expanse of pasture and mountain. The hunchback braved the smoke-filled room with the supper tray. It was time for me to leave, and that moment of what I sensed might be confession was not to come, not today at least.

When I returned in a few days, I discovered I had unwittingly stumbled upon a way to dispel the housekeeper's evil curse. I should have known better. It was her deformity that had thrown me off, but the housekeeper was a woman, after all, and all women love flowers. I had brought a huge bouquet of cut fresh flowers for her, and a box of Hoyos and a bottle of Port for my old friend. "It's a Fonseca," I said, "1976. The clerk said it was the best they had."

"Crack it," said the old doctor. "Life is too short for cheap wine."

"Where were we?" I said.

"I forget," said the old man. He hadn't forgotten, and we both knew it. But he was not about to tell me about the diabetic patient who loved him.

"Your *Last Lecture*," I advanced.

"Oh, yes," he said, "advice to the young and all that. Well, let's see, here's a passage from my favorite book." He reached over to the low bookshelf, extracted a book, and opened it to where there had been placed a bookmark.

"Here it is," he said, beginning to read.

"'The best thing for being sad.' replied Merlyn, beginning to puff and blow, 'is to learn something. That is the only thing that never fails. You may grow old and trembling in your anatomies, you may lie awake at night listening to the disorder of your veins, you may miss your only love, you may see the world about you devastated by evil lunatics, or know your honor trampled in the sewers of baser minds. There is only one thing for it then—to learn. Learn why the world wags and what wags it. That is the only thing which the mind can never exhaust, never alienate, never be tortured by, never fear or distrust and never dream of regretting. Learning is the thing for you. Look at what a lot of things there are to learn—pure science, the only purity there is. You can learn astronomy in a lifetime, natural history in three, literature in six. And then, after you have exhausted a milliard lifetimes in biology, medicine and theocriticism and geography, history and economics — why, you can start to make a cartwheel out of the appropriate wood, or spend fifty years learning to begin to learn to beat your adversary at fencing. After that you can start again on mathematics, until it is time to learn to plough.'"

"That's beautiful," I said. "Where . . . ?"

"Yes, it is beautiful," said the old doctor, "yes it is. You know, you should never forget what it was like to be a student, how you looked at those senior to you in medical school, what you thought of residents, attendings, seasoned clinicians. We should never forget the power we have over the young people in our profession, a power that can shape lives for good or for evil. And believe me, there *is* evil in the world.

"Live your life as a Jean Valjean rather than an Edmond Dantès. Seize the opportunity to do The Good Thing. No other profession will give you so many chances. Don't become selfish.

"Selfishness. You know, when I have been racked with guilt, when my soul is as thin and dry as a chip of wood, when I feel worthless and have nothing left to give —when I get too selfish, I've turned to the cure for this—generosity. I've tried to find someone less fortunate and then was generous to a fault."

I walked into his next diatribe as though he had been lying in wait for me. "You know, only yesterday," I said, " I saw this fabulous movie on television . . ."

"Instead of one hour before the television set," the old man said, "you could memorize a poem. Think of it. Poetry is the quickest, most efficient way into the thoughts and feelings of a culture or a country. The best words in the best order, as they say. Be careful of that television set," he said, admonishing me, shaking his cigar at me. "Life is what is happening to you while you're getting ready for something else.

"Your favorite poem?" he asked.

" 'Dover Beach' I guess," I said. "Yours?"

"This:
'Sometimes things don't go, after all
from bad to worse. Some years, muscadel
faces down frost; green thrives; the crops don't fail;
sometimes a man aims high, and all goes well.
A people sometimes will step back from war;
elect an honest man; decide they care
enough, that they can't leave some stranger poor.
Some men become what they were born for.

Sometimes our best efforts do not go
amiss; sometimes we do as we meant to.
The sun will sometimes melt a field of sorrow
that seemed hard frozen: may it happen to you.'"

"Who . . . ?" I asked. But he was ahead of me. The approach of death heightens the senses, as they say.

"The accessible poets, that's who I've read. Dickinson, Frost, Wilbur. And set aside time each day to think. Philosophers do this. You should too. Thinking is not daydreaming. Learn how to think. Med school has taught you how to memorize, and, one hopes, how to learn. But nobody teaches you how to think. It requires solitude, this thinking does, and you can't find solitude in front of a TV set or at one of your health clubs, or when you're distracted on a busy commute. You need real solitude to give you focus and concentration, which is what you need for thinking."

It was two weeks before I could get back to visit the old doctor again. I have chastened myself since, believe me, over what in my absence I might have missed. Nevertheless, when I went back to see him, the housekeeper greeted me with what vaguely resembled a smile, accepted her flowers, led me hastily to his room, and left us alone. He began to talk about his diabetic patient, as though he had never left off, as though it were the next sentence of his story.

"She stood in my office and just wouldn't leave it alone," said the old doctor. "She said to me, 'I know you, Doctor. I know you very well and I love you with my whole heart. I really do.'

"Lucky for me, I could get called away again and think this thing out. I twisted and turned the whole business around to look at it every way I could. I was her doctor, for God's sake, and I had saved her life after all. Why shouldn't she feel some affection for me? And besides, here I was married to medicine. That's a contract just like any other contract, with rules to follow. You just don't break those rules. You don't allow this kind of thing to happen. You keep your distance. We believed that back then just as you do now. I explained all of this to her and she would just stare off with that wide-eyed innocence of hers and smile and say, 'Why can't I just love you?'

"Well, I didn't give her a return appointment. And she didn't come back to the office again, but something made me drive to her home to see her. I don't know what it was. Or did I? I called those trips house calls at first, but who was I kidding? She was very beautiful, in fact, in a fragile sort of way. I remember being amazed at myself that I hadn't noticed her beauty when I had been treating her disease. Now it seemed that all I could see was her beauty. That, and feel this unwavering love she had for me.

"Okay, I *wanted* to see her. I *had* to see her. I was breaking all the rules, cheating on medicine, breaking the Oath. I couldn't help myself. I drove over to see her every chance I could get. I'd take her for walks when there was time . . . or when her disease would let her.

"I didn't know what had come over me. I would be in my office examining a patient and all of a sudden I'd find myself thinking about her. Or I'd be talking to a family in the hospital and I might be trying to explain to them about this disease their Aunt Martha had and suddenly I'd stop and pause and I'd be off in a daydream again, imagining myself walking in the woods and kicking the leaves with her. I would get irritated with my secretary if she scheduled patients in at the end of the day because it would mean I'd only get a later start driving over to see her.

"My guilt really bothered me. I don't want you to misunderstand that. It was more than just *nice* to be with her. It was *wonderful* to be with her, and I felt almost like I *had* to be with her, that it was something I lived for, something that was keeping me alive. But I still felt that she was my patient, that I had medicine, that I was married to medicine, that medicine came first, that I had crossed a line I shouldn't have crossed. I would tell her these things. I would tell her that I felt guilty, that this was wrong, that I really shouldn't be doing this, but that I couldn't help myself. She would simply ask me what could possibly be wrong with two people loving each other.

"Her disease didn't just go away. You realize that. She had some pretty bad episodes—imagine what it was like having diabetes before we had any antibiotics. Whenever she was hospitalized, I'd go over and take care of her because there wasn't anyone else qualified to manage her disease and because . . . she wouldn't have allowed anybody else to take care of her anyway.

"And she became a different kind of patient for me then, I'll tell you! She would teeter on the brink and I would pace and swear . . . and pray mostly." His voice caught. He swallowed hard, and I could see the tears.

"Isn't it funny that doctors don't believe in God?" he asked me. "But if there isn't a God, who is it you speak to when your patient is doing poorly? Who is it you're whispering to when you are about to stick the chest tube, or send home the LP needle, or shock the lifeless heart? If there isn't a God, then why is it that patients who are prayed over seem as a group to do better? If there isn't a God, why is there beauty in the world? If I have learned one thing in forty years of medicine, it is that there is a higher power, and great things unknown to me."

The housekeeper entered with *two* trays for dinner.

I had arrived.

She left and hastily arrived with a third, joining us for dinner without invitation, without fanfare. She had vased the flowers I had brought her that day and had set them on the sideboard. The fragrance of the paperwhites would not, alas, cut through the cigar smoke. But the housekeeper seemed not to mind. For his part, the old doctor had a full audience now, and although he would refrain from talking about his love, he did not hold back his wisdom.

"How was that meeting you went to?" He gave me no time to answer. "By the way, watch out for organizations. Organizations should serve the common good. But they don't. They get caught up in two things. First they try to preserve themselves above all else. That gets to be its own first priority. And the second thing, its members get bent on self-promotion, when really they should be working to do The Good Thing."

There it was again, that Good Thing of his. He went on.

"If you find yourself stuck on a committee, try to do The Good Thing, shun self-promotion, fight evil. Speak out, stand for what you believe, fight for the unfortunate. Be a renegade, a loose cannon. If you become politically adept, a company man, a silent vote for the majority, you've failed. Oh, you'll get titles and advancement in the organization, but what have you really gained? Remember, there is power in difference of opinion — in democracy in other words. In 'group-think' there is only death of the soul.

"These organizations that you belong to are made up of doctors. You're a doctor so you can care for others. Not to live like a doctor. Not for show, not for privilege, not to own things. Millions on this earth would give everything they have to trade places with you, just for the chance to do The Good Thing. Don't squander this opportunity.

"Fail one hundred times," he said, nodding to me, "but keep trying. Strive for this on your tombstone: 'He tried.'"

The housekeeper had left the room abruptly in mid-sentence and was now returning with coffee. Since I had consumed three glasses of Port, smoked two cigars, and was heady with the old doctor's wisdom, I could convince myself that the hunchback had added something to my cup, giving my mind this remarkable clarity. She left again with the dinner trays and dishes, and as I rose to leave in her wake, the doctor motioned for me to stay. He knew, as I did not, that this would be our last evening together.

"You're wondering what became of her," he said to me. "How it all ended, with me and the diabetic girl. Well, that first winter she was in and out of the hospital all the time, but in spring she was ready for her walks again and I'd drive over to see her every evening. I'd look at my office nurse for some sign of disapproval from her and I knew that all my patients knew something was going on, and I expected the same disapproval from them, but it didn't matter to me.

"We took long walks that spring. She would hold my arm in both of hers and lean on me as we walked. I loved every minute of it. We would talk about the War, about the Brits, about how they were holding out, about how I felt that it was my duty to help them out. I remember the day when I stopped abruptly and turned to her. I held her shoulders in my hands and told her I had to do this thing, I had to go overseas, and I had to do this duty but I would be back, and when I came back I would marry her. If she would have me. I was trying to be all serious and formal and get it right, if you know what I mean. But she just widened her eyes and looked in my direction and threw her head back and laughed and said,

"'*Have* you? *Have* you? Of course I will *have* you!'

"They sent me to a station hospital outside Birmingham. I knew as soon as I got there that I should have married her before I left. War is like dying, you know. It brings everything into focus. It shows you what's important and what's senseless. And what was senseless, I'll tell you, was my worrying about this stupid 'marriage contract' I had with medicine. I mean, lives were ending all around me and the world was falling apart and I wanted nothing else but to be with her. I could only think about her.

"We were very busy at the hospital. I don't think I slept a full night in two years. I managed catnaps whenever I could. They evacuated the wounded over to us — those wounded that survived the trip—and we would patch them up. Believe me, there were plenty of wounded.

"But she never left my mind. I would live for the letters from her, letters she dictated to me, written in her mother's hand.

"We were experimenting with Prontosil, the sulfonamide, you know, treating wound infections with it. The Huns had discovered it a few years before and the Brits had gotten very interested in it. We were using it and having some incredible successes."

He half-turned to me and looked at me and then turned his face and his shoulders to the wall and went on with his story.

"Well, it was ironic that we were using Prontosil, creating

all of these miracles with the wounded GIs, and then I get the letter from her mother. It was sepsis. She had died of sepsis.

"Do you know how I felt? I raged at myself! I didn't want to live. I couldn't think. I blamed myself. If I had only married her, if she had been my wife they would have sent me back when she got sick. I could've taken the Prontosil back and saved her life. And she would still be with me. I blamed myself for her death. I should've married her when I had the chance. They'd have sent me back to the States because of a sick wife. But they won't evacuate you for a sick patient.

"I didn't want to go on. All around me the world was fighting for survival and I just wanted to die. I remember walking onto the wards and seeing the GIs lying there, missing a limb or an eye, all wrapped up in their pain, yet managing a smile for me and saying, 'Hi Doc,' and 'Thanks Doc' and . . .

"I just went on with my life. It wasn't any major decision. I didn't say to myself that well, I'm a doctor and I have Medicine, even though I don't have *her*. I didn't assume that my decision was made *for* me, or anything like that. I just put one foot in front of the other and did my job. That's what you do. You just do your job."

I didn't know what to say to the old doctor. After all, he had enough wisdom for three lifetimes. What could *I* tell *him*? Oh, I said that I understood, that it was human nature to be cautious, to procrastinate. I talked about all the people in *my* life whom I had wanted to open up to . . . be open with . . . whom I had wanted to understand me. I told him about all of the intended "somedays" in *my* life when I *would* relax my guard, *would* allow myself to feel—those "somedays" that never seem to come. I sympathized with him, about how circumstance has a way of slamming the door on you.

I rose, put a hand on his shoulder, and murmured a goodbye. I was never to see him again. When I returned, with flowers, a few days later, there was a black wreath on the door. I handed the flowers to the housekeeper. She nodded a thanks to me silently, and backed in to the darkened house, closing the door in front of her. I was left alone.

I am now given to long walks, and it is at these times I can be with him again — the old doctor who seemingly broke the rules, and so became human. I walk until the hike exhausts me, and I am flooded by the memory of his words, which are these:

"A physician's professional life is threatened by three enemies: arrogance, greed, and intellectual laziness. Hubris is arrogance dignified. Karl Menninger, the great psychiatrist and doctor of doctors once said that he had successfully treated doctors for every manner of illness – substance abuse, marital discord, depression—but had never been able to cure a physician of greed.

"Never ignore a sign or symptom you can't explain.

"Honesty is fitting words to the actions. Integrity is fitting actions to the words. Our actions define us; not principles, not goals, not titles nor academic rank.

"Approach each patient with this thought in mind: I will learn one single new thing from this person.

"Travel. You *must* visit other universities, other medical centers, other countries, if only to gain an idea of medicine's differences and its commonalties. To remain provincial is to become both arrogant and ignorant.

"Study medical history. Find your place in it.

"Cultivate your teachers well. Have them teach you how to learn, not spoon-feed you. Cultivate your consultants as well. Do not abuse them. Send them the baffling case you cannot diagnose by your own wit. Do not, out of sheer laziness or crunch of time, send headaches to the neurologist, chest pain to the cardiologist, or arthritis to the rheumatologist. Finally, cultivate your students.

Do not try to make them into your own image for purposes of self-affirmation. You will harm them in doing so. Bother to find out what they need and want to do, and what they are capable of. For students, as for children, quality time is all that is required.

"Just as you cannot cure all disease, you cannot be a doctor to all patients. For your own piece of mind and for the well-being of patients, you must learn to say "no", and "I am sorry I cannot help you" and "I think it is time you saw someone else". These may be the most difficult things for a physician to say, reared as she is in a world of omnipotence and endless possibilities.

"Communicate. Imagination is the great demon of marriages, partnerships, universities.

"Be on time. Never punish the prompt.

"'If you cannot make a diagnosis, make a decision.' A corollary to this is that most things get better by morning. And its antithesis is this: that if you cannot do something, order a test.

"When in doubt, return to first principles. Take a history. Examine the patient. Talk to the family. Ask the nurse.

"Simplify your life. Thoreau was right. Your possessions will possess you. Measure your worth not in things, but in knowledge and in kindness to others.

"Remember this: 'All that is required for evil to triumph is for good people to do nothing.'

"There is too much to know. Learn what you love and leave the rest to others. Libraries are repositories of knowledge. You are not and cannot be, so don't try to be.

"For God's sake, stop pitying yourself. The Great Plague of our ancestors *killed* doctors. *Ours* does not. Likely you will never be exposed to the Ebola virus. You are not at the mercy of a despotic king. You are not bound by class, nor diminished by poverty. You have great science as a tool, not leeches. The excellence of your pharmacy dwarfs arsenic, antimony, belladonna. Your citizenry in the richest, most advanced country in the history of the world is no more than sheer good fortune. You do not live in Uganda. You enjoy more than an ox for transportation. Your children will almost certainly reach adulthood.

"Do not waste your time. Be sensitive to anything that threatens to waste your time, and avoid it. Friends are not a waste of time. Nor is family. Nor is thinking. Nor are matters of the spirit and soul.

"Let your children, your spouse, your colleagues, partners and students, overhear you praising them.

"Stay in shape. This means more than mere diet and exercise. You need a diet of poetry and literature, and stiff exercise in thinking and spiritual contemplation.

"Being a doctor requires quick reflexes. The occasion *is* instant. Hone your reflexes by a regular habit of exposure to patients, talking to them, touching them, taking a history and doing a physical examination.

"Learn how to listen. You cannot understand another, nor take a meaningful history, by talking.

"Avoid arrogance. In the sweep of human history, what have you to be proud of?

"We exist for each other. Teach others, care for them. Generosity, that's the key.

"When you begin to become overly proud, when you begin to strut and show, ask yourself this: With the tools available at the time, would you have been capable of the observation and description of Hippocrates, the precision and analysis of Sydenham, the auscultatory skill of Laennec?

"Whatever did we do without evidence-based medicine? How did the giants of medicine practice, after all? Well, I believe this: they were inclined to think."

These were great lessons for me. On my long walks, recalling those hours with him, I can begin to believe myself capable of owning a mere portion of them. Even if only a very small portion.

But if there is one certain lesson I have learned from my days spent with the old doctor and his housekeeper, it is this: Commonly, when I return home to my wife, who is a trophy, but whom I did not marry because she is a trophy, I bring her flowers. A lot of them.

*'arched her back'*: a posture sometimes assumed by a patient with severe meningitis. Opisthotonos is the medical term.

*acral paresthesias*: numbness of the fingers and toes.

*amiodarone*: a drug used for dangerous heart arrhythmias.

*anacrotic notch*: a hesitation in the upstroke of the pulse; when accentuated, indicative of severe narrowing (stenosis) of the aortic valve.

*asterixis*: a tremor of the hand when the wrist is extended, indicative of brain dysfunction (cerebellar) of many causes, most commonly liver disease from alcoholic cirrhosis.

*Austin Flint murmur*: a 'false' murmur of mitral stenosis produced with severe regurgitation or leaking of the aortic valve; named for the nineteenth-century American physician who first described it.

*axonal radiations*: tracts of nerve fibers in the brain.

*bolete*: genus of mushroom, most of which are edible; the undersurface of the cap has a spongy character rather than gills. (Some *are* poisonous!)

*Bozzolo's*: pulsating vessels in the nasal mucous membranes indicative of severe aortic regurgitation. In the story Osler, a preeminent physical diagnostician in his day, is finding signs of disease most young doctors of today have not heard of.

*bronchospasm*: constriction of the airways, most commonly found in asthmatics and producing the characteristic wheezing sound.

*Burkitt's*: a cancer of the lymph glands and the most common cancer of children in equatorial Africa.

*C.O.N.*: certificate of need; State regulatory bodies issue these when permitting health care organizations to undergo large expenditures. Meant to avoid duplication of medical care and overtesting, too often they are subject to political influence.

*chemosis*: swelling of the outer layer of the white of the eye; commonly seen in viral eye infections, it can also indicate systemic disease.

*chorovod*: an Eastern European group dance, done in lock-step.

*ciguatera fish poisoning*: foodborne illness featuring all the symptoms found in Tatiania in the story and caused by a toxin found in fish in the tropics – often in the Caribbean. Red snapper is one such fish, and Hankins makes a medical pun in the story – red snapper is also a slang term for tuberculosis.

*Climens*: a sweet dessert wine from Barsac, Bordeaux. Celestial.

*clysis*: administration of fluids under the skin, before the advent of intravenous fluids.

*coarctation*: a pinching off, or narrowing of the aorta, giving rise to "missing pulses" and hypertension in some extremities but not others, depending upon the location of the obstruction. Rare, easy to diagnose, not often looked for.

*COLA*: cost of living allowance.

*coma vigile*: a type of coma where the patient appears to be aware but is not; *persistent vegetative state* is synonymous. The patient in the story has been misdiagnosed, has *locked-in syndrome* and is aware, preserving his sanity by conducting Smetana's Má Vlast over and over in his head. The neurologist in the story is meant to be the great Raymond Adams of Massachusetts General Hospital, who never would have missed this diagnosis.

*conjunctival icterus*: jaundice of the eyes, chiefly seen in liver disease.

*Corrigan's pulse*: bounding, then collapsing pulses, seen in aortic regurgitation.

*corticospinal tracts*: the bundles of nerves running from brain down the spinal cord conducting nerve impulses for muscle activity of the body.

*cyanosis*: bluish hue, signifying low oxygen saturation in the blood and caused most commonly by diseases of the heart and lungs.

*cytokines*: signaling compounds, chiefly proteins, used for cellular communication. When the body mounts an immune response to infection, cytokines have an integral role, for example.

*Dalrymple's*: the stare, sometimes subtle, seen in patients with overactive thyroid gland disease (hyperthyroidism).

*DeMusset's sign*: bobbing of the head in synchrony with the heart beat, indicative of severe aortic regurgitation. Alfred DeMusset, who had it, was a nineteenth-century French poet and lover of George Sand.

*dendrites*: the branched projections of a nerve cell.

*diastolic apical thrill*: a felt sensation over the chest, like a cat's purring, indicative of narrowing of the mitral valve (mitral stenosis).

*diastolic rumble*: the heart murmur associated with the above apical thrill.

*diastolic sound*: a low frequency heart sound heard just as the heart has finished its contraction, usually associated with heart failure (but may be a normal finding).

*dyspnea*: shortness of breath

*ecchymotic*: bruised, usually because of some pathologic process

*ectopy*: extra heart beats; felt by the patient as palpitations.

*Eisenmenger's*: a rare form of congenital heart disease producing cyanosis (qv.).

*endocarditis*: infection of the heart structures, most commonly of the valves.

*endocrinologist*: a specialist in glandular diseases, e.g., diabetes, thyroid problems.

*endocrinopathy*: a disease of an endocrine gland, e.g., underactive thyroid, tumors of the pituitary gland.

*endorphins*: naturally produced by the body, they produce opiate-like effects, such as the runner's high.

*enkephalins*: cytokines (qv.) having to do with regulation of pain in the body.

*entoloma*: common, usually pink-gilled mushrooms, and usually poisonous and dangerous.

*Ewing's*: a rare type of bone cancer found in children and young adults.

*falciparum*: the more severe and sometimes lethal form of malaria.

*festination*: an involuntary tendency to take short, accelerating steps when walking, commonly seen in Parkinson's disease.

*fetor hepaticus*: the fishy odor on the breath of patients with severe liver failure.

*fields of Forel*: an anatomic area high in the midbrain, below the cerebral cortex.

*foley*: bladder or urinary catheter

*fundi*: the back of the eye, where the retina, optic nerve, and retinal blood vessels may be seen; useful in physical diagnosis.

*gomer*: a pejorative term for an undesirable patient; no more should be said about it.

*Graham Steell murmur*: a heart murmur from leaking or regurgitation of the pulmonic valve, usually produced by hypertension in the lung arteries.

*hemochromatosis*; a disorder of iron metabolism, usually genetic, more common than is diagnosed, where iron accumulates in the body, causing pigmentation of the skin as well as disease of multiple organs.

*Hodgkin's Disease*: a type of cancer of the lymphatic system and in most stages usually cured through radiation therapy and/or chemotherapy.

*hydrocephalus*: blockage of flow of the spinal fluid producing in infants and young children abnormally large heads, convulsions, mental retardation, and death, that is until surgery was devised to treat early in the disease and prevent these disastrous outcomes.

*hyperpigmented palmar creases*: the type of pigmentation of the hands seen in hemochromatosis (qv.).

*hypothermia blanket*: hospital device used to lower body temperature in cases of severe fever.

*infarct*: heart attack; damage to heart muscle most commonly from occlusion of a coronary artery.

*IVAC*: automated infusion pump, used in hospital to control rates of intravenous infusions.

*Jenner's discovery*: smallpox vaccination, first used by him in 1796.

*Joffroy's*: absence of wrinkling of the forehead when looking up, seen in overactive thyroid disease.

*joust*: slang term in medicine, when one physician disparages the patient care of another, sometimes provoking malpractice suits.

*ketoacidosis*: a build-up of acids in the blood, seen as a part of diabetic coma.

*Kreb's cycle*: the citric acid cycle employed by all living cells to use oxygen to produce energy; all medical students memorize it, and most then forget it.

*Kroenig's isthmus*: the narrow straplike portion of the top of the shoulder which is normally resonant when percussed by the fingers, unless diseased by tuberculosis.

*kyphotic*: severe forward curvature of the spine.

*laetrile*: a compound isolated from almonds and purported to be a cancer cure, but labeled as quackery by the American Cancer Society.

*leishmaniasis*: a parasitic disease of the tropics and subtropics spread by the bite of the sand fly. It is present in Iraq.

*leukotriene*: compound naturally produced by the body central to the inflammatory response and involved in asthmatic and allergic reactions. A cytokine (qv.).

*Levine*: a type of stomach tube inserted via the nose or mouth and very uncomfortable for the patient.

*locked-in syndrome*: stroke producing total paralysis and inability to speak; otherwise, the patient is aware. In contrast, see also coma vigile.

*LP needle*: lumbar puncture needle, used for spinal tap, in this story to diagnose meningitis.

*mandibular ramus*: the jaw.

*Means-Lehrman scratch*: a scratchy sound heard over the heart with the stethoscope, in hyperthyroidism (overactive thyroid disease).

*medial longitudinal fasciculus*: nerve fibers in the brainstem controlling conjugate (or coordinated) gaze.

*metastatic*: usually referring to cancer, indicating spread from its primary point of origin.

*milky fluid*: normal cerebrospinal fluid is clear; milky fluid in this story indicates the presence of meningitis.

*mitral rumble*: the heart murmur of mitral stenosis or narrowing of the mitral valve.

*nephrons*: the basic structural and functional unit of the kidney, seen at the microscope.

*nitroprusside*: an intravenous drug used to lower extreme high blood pressure.

*ochronosis*: a rare inherited disorder with multiple organ dysfunction and pigmentation of the skin, often of a bluish color.

*oncologist*: cancer specialist.

*opportunistic infection*: infection occurring in patients whose immune system or resistance is compromised, either through another disease (e.g., AIDS) or because of medication (e.g., cancer chemotherapy).

*osteotomy*: bone surgery of any kind.

*panhypopituitarism*: complete failure of the pituitary gland.

*parturients*: herbs or medicines stimulating labor.

*PDAs*: patent ductus arteriosus, a type of congenital heart disease.

*persistent vegetative state*: coma vigile (qv.).

*plaque-formation*: deposits of cholesterol in arteries which may lead to stroke and heart attack.

*pons*: the knob-like anatomic process of the midbrain, vital for a number of brain functions.

*pre-excitation*: a disorder of heart conduction, often leading to very fast heart arrhythmias. Uncommon.

*ptosis*: drooping of an eyelid, possibly indicative of disease.

*puerperal sepsis*: infection contracted during or shortly after childbirth.

*pyloroplasty*: an operation to relieve obstruction in the lower stomach, most commonly in children.

*Quincke's*: abnormal pulsations in the blood vessels of the fingernails, once thought indicative of aortic regurgitation.

*redspot*: the Eastern brook trout; the local Maine term for that prince of fishes.

*regurgitation*: leakiness of a heart valve.

*reticular activating system*: the part of the brain controlling arousal and wakefulness.

*rheumatologist*: a specialist in joint diseases

*rumble*: heart murmur, usually referring to that of mitral stenosis

*S-2-P*: a component of the second heart sound, produced by closure of the pulmonic valve and when accentuated, indicative of disease.

*sarcoma*: any cancer of the connective or supportive tissues, i.e. bone, cartilage, muscle. Osteosarcoma is a bone cancer.

*sentinel node*: the first lymph node or group of lymph nodes reached by a spreading (metastatic) cancer.

*serotonin*: a central nervous system messenger chemical, involved in mood, sleep, appetite, body temperature; antidepressants act by increasing serotonin availability in the brain.

*singer's nodules*: calluses on the vocal cords, common in opera singers. Not cancerous.

*spider angiomata*: abnormal spidery blood vessels on the skin, indicative of liver disease.

*squamous cell cancer*: a type of cancer of the skin, mouth, and respiratory tract; except for skin squamous cell cancers, often related to smoking.

*Stellwag's*: infrequent blinking, seen in overactive thyroid disease.

*suprasternal bruit*: the noise of blood flow heard in the overactive thyroid gland, in the neck just above the breastbone.

*Terry's nails*: the pale white nails seen in patients with low blood protein, most commonly in liver or kidney disease.

*tetrologies*: a severe form of congenital heart disease.

*the Match*: the computer matching of medical students with internships; occurs in mid-March every year.

*"toasted him"*: slang term for radiation therapy.

*TNK*: Tenecteplase; the clot-buster used to treat heart attacks.

*trachoma*: eye infection from a bacterium; the world's leading cause of infectious blindness; eminently treatable with hygiene and antibiotics; endemic in the poorest regions of Asia, Africa, and the Middle East.

*transposition*: severe form of congenital heart disease.

*Trendelenburg*: head down position, used to treat shock.

*trypanosomiasis*: parasitic infection transmitted by the bite of the tsetse fly; the cause of African sleeping sickness.

*ventricular gallop*: sound heard in the resting phase of the heart cycle (diastole) which may be normal, or may indicate heart failure.

*ventriculoseptal defects*: hole in the heart, in the wall separating the two lower chambers of the heart; usually congenital.

*vivax*: a less virulent form of malaria.

*von Graefe's*: lagging of motion of the upper eyelid on downward gaze, seen in overactive thyroid disease.

*VSD*: ventriculoseptal defect (qv.)

*Wegener's granulomatosis*: a rare disease of blood vessels with inflammation involving multiple organs.

Michael A. LaCombe, M.D., is a graduate of Harvard Medical School. For eighteen years, he practiced primary-care general internal medicine in western Maine. For the past twelve years, he has practiced cardiology at MaineGeneral Medical Center in Augusta, Maine. The first author to write fiction for medical journals, he has published over 100 short stories and other literary pieces.

*Bedside* is Michael LaCombe's twelfth book. Five previous books by LaCombe on medical humanities topics have been published by the American College of Physicians Press. LaCombe's collection of medical writing by the well-known Canadian physician Sir William Osler was recently published by ACP.

Michael LaCombe has given readings of his stories at over fifty major universities in the U.S., Canada, and abroad. His chief accomplishments, however, are his marriage to Margaret Mary, his five great kids, and his three grandchildren prodigies.